Nothing for You Here, Young Man

MARIE-CLAIRE BLAIS

Nothing for You Here, Young Man

MARIE-CLAIRE BLAIS

Translated by Nigel Spencer

ARACHNIDE

© Éditions du Boréal, Montréal, Canada, 2012
English translation copyright © 2014 Nigel G. Spencer

First published as *Le jeune homme sans avenir* in 2012 by Les Éditions du Boréal
First published in English in 2014 by House of Anansi Press Inc.

This edition published in 2014 by
House of Anansi Press Inc.
110 Spadina Avenue, Suite 801
Toronto, ON, M5V 2K4
Tel. 416-363-4343 • Fax 416-363-1017
www.houseofanansi.com

Distributed in Canada by
HarperCollins Canada Ltd.
1995 Markham Road
Scarborough, ON, M1B 5M8
Toll free tel. 1-800-387-0117

Distributed in the United States by
Publishers Group West
1700 Fourth Street
Berkeley, CA 94710
Toll free tel. 1-800-788-3123

18 17 16 15 14   1 2 3 4 5

Library and Archives Canada Cataloguing in Publication
Blais, Marie-Claire, 1939–
[Jeune homme sans avenir. English]
    Nothing for you here, young man / author: Marie-Claire Blais
; translator: Nigel Spencer.
Translation of: Le jeune homme sans avenir.
Issued in print and electronic formats.
ISBN 978-1-77089-357-3 (pbk.).—ISBN 978-1-77089-358-0 (html)
    I. Spencer, Nigel, 1945–, translator II. Title. III. Title: Jeune
homme sans avenir. English.
PS8503.L33J4813 2014   C843'.54   C2013-907036-2   C2013-907037-0
Library of Congress Control Number: 2013918887

Cover design: Marijke Friesen • Text design and typesetting: Laura Brady

We acknowledge for their financial support of our publishing program the Canada Council for the Arts, the Ontario Arts Council, and the Government of Canada through the Canada Book Fund. We acknowledge the financial support of the Government of Canada, through the National Translation Program for Book Publishing for our translation activities.

Printed and bound in Canada

For Marie Couillard, in friendship and gratitude

. . . once again my thanks to a remarkable artist . . .
Sushi

— M.-C. B.

So this is how it would always be thought Daniel, this rush of painful sounds and images pouring through you, whether it was the fate of the sparrow, the chick swept by dust from the streets and calling for its mother, or anyone tiny and young in this distressed universe that laid claim to Daniel's heart and even his failing breath, his futile, seemingly infinite patience in the face of suffering, no matter how small the creature that struggled, even in this airport they had just closed, nothing flying in or out till who knows when, yet Daniel, a man of his time, was accustomed to this, a lightweight in the balance of things he thought, even if it all seemed so ponderous to him, making his own particular rotations around the Earth like the bird's feather, still no flight, what was it though that kept bringing him back to that bird trapped among the cables over a station platform in Madrid, what was it, oh if only this kind of delay wasn't happening just when Mai, away at college and so far from them, was coming back for a visit, you can never be sure of course, not even sure she was still his daughter, what he did seem to know was the wild sparrow in Madrid, chirping in despair like the chick this morning, endless cries ignored by merchants, standing with cross-armed in front of their shops, and about to sweep it away with the street dust under its golden newborn feathers, when would all this stop drumming in Daniel's ears like the sparrow he'd left to its fate among the cables of the Madrid station, and this is what we all do without a clue how it leads to our undoing, unknowingly building airports, stations, steel and concrete deserts, oh but this one gets us a view of the beach and the calm sea, so why are all flights cancelled. At this moment squinting from his bed through the half-open door, Petites Cendres could see Mabel out on the veranda talking to her parrots and getting screeches in reply that seemed to say, the rent, you're behind on the rent, he could see their beaks hooked against the shadows, and soon Mabel would go downtown to put them on display or sell roses, well aren't you the lucky one she said as boss of the rooming house you got someone nice to pay your board and lodging, but Lord Jesus, you haven't been out of bed for almost two weeks Petites Cendres, now you've got enough hair for plaiting, and nails so long and dirty, I daren't say, you're no better than the next man, whilst I break my back showing off these parrots to folks, selling roses and all, oh yeah and what do you suppose you got inside those scarlet petals now, Mabel, what eh, maybe some powder for me or do you keep that specially for your customers, not for me though, no way, Lord Jesus no said Mabel, not for you, you got no idea what that stuff costs, and you living here in my respectable house like some trash, you sunk as low as a beggar, and if it weren't for that nice anonymous donor of yours, you'd already be out there dragging yourself round Bahama Street, you're just lucky this nice person gives me the money for you Petites Cendres, so my lips are sealed, no way you going to know his name, he watched the hooked beaks in the shadows and the downy white eyelids of one asleep on her shoulder, now the whites around town, Mabel went on, they mistreat these birds showing them off the way they do, stolen from Brazil too, why I saw one, pale pink, that looked like it had dengue fever, head flopping from side to side, whoever was it said hurt something smaller and you hurt me too, maybe some fat-bellied comedian, just watch how they treat you my darlings, no respect, just yelling out to tourists, hey ladies and gentlemen come take your picture with these birds from the tropical savannas, that's how they treat you, charlatans that stole you out of the jungle, Mabel went on, and you Petites Cendres, you haven't forgotten we're throwing a party for your Doctor Dieudonné, oh yes, soon as he gets back, the entire Black Ancestral Choir's going to celebrate Dieudonné, man of God taking care of the poor and never asking for one cent, why did he have to go away said Petites Cendres, carefree in the comfort of his bed, wasn't his clinic enough, he mumbled into the dishevelled folds of his sloth, I mean why go volunteer there when we're holding a party for him right here, Mabel's singsong voice cut in, going from deep to nasal, he's getting the town's medal of honour for doctoring all you lazy layabouts and lost souls, and running two hospitals and a hospice, our very own choir director's going to give him his plaque with those same fingers and long thin red nails of hers, the ideal man, says the doctor, is not one who piles up money but one who saves lives, why he's even helped our Ancestral Choir a whole lot too, he's going to need a nice black tuxedo, just what he hates, and Eureka, the head of the choir, will be so proud that day when Reverend Ézéchielle invites us all to sing in her church, right where all those good-for-nothings and scoundrels wash up, the only church or temple that would want them, no other would take a one of them, just the Reverend, she'll help anybody and take on anything, her heart's that big, everybody knows she can remember the young Dieudonné, an immigrant from Haiti tossed out of universities along with those first black students, and the white student who stood beside him, both of them later becoming doctors, in those days when the burning crosses were planted in front of dormitory doors, he was forever there, as if to say I'm always going to be with you, I'll even burn with you from the fire of those torches or the acid tossed in our faces, because there needs to be someone by your side Dieudonné, yes Valdez would always be there, right by his side and honoured as well, you're too young to remember all that, Petites Cendres, either that or you're just being thankless and indifferent, oh shut up was his answer, of course he'd be up to celebrate the doctor's return, Mabel would be there first though, parrots clinging to her shoulders, her full round silhouette proudly floating past the gaping sprawlers on Bahama Street, he thought, dirty young hands on guitars, dogs sitting beside them, worn out, mournful and lazy, get to work Mabel would tell them, no-good loafers, whilst me who's three times your age, right, me, me, shrieked the parrots in mock repetition, hey we want a taste of that bitter stuff in your roses said a boy with an earth-coloured face through a cobweb of hair, don't you got nothing for us, hey listen to me said Mabel, these roses I'm selling tonight are honest ones, their petals, their pollen and not a thing more, no way I'm going to prison like Marcus, poor dumb kid, all he wanted was to help his friend Herman, going crazy up there onstage, too bad he got searched and locked up, poor Marcus, that's what happens when you want to help someone in this world, you get punished, Petites Cendres was still not up, the boy with the cobwebbed hair-straggled face asked, want me to bring the band into his room and wake him up, nah he's not sleeping said Mabel, when you play your flute nice like that he can hear you where he is, those sonatinas get him crying you know, and he wonders where you went so wrong, Fleur, because you did you know, like I told him this morning, I'd be forever grieving if I was your ma, Fleur listened thoughtfully with his flute in his lap, one hand stroking his German shepherd, when I think how you used to be, Fleur, I really got to wonder, but Mabel couldn't divert the boy's gaze from under that overhang of hair, and just as well he thought, so she doesn't see the anger in his eyes, the rage shaking his body, furious with himself, and though it was a warm autumn and hot at noon, he was glad to retreat deep inside the hoodie that hid his chin but couldn't stop the piercing words that went straight to the young musician's heart, Mabel's voice was like his own, what exactly have you done, Child Prodigy Fleur, not to be that flower crushed in the street, just a raggedy stuffed hoodie, what, what, geez you reek of alcohol, the cocktails your ma serves in the pub by the ocean when the illegal families come out to dance on the beach on Saturday nights and your ma gives them free drinks that knock them out right there, while ever since the divorce, your pa and grandpa stayed on the land, poor land back in Alabama, and haven't they all just driven you backwards, shrunk you down to their own size, you could have gone to study in Vienna, attended the greatest conservatories and music schools in the world, but no they said, no don't go Fleur, don't go, you're so young, a boy can't just up and leave his folks at eleven or twelve, your only shot, Mabel went on, is to get yourself into a music-teaching pro-gram right here on Bahama Street, yes, I know, you wouldn't get anything for your cello and flute and piano lessons, but at least you'd eat every day, child, Garçon Fleur, you remember that don't you, that's what they called you when people came from all around to hear you play a Bach sonata on the piano or conduct a jazz band that Garçon Fleur is dead though, just a fake, an illusion the boy murmured sombrely, or perhaps he didn't and the words simply weighed on his lips and fore-head without the strength to force them out of the unseeing shade inside the hood pulled all the way down to his brows; and soon night would fall, time for him to fall asleep like Petites Cendres, his dog stretched out beside him and the flute hidden in the folds of his coat, sleep, thought Fleur, just so I don't hear or see them anymore, at least not till tomorrow, so even if I play well on any instrument, just a fake, an illusion, it's because I love it that I can't get free, now it's become merely a mechanical longing for the loftiest sounds possible, Bach and Schubert, planted in me like it wants to kill me, his thoughts ran to this as he sat slumped against the wall out there on Bahama, same age as the young Korean violinist, both of them the great revelations of the year on the New York concert stage, but at least she didn't have to scrap her career because of ignorant parents who loved her too much, oh no, she was still listened to with respect, veneration, a grown woman now, dazzling to hear, said the critics, in a world where talent is worn out and used up so quickly, the stars perfectly aligned for some and not for others, they aligned for Ky-Mani Marley though, son of the legendary musician and not devoured or blotted out by his father's passing, the exact opposite perhaps, Fleur's father knew nothing of music, just a farmer toiling on an arid plot of land, so the stars, well maybe for some like Ky-Mani Marley, I'm going to hear him tonight as a matter of fact, to hear him sing "Dear Dad," we wear our hair the same but I've got no beard, now that's music come alive "Dear Dad," I could perhaps try and play at the New Music Festival or reunite the guys I used to play with for my *New Symphony*, if I had some willpower as Mum used to say, you've got to want to, son, you've got to want to, and now out of breath, the fat lady in the pub is rushing over to her customers, still beautiful mind you, they flirt with her though she doesn't like it, no man, not one since the divorce, just her son and his bad reputation, Garçon Fleur she still calls me and never has caught on that it gets on my nerves, Fleur's enough Ma, blossoming up from the spit in the streets, you just don't get it do you Ma, it's all an illusion, a put-on, he can hear the din of street noises, the chatter of Mabel and her parrots, the one called Jerry says Mabel let's get out of here, Mabel says over towards the docks and stop scratching my head with that beak of yours, no, no Jerry says, let's go, let's go, hey it's an old head so don't mess with it Jerry, okay, and Fleur can see Jerry's blue-rimmed eye staring at him as the bird repeats softly, let's go Mabel let's go okay Fleur carried a torch for just one woman, love them all as he might, it was always her he thought of, the young Korean violinist, the revelation of that year's contest, she, not Fleur, would be crowned and she would go to Moscow, for his parents had decided, isolated, Fleur would stay at home stranded like a pebble on the edge of a brook, too young his parents said, you can't let a child just go off like that, besides he'd need a new suit, the chubby kid who'd sat playing the piano with bare feet, not laced up to the neck in some outfit, no you wouldn't be happy that way his turbanned mother said, just a jean jacket without sleeves and jean shorts she'd embroidered for him, stringy at the bottom, his hair combed flat and brushed with a motherly love that intimated his destiny, wasn't this how she'd dressed him for the concert in New Orleans, complaining even that was too far without her by his side, oh he's not going to be alone, there's the drummer, guitarist, and bass player too, and yes, he would have grown up to marry her, the violin virtuoso friend with flying fingers whose name in her own language was Fleeting Dawn, but she'd rather be called Clara, as in Clara Schumann, an integral part of the music itself, Fleur, well perhaps he was too simple for her or the exotic air of such a distant culture, it was far too complex for a background like his, stooped over the piano, stripped to the waist but for a short embroidered vest, a primal child not about to cavort as a trained curiosity on the world's concert stages he thought, down-to-earth and devoid of imagination, they always got it wrong and took the boring, purely common-sense route, though Grandad would have sold his barren land for me, yes, he'd have done that for his grandson, and Fleur would have grown up, the childlike boy in him torn away so he could grow to manhood in that little cocoon of lies, with shoes on his feet before this, even now here he was out in the street, barefoot under his overcoat, he'd have worn a suit too for Fleeting Dawn's triumph at the Moscow competition instead of remaining captive like a netted fish, its throat finally cut while his parents said they only wanted what was good for him, and wasn't it enough to be well-known as a virtuoso at home and in the towns nearby, surely that should be enough for a young lad, still a boy, we'll see later on, his father told him, but Fleeting Dawn was already married to a pianist, he was on tour though and rarely at their home in Paris, well actually they had several places, still one day Fleur would catch up with them, new shoes, tight-fitting black suit and all, and then he'd say to her, well he'd say hi it's me, Fleur, remember that sonata we practised so hard, well would you like to hear it now, and he'd give his dog a shake and get up with his flute, and he had the impression passersby were listening, whether they stopped or kept on walking briskly, still they clapped, but it was really Fleeting Dawn or Clara he thought of, the daylight that shimmered in his heart against his nocturnal haunts, kind but unhappy, he'd be off to his mother's for a shower tonight, and maybe she'd even wash his feet and hair like when he was small, such nice hair she'd say, but look what you've gone and done to it, let me at least brush it for you, her gaze melting into the hesitant look of this errant, ill-famed child, you mustn't hold back from your mother, she'd say, but the island would close in on him like a net over the exposed skin of a fish, even a shark and he couldn't escape, eyes rolling skyward, gone forever those playful vacations at his grandfather's, running with goats through the fields, sitting on his knee, so what about music he'd ask, well I don't know much came the answer, but I do know you can't do only that in life, this is an old man speaking and he doesn't know anything, but music, oh don't listen to me he said sipping his dark beer, listen to what God tells you, after all He loves music too, now I'm a man of little faith but I do know this, they say there's lots of music in Heaven, angels' music, and without it I don't think too many people would want to go there, though as I say, I'm not long on faith, but no, ascending to those heights for some boring human voices, or even the memory of them, celestial or not, I doubt the gates of paradise would be open to me anyway, nope, not me the doubter, c'mon are we going asked Jerry, one of Mabel's parrots, she's got big teats like Martha my mother, also good for a show out on the docks, oh she's got herself all prettied up too, several layers of clothing and that hair, thought Fleur, yes it'll be cool out there by the sea tonight, and his fingers mechanically played the sonata he had so often rehearsed with Clara when they were very young, it's beautiful said Mabel, beautiful like in church, you know the Reverend's going to pay for my trip, plane and all, so I can see my girl in Indiana when she has her third baby, Mabel was wearing a worn pink velvet vest and a tight red top that Fleur thought pushed up her breasts, plus a white skirt and shoes, with a handbag that seemed heavy with the ginger beer she said she was going to sell out on the quays, she said it would do him good to have some himself, it could cure pretty much anything, and she made Petites Cendres drink some every single day, though it didn't do anything for his dejected look or his sinful laziness, I have to appear worthy of seeing and hearing him, I have to go freshen up at my mom's Fleur thought, he's going to have three other bands there with him, oh the stars are all aligned magnificently, uh-huh Ky-Mani Marley, what's the idea of having so many babies anyway, said Mabel, my stomach's empty, I haven't eaten a thing since yesterday, but at Mom's I'm gonna get nachos and brown ale, then get into fresh jeans and go out, Fleur's breath flowed abundantly through the flute, even though he'd begun to feel hungry, and there was the sharpness of alcohol sliding past his lips, yes, he ought to have followed Fleeting Dawn to Moscow instead of listening to them all, simply taken the money and gone, as someone had suggested. Then the metallic-sounding Voice announced they'd be held over, but you can't leave here the Voice kept saying, and Daniel obediently listened, the same as all the other passengers, and already two hours had gone by, one of them got to the bar before Daniel, I guess we have no choice but to drink, she said, I really need to talk to someone mister, I can't go outside for a smoke so I guess it's you, boy what a world and what strange times Daniel said, as though sensing her crisis and trying to soften her tremors, the flight's delayed, that's all, he said, but not for long, look, the sea's calm and the sky's blue and cloudless, that only makes me worry more said the woman, think of it, I could be having a smoke on the beach and here we are all piled together and for god knows how long, oh it won't be long now said Daniel with a doctor's reassuring tone, already dismissing her in favour of Mai, his daughter, can I buy you a drink he offered with what seemed a pontificating tone of indifference, one that strips one of one's habits, no, too cruel she said to herself as she watched his gaze surf elsewhere, oh that was men for you, still this one seems more attentive, even affable, and he thought about youth and nothing else; unknown barely a moment ago, she had already disappeared from his radar as it swept on into the limbo of anonymity, oh sure he'd offered to buy her a drink as his eye settled on a group of college girls pouring into the seats fully armed with computers and identical jackets, so there you have the mind of a mature male, the woman thought to herself, carbon-copy girls on borrowed time from carbon-copy parents, compact, dense, and cast from a single mould, the woman wanted to phone someone like everyone else, cellphones at the ready, hers too, but she had no one, no, absolutely no one right now to whom she could report her delayed flight for instance, no, off on vacation all alone, pleasing herself and no one else, delayed flight or not, what did she care, no, her sole obsession was this habit, these colourfully wrapped little packages in her bag, not to be touched, and oh the smoky taste right down deep inside, did she even have the right to dream of them, so why was this man eyeing those girls anyway, was he seeking out someone special among these untouchable, well brought-up, well-nourished offspring, densely packed into their mini-skirts and short shorts, all pink and healthy, not like Mai at all, thought Daniel, well maybe a bit in that physically poised way of looking life in the face, that slightly unaccomplished grace in their movements, looking askance at adults like aliens, no wait, Mai wouldn't do that, not create distance like that, cool and inaccessible, safely confined within her parents' class, smiling at you dismissively if at all, no, I'll be late for Mai's photo exhibit at college thought Daniel, glad that she was headed for arts instead of science, no longer sharing a room, the way she wanted it without the distraction of a roommate, Mai being Mai of course, she had plenty of friends, sociable as always Daniel reflected, oh I agree sir that these are indeed mysterious times we live in, said the woman trying desperately to hold Daniel's gaze, grey and dark, ruthless and pitiless she said, aware of him slipping beyond her grasp, Daniel, my name's Daniel and I'm on my way to see my daughter, it's been six months he told her, I guess this is how they slip away from us bit by bit, so he had a family, worse luck, fathers, all they ever do is talk about their families she thought to herself, what narcissism to think anyone was interested, wife and kids and all that, domestic defeat so inimical to a woman who enjoyed living alone with her own habits, her own freedom, although law and order would inevitably invade that too, invade everyone's retreat, no smoking in the apartment ma'am, look at the colour of your face, listen to the cough, your health is not good, so we will take you hostage, the imperious voice of authority, the Voice in airports announcing delayed or can-celled flights, nothing leaving here today, the absolute Voice impartial and infuriating, subjugating all to its will, impervious to any resistance, like these passengers and baggage suddenly corralled, young and old with no escape, not even a hallway or a smoking area thought the woman, no living space, just walking in circles in this hateful homogeneity, sky and sea so near and yet so far, unreachable beyond a sliver of glass, a bay window onto a calm sea and a blue heaven Daniel was reminded that Augustino had written that in one of his books, too much, perhaps he writes too much, his father wondered, and how was it he wrote so much about a time long before he was born, a frantic force driving him to see the world in its totality, every bit of its turbulence and tragedy, never mind when things happened, now or decades ago, perhaps it was simply today as it would be tomorrow, right here on this beach, Augustino had written this one Thursday in October as the military installed their missiles, putting up a barbed-wire camp, deployment today or deployment tomorrow on this gentle beach called Repose, up in an instant they were, the camps, Eagle missiles, and for hours, even days, not a bird was to be seen in the sky, darts ready to be launched from the missiles perhaps, no, wait, was it in November as the fog rolled in Daniel wondered, maybe not, maybe only a flying exercise, the usual Caribbean practice runs, nothing out of the ordinary, the young president had, after all, said no to the missile shield, no to the fiery darts, perhaps thinking of his own children, Augustino's brothers and sisters and a genera-tion that might never see the light of day, with an eye on his own progeny and the generations after that lingering for now in an antechamber of limbo, he said no, that is what Augustino wrote, though born long after this miracle of a man with the brass to say no, Augustino himself a young man with nothing here for him here, Daniel thought, nothing, just torn prema-turely from the tree like a dried-up piece of fruit, a strange son, strangely grateful that by saying no they had conceived and borne him, strangely grateful in his impulsive, virulently spontaneous writing carried away perhaps by his all-consum-ing desire to scramble up, over, and beyond the lip of History's crater, Augustino pointed to the tortuous twists by which countries could swallow without themselves being swallowed, Augustino's existence and his parents' could so easily have been evaporated by an almost casual lick of fire, that was how he described it, no city or its people, no matter how distant, would have survived, every one of us betrayed in a day by that voice saying so fast and without hesitation, yes, quick, take the offensive, we've lived within close reach of unimaginable betrayal, that October, for instance, when we very nearly ceased to be, when Repose Beach, with its white sand, its whiter herons, egrets, and doves, was invaded and encamped by troops, barbed wire everywhere, the trumpet sounding to herald this very betrayal, each one glued to the radio not for this story of battalions and artillery ready to put an end to life, no, but to witness the fall of the San Francisco Giants in the seventh game of the World Series, others nibbling popcorn before movie screens, cinema and TV providing the drama that was lacking in real life, the radio telling them that it might have happened during the night, but with daylight, afternoon, and evening past, no point in getting all worked up, after all, trains were running, no steel-clad Eagles were on their unerring one-way flight, no, here on the island, the sea was calm and a brand-new blue sky stretched over them, Daniel in his thoughts had no inkling today, any more than he did yesterday, that this October's make-believe beauty masked an occult world of warlike laws bound to endanger him and his own. You've got to be there in time for sunset on the sea tonight said Robbie, begging and laughing as he knelt on Petites Cendres' bed, oh yes, tonight's the night, there, you hear Fleur's music out in the street Petites Cendres said melancholically as he pulled the sheet over his head again and made sure Robbie knew there was no way he was going out, come on get your underwear and jeans and vest, you have to be there, all our friends are coming, I'm going to have a gold crown like this Robbie said sporting a paper one with "Queen" written on it, it was his year to be crowned and honoured and kowtowed to, I'm even going to stand by the Christmas tree and give out presents to the kids on Bahama Street, and come nightfall I'll dish out condoms and other cool stuff at the Saloon, cinnamon cookies and chocolates, 'cause I reign supreme, see this mole above my lip, well it's sexy and I've decided I'm keeping it for my coronation, oh and they're building a stage specially for me out in the street, all the former queens and princesses will be there, parading and sparkling, oh and my calves will be in such a knot, I know it, I'll be so afraid of tumbling off my glory ladder, and Yinn behind me in one of those grandiose outfits she brought back from Asia, maybe a beaded blue tux, narrow-waisted like a bouquet of lilies, buttocks and legs practically nude underneath, glass-heeled pumps too, makes you giddy, doesn't it, to say Yinn's name out loud, and Petites Cendres stirred under the sheets and Robbie said enough already and dragged him by the hair then the afternoon silence and you could hear it fading into colours raining over the city, yes there it was, Fleur's sonata, or was that just the sound of Petites Cendres trembling under the sheets and refusing to get up even when Robbie cried victory, here put on your jeans and Jockeys and tank top, Mabel got them ready for you over at the laundry, what a saint she is, always praying too, praying for you and me brother, what a pair of sinners, that's a tall order for a simple woman with no husband, tossed out the good-for-nothing just like that she did, the slacker said he was on unemployment, crack dealer more like it, says he's going to open a vending machine for the school kids on Bahama, one more nut-job, so yeah cried Robbie, victory, got them right here, Jockeys, jeans, and sleeveless, come on brother, up, why you lying there rotting away on that mattress, how many days you been here anyway, your landlady Mabel came and got me, and Yinn, no never mind, I told you already, look no man's got a broken heart that can't be fixed, that's the way it is, indestructible, look come on and get dressed brother, oh and Fleur's beautiful music out on Bahama, that'll get you back to life, sure the man's every bit as lazy as you are, languor and sloth bring shame on an unhappy man, told you already didn't I meanwhile Mabel tramps up and down the docks with those parrots Jerry and Merlin, she says Merlin's tail feathers are as orange as a ray of setting sun, and when he spreads his wings oh that's something to see, yep that bird'll outlive me by years, he could make it to eighty, and who'll his master or mistress be when I'm gone, eh, I already went to so much trouble training him not to think about his former owner the way he did, any male voice would make him jump, his old master's voice maybe, well no, he'd look at me like a disappointed lover, that mask of a face looking down black and white, brown lines around that piercing yellow eye, come on down and see Merlin and his lost-master blues, the guy who gave him to me was a ship's captain before he died, sometimes when he's being good he calls me Mama, my Mama all blue and gold this Merlin, but Jerry now he's white as snow all over, Robbie said, and Mabel's weaving through the dream merchants on the wharves, oh yes, and she stomps and frowns about you Petites Cendres, wanting you to get your love of life back, ambling among the fire-breathers, the trained animals and acrobats, yes you, Petites Cendres, and selling her lemon-and-ginger drinks while Merlin, with his orange tail, wonders what's become of the old master gone before him same as Mabel will, 'cause he's the only one who will last forever, just old nostalgic Merlin pining over his past loves, and in this perilous uncertain moment Mabel loves him oh so much, totally devoted to him and to Jerry the reasonable one, see it's a bit like you, Petites Cendres, hobbled by these silly regrets of yours, dreams or whatever, but outside it's all music and dancing and singing, do you really want me to go get Dorothea the doctor of stooped shoulders and broken spirits, wait till she flips you over like a pancake and massages those bones the way she's trained to do, a miracle cure, her gift from heaven, yeah they say she's gotten the paralyzed to walk again: I remember now thought Petites Cendres, once when Mabel wasn't watching over me, when she was out of the house, I did walk to the veranda, the whole town was baking under the sun during those summer days, bathing in it, suffocating from the jasmine in the gardens, corncobs on the grills along Bahama Street, and there he was collapsed in Mabel's hammock, no I never saw him, not even a glimpse, goddess of obscure temples, he saw me as he drove by and maybe soon would give me a lift too, strong as he was, was it the dark approach of some deathly convoy coming for me under sweltering sun, or just him, Yinn, giving me a friendly wave and nodding as he drove by, smiling in the shade of a blind, did I really see him wave to me, saying hi wordlessly there in the street, or was he only passing by oblivious, maybe let down or sad the way he often was at the end of the night, when he'd roll Robert's T-shirt up over his virile body, saying look at this god, let me caress him, he's grown up hasn't he this Robert from Martinique, one day he washes up here at the saloon, the next here he's all cuddly, 'cause on the outside he's music and song, Robbie said once again knowing Petites Cendres wasn't listening, undaunted Robbie went on, your clients are wondering where you've got to, you're not in the sauna where you used to be, nor on the hotel terraces at night, not in the Jacuzzis or men-only pools or gyms you used to go to so often, and the erotic video parlours where you used to pick them up, boy what a life you've lived Petites Cendres, gym, sauna, bar, you were all over the place, you charming, shameless, crazy half-breed, it's time you got cleaned up again, cut your nails and hair, he pointed in Yinn's direction and imitated him, better arch those eyebrows brother, I want you front and centre for my coronation tonight. Oh yes, the stars were aligned for him tonight Fleur was thinking as he played his flute in the street, the music slicing out of him and right through those rags as though bringing on a sudden spell of dancing, yeah all night at the Sunsplash Club he'd be listening to Ky-Mani Marley, got to get to Mom's for a clean shirt, yeah and some hibiscus in my hair like the old days, a man of flowers like when I played concerts as a kid, the flower was me, I blossomed the instant I sat down at the piano, splish splash, flowers falling in bits and withering like rotten teeth in the back of my mouth, hey what is that I smell, jasmine or something even more extravagant, the rare flowering from corn, suffocating, and who knows, maybe on one of those tours Clara might actually show up in one of the halls for a master concert, yes, appear she will and I'll see her bring the violin towards her face, pallid under the stage lights, yes, it will be a Beethoven concerto, so if I want to get in to see her and hear her I'm going to need a new suit, oh and they'll all know me in the orchestra, they'll wave, then splash, how it all just breaks up and shatters, I'll go to the Sunsplash Club tonight and listen to him sing, the man from the stars, *dear Daddy, Daddy dear, oh where are you,* yeah I could conduct that orchestra, could've, could still, in a brand-new black suit and shoes nicely shined, not like before with my parents content to let me go barefoot, playing the taverns while people stuffed themselves or just nibbled something, sailors and nasty captains with their drunken wives yelling bravo at me, oh he'll go places that Garçon Fleur kid, bless him, and there she is on the podium my sweet flower Clara, Fleeting Dawn, face pressed to her violin for the Beethoven concerto, listening to its celestial music, oh it makes me cry, yeah, I'll be there to hear and admire, but I don't know if she'll even recognize me moments when suddenly devastated by deafness in the middle of a composition, young Beethoven there in his miserable rooming-house covered his boiling brows with pots of water that filtered through the floorboards and set the neighbours to howling scandal, and who'd have known that youthful bellowing maniac upstairs would be the humble author of such music, so undone and so wounded, yeah thought Fleur, he wrote in blood and under showers of freezing water, it shows doesn't it, life, I want it back, and tonight I'll be there to listen to him. Oh may those stars be aligned said Robbie ripping the bedclothes off the mummy that Petites Cendres had made of himself, come on, up brother, I'm not going to let you live in this mess between the bed and the bureau, think about Fatalité, always the hero, always on his feet, bold even when he could barely stand, I remember the last trip, it was to Mexico and they'd invited him to dance and sing at some ball they were having, so Fatalité said come with me, 'cause he didn't want to be alone with the shadow hanging over him that first time he had pneumonia, nope, no way, we'll have a ball too he said, dancing and drinking and all that, stoned and drunk the whole time, it was his last hurrah, exalted and supercharged with nothing in his head but the finish line, yeah sure stoned and drunk all the same, even on the plane they were taken aback by how grandiose he was, especially with all those plumes and feathers and hat, splendid in his decadence and saying I am noticed therefore I exist, and when that's over, well there won't be anything to see, nothing, for two whole weeks we did nothing but laugh and dance and sing in club after club swilling martinis, and to turn on his fans Fatalité showed himself off in all sorts of weird and insane disguises everywhere in the streets and later on the beaches, he'd say here's my audience tonight right here on Los Muertos Beach, what PR, we ate out by the ocean so happy and pissed, yeah okay stoned as well, still with that trace of pneumonia casting a shadow over it all, nothing too serious though, not enough to stop him from having fun, then out of the blue in that romantic setting Fatalité says to me, I wish this could last forever, you and me, this is the life isn't it, nothing to do but smoke weed, so much happening, so many adventures while we're still young, look at that sky and that ocean, oh how majestic, really, if only this could last forever, hey tonight you perform at the Atlantic, don't forget, I told him, a table for two by the ocean and forever stoned and drunk, the two of us, as we pondered the riches of our existence, a virtual treasure chest, ah this is the life, Petites Cendres, fighting on fearlessly, saying whatever happens tomorrow, today's the day my senses are aglow, so what do you say Petites Cendres, but he just shaded his eyes and said nothing. Daniel saw one of the college girls move away from the others and undo the team shirt she'd tied round her waist, just as Mai would have done to unburden herself, they were all loitering around the airport with their video games, must be from some private school, and Mai too had gotten out of the uniform that marked her as a member of the elite and impatiently tossed aside the shirt, without which she seemed almost undressed, her belly piercing on display amid the light white summer clothes she had on underneath, then the girl sat on the ground with a book titled *Scientific Discoveries*, and of course Daniel realized it meant women's scientific discoveries, he'd dared assume that Mai was interested only in the arts, but maybe not, perhaps he was shut out of this new growth into womanhood a very few years from now, like this college girl bent over her book and drawn in by the demands of knowledge that he and his generation had no right to, as his kids were always reminding him, he was a relic of the past rather than a forerunner of the future, he needed to realize this, unfair maybe, as unfair he thought, as our children judging us like enemies, so here she is this diminutive college girl studiously glued to her book beneath a crown of golden locks, he could have lifted her into his arms and cradled her the way he had his own daughter, yet beneath that forehead were eyes like Mai's, so pitiless and inquiring, and who knows maybe this girl would be the great one to make or apply new discoveries; this was Daniel, but he was also a man who desired women and managed to hold on to what his children called his writer's youthfulness, nevertheless when they recorded all the discoveries to be made by these young people still in schools, colleges, and universities, boys and girls on the verge of tomorrow's astonishing creations, Daniel had slipped past that beatific summit of his life, and like it or not, he'd have to accept old age regardless, this was the heart of the huge injustice that separated women and children, he thought, the clash, the rage, this thought saddened him the instant the woman told him her name, Laure she said, elbows on the bar, funny that was my mother's name, he replied, Laure he said again, sorry there's no place to smoke here, yes she said, and I'm not the only one, if only they'd let us out for a few minutes, it really is an assault on our freedom to deprive us like this, no, really, Laure went on, there's no one you can go to for any kind of recourse, no one, they're all against us, me, she said, it's like stopping us from breathing whatever makes us relax, a cigarette, now how harmless is that, they think they're the guardians of our health, our ventilation, the air in our lungs, the reproduction of our cells, our fight against bacteria, when all they're really doing is ham-fistedly stopping us from breathing, that's how it's going to end for real you know, it'll finish me, and Daniel allowed that yes it was a cruel situation to be in, offering her some mineral water, thinking all the while about his daughter Mai, like this young college girl with a book of female scientific discoveries open on her lap, a look on her face every bit as uncompromising as Mai's when she looked up at him, Mai the engineer perhaps out to save an endangered planet, even included in the book this girl had in front of her, converting India's grain to flour in an incubator that functioned without electrical current, an innovator in the labs where such devices were created, and aiming to produce them locally in Africa, inventions that were her gift to the world, offered with an elegance that was pure and natural as her philosophy, rooted in the needs of others, simply arrived at and wholly her own, if not this, then perhaps a reform-minded financier, an economist whose career was entirely free of corruption, maybe a troubleshooter on the hunt for young disaster victims with her humble cellphone, or part of a network reporting on the countless cases of malnutrition and malaria, she, all of them saving thousands who might die before they were five, a dream thought Daniel, maybe a dream that all these little ones might not grow up amid ruins, his greatest wish for the disinherited of the Earth, for this, for Mai he had partially shelved writing for ecology, there were still the conferences, signings, and readings that connected him to literature, but the Earth is our one vast muse, isn't it he thought, still nothing flying out of this place, perhaps he was stuck here all day while colleagues and others awaited him at the university in Ireland, and he wouldn't see Mai till he returned home, or was that a dream as well, a hug and reconciliation with Augustino, cool and cerebral, not the emotional kind like me at all thought Daniel, no, he wrote unsentimentally as a bringer of justice to a generation of scholars, researchers, and physicists who'd thought the neutron bomb would be a betterment for humanity, the men, women, administrators, and politicians behind this project, oh yes he judged them, all those spectral squads like criminals in a war of shadows, a war chilled by its own fixation on horror, and how could a renowned physicist on his deathbed face designing that monstrosity and calling it the most moral of weapons, so wrote Augustino in his book *Letter to Young People Without a Future*, how could a man who had designed this bomb for ripping enemy troops to shreds without the slightest harm to buildings and installations, the moral model of the perfect nuclear device, invented and designed to spare all things inanimate: tanks and helmets would not be obliterated, just those who sought protection in them, the killing fire beneath their feet reduced just enough for that, such a fine calculation made by a man who at forty-nine would take this secret and unutterable betrayal to the grave, leaving only the controversy of a weapon yet to be used, as this great mind lay dying and dissolving into madness, wrote Augustino, the world needed proof that the ignition of invisible particles made this machine into a model of morality, living organisms consumed in seconds, yet not the stones of our houses or the metallic frames of our cell phones, this much revered man with a gnarled face that bore no hint of criminality, how would he spend his last hours, struck perhaps by the lightning of conscience, mightn't he feel damned without redemption or any way to reclaim what he had erased from the face of the Earth with the very pencil strokes that had laid out the foundations and intricacies of this indescribably demonic project Daniel responded, would an abrasive youth like Augustino have been able to inflame the wound of his cowardice as it tried to close over the satisfaction of a job too well done in the hope of making his country safe, a cleansing disinfectant bomb as he thought of it, his very own discovery, neglected and wrapped in its own Machiavellian mystery, a device intended for purification, he alone perhaps felt no blame in seeking a defence for his country, alone in knowing that grey zone where inventors like himself might commit the worst crimes and always be pardoned for defending their homeland, thus erasing all notions of good or evil amid the exaltation of their scientific epiphanies, Daniel told his son, perhaps at the close of his life he may have felt the light at the end of the tunnel casting some of its first warmth over him, long sought after throughout his research, no need at this stage to question any of it, perhaps seeing in all those pages of calculations an answer he could call God, well so much the better then after finding consolation in the Bible and prayer each day, at the gates neither of Heaven nor of Hell, but merely doubt, declaring himself a man released from his most hard-won accomplishments, feats that would destroy the Earth, ah now at last to sleep and think no more, for that door opened slightly onto a much sought-after nothingness. And Fleur remembered the foreign teacher forcing him to do exercises for hours, oh yes my young friend, work and work some more, we could work a whole day without one transcendent sublime note rising from the piano, your skill may be phenomenal but it is not the gift of music, think of Rachmaninov sitting for hours at the piano, think back to them every one, and Fleur would hear that strange voice carry him back to those stormy December nights of Lenin's putsch and revolution, when one composer tore himself away from his much loved native soil, his house sleepy under snow-laden trees, nights near a river murmuring beneath a thin skin of ice, ripped away from his homeland with his wife and children, so beautiful and so far away thought Garçon Fleur, he too would be leaving father, mother, and grandfather, although deprived of October and revolutions and Lenin's putsch, no one even waiting on a train in St. Petersburg to gather him and his family and whisk them away to Sweden where the voluntary exile, his heart contrite, would play concerts, having fled forever, his house probably burnt behind him, his forest, all of it a blaze to be fled with infants in arms and a thin suitcase with his sheet music and orchestral parts, nothing more, just a basket of food brought by a friend with warm clothing, chubby young Fleur had listened to three of these piano compositions, reaching towards the piano, and soon he too would be gone, he and his teacher together, oh how the notes rippled beneath his fastidious fingers as he practised without any of the sublime resonance and transcendence his teacher talked about, content only to say let's start again, then you can play the sonata, how difficult indeed to get a child to feel the music when it was written for grownups, first you must loosen the fingers, but then there were the insensitive parents fiercely opposed to so many hours of practice, but alone in Russia with his teacher, Clara and his agent, they said their boy would not be the same, his cheeks were growing pale and he slept badly at night, no, no, he would stay here with them in town, on the island, he was just too untamed to land in the middle of a competition like that, and so far from them too, he still heard his teacher's goodbyes in the pained notes of the flute when he played in the street, goodbye, what a shame, a real shame the German shepherd growled softly at the wall as Kim and her big mongrel showed up, not even on a leash like Fleur's shepherd, only a bit of rope, this girl so young with flowing curls, a backpack, and black boots, but why was she always stalking him like this, usually so bad-tempered and smiling at no one but him, one of the very few who dared sleep out alone at night, though of course she avoided the really dangerous beaches and knew how to snarl when she had to, everywhere I go thought Fleur to himself, here she is now as he plays, sitting right next to him on a drum she taps languidly, Fleur wanted to yell get out of here, go on, that's enough, but courage failed him, oh he could have run off one December night with his sheet music under his arm, could have caught some train or plane, simply got away that's all, he was eleven or twelve when his fate was decided, either get out or let everything go, fade away. What Daniel had to himself here in this airport during the long wait for a flight to Europe, what he had was time to reflect on Augustino and Mai and Samuel and Vincent as though they were right there with him, watching him and not without irony either, as if to say okay Papa, what is it you really think of us eh, he remembered that Augustino, steeped in his books, wasn't always the same avenger, with something approaching tenderness he recounted the loss of Jessica, a life snuffed out in the crash of her cardinal-red Cessna, and whether it was the rain or the mist, the twelve-year-old pilot had not managed to break the record, flying as she said, flying my Cardinal till it dies in flight, like the bird, perhaps it was at seven she said, I'll cover five hundred kilometres in three days, then her name would go up next to John Kevin's in *The Guinness Book of World Records*, never done before, and it said right there on her cap, "Women Fly," ever since, Augustino had written, each day and night a whole line of them took off in Cessnas they'd learned to fly for that very same trip with

Jessica's words on their hats —"Women Fly"— and she'd flown, not died, just flown somewhere to beat every record, saying to all who followed her, the sky is yours, don't get distracted or afraid, keep a close eye on your controls, if you wander for a moment, and above all don't listen to the sound of the rain, ignore its spatter and fly over it, she knew that instructors had taken back the controls, though not hers, now calcinated beyond recognition with her, her angel, unrecognizable but beside her always, as every one of the girls following her lead, their instructors saying Jessica needed three cushions just to reach the pedals and still see the dials, two minutes to takeoff he said, and she'd had only forty-eight hours of flying time, I told her it wasn't enough, it really wasn't, but she said it will do, she was morose and hadn't slept well the night before, so that made things worse, fearless little girl didn't listen but still, but still he was sorry he hadn't convinced her that forty-eight hours wasn't enough, he heard the applause out on the runway before takeoff, people yelling come back soon, and Jessica smiling at her little sister in their mum's arms, both of them so small below, later over the cellphone, her mother heard Jessica's desperate complaints, I think I hear rain outside Mum, it wasn't supposed to rain, she went on as though she were still beside them, why didn't they cancel, but the rain went on and on, her instructor forever beside her, calcinated and unrecognizable, and no he hadn't cancelled when they were on their way to Route 30 for Cheyenne Airport, there was still time to stop this and save them, intact and not disfigured nor obliterated, a curse on the transcontinental flight she had set her heart on, the instructor thought, the pride and wilfulness of a child had led them astray, after all storms had been forecast for Wyoming while they were still over California, storms, big ones in Wyoming, he'd told her, but she said one minute to takeoff, and that's when he felt his strongest regrets, knowing she'd slept only two hours, knowing all he did, why didn't he snatch her hands, so frail in those black gloves, from the controls, what equanimity was it that caused him to do nothing, to listen to what she said over and over again, five thousand kilometres in three days, what a celebration there would be, what praise and admiration, too late to turn back now, and now here it was, the thunder and lightning leaping across the sky and tearing into the plane's aluminum skin, no, no it's okay, rain, that's all said Jessica, only rain she said at 8:23 a.m., flying too low over Cheyenne Airport, definitely too low, he'd have to wrest the controls from her, much too low he thought, no more flying now, a smudge on the smoke-coloured clouds, rocked by explosive thunder, the wing tip poking through the thick of it, frozen in awe, he heard her say into the phone in fright, it's raining hard Mom, and we're coming down, don't worry her mother heard her say, we're on our way back, gone in a deluge of fire, thought the instructor frozen dumb, that's how it will read, oh God, how could I, both of us like an engaged couple as both of them closed their eyes just before the crash, forever in an embrace circled by clouds of smoke and fire, so that later on, when the other young girls flew over that spot in Wyoming in the same model of plane, they felt a tremor in the air and with it the exaltation of flying and flying till death overtook them, that was Jessica's last rejoicing, her last cry of passion and happiness this, Augustino wrote, it was for this she lived to the last, to be an offering to freedom of the skies for all the others, though not for Jessica's little sister to whom she'd waved goodbye through the window of the cockpit as they took off, now grown, the azure blue into which Jessica and her Cessna seemed to bounce playfully but Icarus-like too close to the sun, enjoying it all so much, taking to it so naturally, to her sister though, the sky seemed more muddied and dark than clear blue, so absorbed was Jessica with her instructor beside her that her father behind in the third red seat barely registered along with the smoky sky, so he'd scribbled her a note, or perhaps he'd merely wanted to, and slipped it on the end of a piece of string next to her ear, this is it sweetheart, we'll never meet again, or perhaps it read there's no hope, soon all three of us will be dead, then again maybe she never even got the message, or there was none, only one her younger sister imagined afterwards, there was so little time, but when as a teen she looked to the sky, it was in hatred, oh so blue it was, then it was covered with clouds that piled up and shed their jagged rain, three red seats spinning and spinning forever, and the ghostly cries from them, a pilot's heaven had snatched her sister and father away and the instructor, a heaven she hated, a heaven of their parents' ambitious gamble on Jessica's life, for that's what it was, a tragic error of proud overreaching, alone now with her thoughts, the sister still saw the three red seats twisting in the sky over the wreckage on the runway, and perhaps Jessica's voice came to her, sorry little sis. There was no point, no point indeed thought Daniel, for his son Augustino's writing bore out all his contradictions, his multi-faceted being, the multitude of resources at his command from all corners of the universe, while his father held to one subject, a single overarching description of his thoughts, or was that Daniel's perception when he himself might be inclined to say and portray all in a single stroke, though without his son's singular ability, Laure meanwhile withering the earth with her recriminations because she couldn't have a smoke, finding herself always accompanying Daniel, and dead set on following him wherever he went in the airport, Laure the smoking degenerate indecorously dogging a rather likeable married man was how she saw herself, though not without a hint of self-indulgence, as she later confided to someone, for apparently he was the only one who felt any empathy at all for her, of course that was a writer's occupational hazard, and she sensed this clearly, so better to tag along with him than another who might lecture about her dirty habit, it's actually pretty cool but everyone gives you grief about it she thought, and though she followed

in his tracks, he was the one who led her to the large pan-
oramic window and pointed to the nearby beach and on it a
solitary bird, a plover, scratching away the sand with its long
legs, a plover, not such a small bird as the one caught among
the cables in the station, he explained that long-legged birds
didn't usually come to this beach because of the sound waves
from planes coming and going, and this oversized one was
freer to explore the wet shores, all at once Daniel saw all of
them in this bird, everyone close to him, the sparrow hemmed
in by cables in the station in Madrid, the hatchling fresh-born
on the morning sidewalk, every bird he'd ever had to leave
to its fate, and so he stared tenderly at the plover, perhaps
recognizing in it a beloved creature at this point Laure sighed
self-pityingly I've had it, why, she wondered, had she bothered, especially given the way she was feeling, Daniel's empathy with this bird, just an ordinary plover on a beach, and she
turned away to the first-class passengers all sitting as though
in reserved seats already, not one of them smoking of course,
and she decided to despise them all, knowing they'd probably
found a way to sneak a smoke before they got to the hotel in
their limos, all very smug with a smoke already under their
belts in some space specially reserved for them, the steward-
esses were now addressing their announcement directly to
them it seemed, ladies and gentlemen we apologize for the
delay, all flights have now been cancelled for a short period,
refreshments and magazines are available for your enjoyment,
we are here to make your wait more comfortable, oh boy,
Laure could feel the rage welling up as she looked around,
she could rejoice over all this with just one little cigarette, its
sweet smell would restore respect for all around her, not that
she was cynical really, her mind was taken off her anger,
unjustified perhaps though still justifiable, as she saw latecomers sealed in by the closing glass doors with no other way to
go, Laure glared at the eccentric family, filthy rich of course,
the star-like mother trailing bracelets and necklaces in her

wake and young handsome hubby looking obsequious, a kid dressed up like its parents and much too old for the teddy bear protruding from its backpack, that was the real surprise though, kid and bear looking equally glassy-eyed with boredom, but what really struck Laure was that over her chic blouse the woman had on a jacket made from wolfskin, thrown on as if by a whim, the head of the wolf lolling back empty-eyed down to her waist, now how, thought Laure, could anyone wear such a thing, and she said so to Daniel, who was still contemplating the plover out on the beach on the other side of the huge slab of glass he felt a jolt when he saw the torn and butchered wolf the woman had on, you could almost see it bouncing and recoiling from the blows it had taken till it finally settled into this abject and tormented position, was this woman in the grip of sadistic vanity and wholly unaware, maybe having received this gift somewhere in her travels and parading it with a kind of rebellious and barbaric pride as though somehow transformed by it from her svelte, almost fragile, former self into the ferocious wolf whose strong, resilient soul she had stolen, or perhaps having shot it herself at point-blank range Daniel thought, all the better to give herself a new look, own it inside and out, the wolf with all its woods, forest lands, and lairs, fuse them all into her selfish little body with its pallid air, perhaps making it a little less breakable in the process, less transparent under the smooth fur cloak of humiliation, her sickeningly servile hubby sometimes screwing up his courage enough to stroke her ever so slightly, over the once-pricked ears now blasted flat, down over its bushy tail and his wife's lower back, itself bloodless white under the decimated grey tail, carnivorous and savage, no hiding place left, borne in plain sight, open shame on this woman's back, a public sacrifice to extravagance, Daniel pulled away to look at the plover by the shore once again, but his heart pounded at the sight of this lone stilted young creature pacing next to the waves so peacefully, how long does it have left before we bring everything down around it, ravaging the seas and killing the oceans and shorelines, what have we done wrote Augustino, from Atlantic to Pacific, we've created floating cemeteries for the most beautiful herons, albatrosses, doves, all of them choking on our plastic waste and glass, hecatombs, yes cemeteries afloat on the high seas he wrote, and if he's right, thought Daniel, if it's true there is nothing left for them, and yet he'd never have thought it Daniel quickly buried this reflection that so desperately needed his attention, and still the Voice announced neither arrivals nor departures but merely advised against wandering off too far, fresh announcements would follow, so there was plenty of time for Daniel to be alone with his plover out on the sunlit beach under the blue sky on the other side of the glass — heat, sun, a seemingly limitless beach — but inside the terminal and inside himself Daniel felt a very real chill, he'd probably done like Mai and dressed too lightly, white shorts, blue shirt, sure that's the reason. Kim sat on her large drum holding a thick rope with her guard dog at the other end, Fleur could put up with the rancid smell that branded her a street person because he had on a whiff of grasses and pine, and his skin wasn't scabby like hers, she wanted to say she showered every day on the beach when no one was look-ing, well almost every day because someone was always watching, but how dirty and awful it was when the menstrual blood ran between her legs and out into the street, hey this isn't here for you girls, and the black kids from Bahama Street she used to fight called her disgusting, hey you got blood on your skirt from your panties on down, want someone to lick it for you, and off she went with her army surplus backpack, same place she got her jean skirts and hobnail boots, khaki tops and matching cap for winter, Fleur went on playing his flute without a glance at her, not to be seen or smelled she thought, and he couldn't bear her presence, oh she'd have loved to tell him she fought with the kids because some of

them had been poisoning cocks and hens in the neighbourhood, some had even been locked up, but others kept right
on, and Kim was going to turn them in, and that was the main
reason she fought with them, to protect the local chickens,
but there was a new boy in their midst, the Shooter, air pistols
were his firecrackers, he shot randomly, and she had to turn
him in too or someone would get killed, not just the poultry,
she couldn't tell Fleur all this though, he never battled the
local kids, never swam with them in the pool the way she did
on Sundays, no one ever fought before or after temple, it was
a day of prayer and none of the mothers let their sons out in
the street, but she had a dog and hobnail boots, so she wasn't
afraid of anybody, and there under the shower by the sea with
her dog prowling around she'd wash her skirt, rubbing and
scrubbing till the blood came out, and she'd sit in the sun
waiting for it to dry along with her G-string and khaki wool
socks until some busybody told her to get dressed before the
sheriff rode by on horseback, though many times her skirt was
still damp, so that's probably why she always smelled bad and
Fleur didn't even if he lived in the street too, no, he smelled
of grasses and pine, the battle of Bahama Street made the day
a long, dirty, and painful one, what with the black kids in
yellow vests chasing the hens and roosters in and out among
the cars, yes Kim was going to get those delinquents busted,
but first she needed something to eat, maybe a slice of pizza
or even a sandwich from the trash can, which was tricky and
awkward because Kim didn't want anyone to see her and it
didn't help her rancid smell any either, Fleur of course had his
mother to feed him in the pub, maybe washed and spruced
up once a month too, but he still had no shoes, so his feet
were always dusty and brown, he used to fetch us beers that
we drank in paper bags under the pine trees on our beach
when no one was watching too close, or at least they pretended they didn't see us, specially the younger cops, they
didn't care about us except when it came to crack, but that

was the Bahama Street bunch, I wanted to tell Fleur this but he wasn't going to listen to me anyway, him and his music, nothing else, boy that could get old, specially when I was always so tired by the time I got here at the end of the day, I told them straight out, you don't even know what a girl is, it's not my fault the blood starts flowing, I scratched them when I could, so they said wait till the Shooter gets back at the whites for putting Marcus in prison because of one of you, the Shooter will get even, still we don't even know who he is, that's what I wanted to tell Fleur, be careful when you play out there, Mabel I wanted to warn her too, but she's already on the wharves with those parrots of hers, so all I could do was wait for sundown, wait is all, Fleur won't spare even a glance for me or my dog, not a one eh Max, she said, and Max raised his massive head in response, like we didn't even exist, told you didn't I, we should never have come, either you're smelly or I am, way too tired to walk any more with that bag digging into my shoulders, we oughta go see Bryan, Brilliant he calls himself, ha, stuck-up 'cause he writes books no one ever reads, not a one, oral tradition he calls it, he recites them out loud without writing them down, doesn't trust computers and geeks who might steal his ideas, he's been a crazy liar ever since his fourth hurricane, works mornings for the breakfast rush at Café Español and maybe some sidewalk cafés at night when he isn't too drunk, but in between he sits around in bars doing oral poetry and composing books if no one's listening, maybe if *Brilliant's* not too drunk, we can sleep with him in his boss's convertible and put the top down if it's too humid, nice eh Max, he's got a room but he never sleeps in it, afraid the floods'll come creeping up the steps, winds whipping away his head like the palm trees, his friend and half-brother Victor, the black giant, never made it, he says he'd never be what he is if Victor were still around, nope I wouldn't, he says, he was my brother, and we were together on the roof yelling for help and waiting for a copter to come by and save us, that was our first hurricane and a plank of wood took him out and he couldn't swim, he sank in a river of mud with all the other planks and fallen branches, my brother my bud, our big house in New Orleans, his family, his mother my nursemaid, his brother all locked away for thieving, but our Nanny said I've got one good son, Victor the giant, and it was true too, the others were mistakes, she knew even whipping wouldn't change them, they were already too hard-boiled from beatings, and Nanny had quite a hand on her, she was our very own Nanny for my sister and me up there in that big white wooden mansion, and Mama before she got converted used to go out a lot on my dad's arm, a queen of mothers, the *grande dame* about town, patroness, then the evil fell on us and she got religion and cursed us for our sins, you didn't save Victor when you could, he who grew up with you, the one good son Nanny had, she was strict even before she converted though, she wouldn't let me out of the house, and only Nanny would babysit me in case I disappeared she said, ever since I ran away on a train when I was twelve, she wouldn't even let me out of the house or past the garden fence my getaway on the train lasted two days and nights and it got me a lashing, Mama wouldn't do it herself of course, too high-class for that, she'd watch Nanny do it for her, and Nanny kept saying with pity, isn't this enough, but Mama still on high said no keep it up till he starts crying, but I wouldn't, see these scars Kim, still got them, but it wasn't really Nanny that did it, it was my mother through her, and she saying the whole time, please ma'am I can't bear to hurt a child, madam, not mine, not yours, the Lord will surely punish me, our family's suffered enough and it will suffer some more, but still my high-and-mighty mother, don't pity him; the first storm that comes along and Victor not knowing how to swim in such filthy water, Nanny was sure her punishment had come for listening to my mother and beating a white boy, sure it's true Nanny said, the second storm came but I wasn't there, it was like I flew over the dips and waves as they came, but it finally caught up with me, and there I was on a rooftop again yelling for help, but no Victor this time, nope, no Victor, gone, drowned, this is what Brilliant's first book was about, the spoken-out-loud one, first I gotta buy some paper says Bryan, otherwise it'll never get done, but when he got back to his room he was so drunk he fell asleep, so it got put off till the next day, second book, second hurricane. But in the second one, thought Kim, everyone died the same, that's what Brilliant said, if he hadn't been able to save Victor his friend and brother along with the three dogs he brought from New Orleans, all dead in what he called the Second Great Devastation, two of his dogs were never found, the third still on the mend at the vet's, in shock like Brilliant himself, terri-fied by the wind and the waves, but the minute he was better, Brilliant would go get him and they'd never be apart, never ever, yeah that's it, Kim would go and see Brilliant, there was a brain for you, okay so a bit cracked after all the storms and cyclones, but still, who knows, maybe it's true and he did get it all written down, Kim thought, scribbled out fast and exult-ing, like the things he published when he was young that won him city prizes, all of it gone for good in the Second Great Devastation, or was it the third, so it had come to this, no more notebooks, not a thing written down anymore, and he figured by the Fourth Great Devastation there'd be nothing left of him anyway, so the only thing to do was get back to that oral tradition, writing by talking, talking endlessly so that and that alone would never be over, and he speechified, orated, not giving a damn whether anyone in this crazy-house of a world heard him or not, he just sowed his poetry wher-ever he went like balm on the wounds of the Earth, he did write a lot to Isadora his sister, trust our mother up in her ivory tower to give you a name like that sister, my painter sister, why just be a kids' book illustrator, okay a great one, for some New York outfit when you could be painting the way you used to paint while I sat beside you in the nursery, remember I used to tell you what to paint while I told you a story, remember the one about the striped cat that Mama brought a long way just to get rid of the mice in the stable, more a tiger than any ordinary cat, she got him from India, then we discovered he really was a tiger when he got out in the field and swallowed the cow with one bite of his massive jaws, you never did believe that one, but you did do some childhood drawings of it, still I swear it's true that nobody ever saw a cat like our Tiger, what a huge appetite, oh Isodo my dearest big sis, I've got no one else in the whole world but you, please come back or phone or something, and don't say I'm to blame for Victor's drowning, Mama goes on about how I could have saved him by pulling on the beam that carried him away, my brother, my friend, dragged under that dirty water full of bodies, I could've, I could, she blames me ever since she got religion, the only mother we ever really had was our black Nanny, she brought us up Iso, you know it Iso, our only real mother, Victor's too and his brothers' and sisters', the guys in jail up there on the hill during the festival, we can eat and drink and sing in the street while they're in their spotless white building yelling and screaming through the bars in their prison city, we can practically touch and see them on festival days, yup just one mother for both of us Isadora, and what do you think our hoity-toity Mama would say if she knew what her son Bryan the Brilliant was thinking, contemptible reject that he is, maybe he should've been left there in the straw when they found him on the train two days and nights after he ran off, better if they'd never seen him again, or maybe surviving one hurricane after another because he was so small and nimble, had his head whipped off by the deadly winds, that's what our Mama would have said, and Isadora told him not to be so outrageous, after all he was supposed to be a grownup now and maybe he should get back to his writing, she even promised to illustrate his first novel, well she promised everything to her nimble little brother, so much that he flitted from one catastrophe to the next like a butterfly, she said, adding that their mother prayed for her son now she was converted, her nut-job son, though it wasn't his fault, no really not Bryan's at all, he even got shards in his forehead while trying to save Victor from behind that beam, then after he came to he babbled senselessly for days from the time he was in the helicopter, describing in detail how he saw Victor face down in the river filled with detritus and bodies, his blue overall swelling up over the foam, yes he could see it all, all he said, so they gave him a sedative but he would never be calm again, so please Brilliant, please, she wrote, I'm hoping you'll send me your first novel, the one about your exploits and adventures, what's more extraordinary than your very own Brilliant life, oh do let me put my drawings to it, flamboyant pictures to match what you've seen and been, your escape on the train for instance, two unforgettable days and nights towards the ends of the earth, and how skinny you were when you came home, Mama had to get Nanny to spoon-feed you, don't commit a sacrilege Brilliant, we have one mother and she's our darling Mama with all her faults, every mama has them, she loves and forgives us for everything Bryan, she sends you money doesn't she, so you can live properly, okay maybe you're not crazy about your job Brilliant, so go get another one, but most of all live a good life, a thousand hugs and kisses dear brother, same as before that beam ever fell and despite all that has kept us apart, if you were here with me on this new island I wouldn't be who I am he replied, battered by winds and storms, 'cause it's here the Third Great Devastation happened, here I really thought I could at last find refuge with my dogs and my books and my writing, nope I'd be different if you were still here with me, and Victor, still here forever, Mama sends me money to make sure I stay away, anywhere, nowhere, just so I'm gone, but I wouldn't be what I am, my dog too, homeless, shattered, in shock, waiting for someplace to settle, no I'd be different if you were here sis, and that, Kim thought, was how Brilliant wrote to her often at nighttime in his boss's convertible, when he'd pull all the ballpoints out of his shirt pocket and write on paper napkins from the Café Español where he served morning breakfast to the tourists, Kim next to him finally lying down to sleep on the back seat, but again she heard the angry voice of Fleur pausing for breath in his flute-playing because his mouth was dry, he said that he needed a drink, always bad-tempered, anyway it was time for Kim to start drumming while he took a break, this part of the sidewalk was his turf, so play your drum or get lost, Fleur said, disgusted by her smell of course or her dog's smell or maybe both of them reeking of the alleys and backyards, when she washed she really went to town and when she took the dog to the dog-walking beach it was still repulsive for the swimmers who moved farther off, it hurt her feelings, but maybe she had imagined it, Max looked all shiny like her hair, which she brushed every day, you both have real nice hair Brilliant told her, yeah Max looks like a real somebody's dog, not some street mutt, when Brilliant rambled like this every detail mattered because he was brought up in a family with principles and good manners, even if Mama was too tough on them, he used to say, but Fleur was so scratchy and unbearable Kim thought, he wasn't so different from those Rainbow Kids who'd invaded the town, once rich and the worse for wear, rebellious papa's boys still with their credit cards and cellphones and laptops, materialistic one way or another, all of them from overseas or elsewhere in North America and here for the winter, Rainbow Kids, the flotsam of an itinerant subculture was how Kim thought of them, Fleur was really more like them, a spoiled brat tied to his mother's apron-strings, plus the credit cards and the cellphone he never used, the chief of police had busted some of them squatting in an abandoned school, it was a historic building and vandals had wrecked the place, even the walls, doors, and windows were pushed in, ignorant vandals said they were non-violent but they broke everything for fun all the same, thought Kim, but Fleur was neither a vandal nor a dropout, he was something nobler, a musician, Kim put her stick on the drum as he stroked his dog, a German shepherd called Damien, a short break he called it, maybe now he was relaxed he might finally smile at her, that would sure lighten a long and stupid day. Petites Cendres stayed wrapped in his sheets refusing to get up, and Robbie told him about Yinn's triumphant success as a drag actor, singer, and dancer in Japan, then in Thailand where he was born, so hot that young people flocked to applaud his shows in nightclubs and even theatres, so this proves it can be done, and we're going to have a retirement home for drag queens after all, this was Yinn's dream, he'd already talked to an architect about it and it would be ready for spring, don't ever forget this terrific career won't always be here, I've wondered, Petites Cendres, if we, had it before, maybe Fatalité wouldn't have died alone at twenty-nine in an apartment with the lights blazing, she hated the dark with no stage dressing, really too bad, it really is, so young, so weak, too weak to go on singing and dancing, no funny, ironic laughter, Fatalité like before, no cozy rooming-house with friends around, barely standing like a horse on its last legs, hopeless maybe but still upright, and having to inject that last dose herself, but in Yinn's retirement home for drag queens they'd be surrounded by love, compassion, tenderness, and everything a soul could want on its voyage to nowhere, Robbie said, none of this preparing-the-way stuff for me 'cause I'm not a Buddhist like Yinn, Yinn whose mother protested with vehemence, the minute you get a bit of money you have to go out and spend it son, just one moment of success and glory and out you go spending money on someone else, while you and your poor mother who needs shoes, yes poor Mama, I'll have shoes and you'll have shoes, he answered, yes but don't get them so tight that you have to cram your feet in, okay Mama I won't, thinking about Fatalité I had the idea for young retirees, they don't like that word actually, it sounds too final, too headed-off-into-limbo, uh-uh we'll call it the Rehearsal or Comeback House, now that's nice, isn't it: the Rehearsal, Comeback House, and one day it'll be your turn to move in teased Robbie as he tugged at Petites Cendres' hair, why not next spring, I mean like a lot of them you're not so hot on stage, nor the liveliest, but not one of the dying either, more like, well, getting ready or rehearsing, what do you think Petites Cendres, and I probably won't be far behind, maybe a few more years, that's all, Herman too and a whole lot of others, sprained ankles and all, so often perched on heels that were almost stilts, but Petites Cendres was turned off by Robbie's monologue, he wanted to steer the conversation away from Yinn who dropped into it too often like so many lightning flashes, so he said, met any sugar daddies lately, not a one Robbie said, I'm tired of them, not enough time for sex, but the other day I lured a young one into my lair under the edge of the veranda, piercings all over his face, here for a weekend at the hotel with his folks, imagine that, twenty and still living at home, he said I want a fling, nothing complicated, it's my first night out without them, I said boy have you got some catching up to do my friend, isn't it time to loosen up the apron-strings a bit, so pretty boy, you know under this makeup, sexy dress and black curls, I'm no girl, I'm a guy, so are you sure that's what you want — a guy — or are you so innocent you haven't a clue, uh-huh I know what you are, but I'm not experienced or looking for anything, you know, complicated, just a good time, see the condom I got, I mean it's like candy, appetizing, and you've got real soft eyes, so I took him home, and Yinn finished his last show of the night then came over to me and said, he's underage your kid, isn't he, I'm not a minor, no way, the pretty boy yelled back, oh he was experienced all right, a full moon and Robbie's sweet eyes did him in, no nothing complicated he said but at

my place pretty boy fell asleep on my shoulder, and come
morning he told me it was the sweetest thing he'd ever known,
Robbie's shoulder, boy I must be getting old playing daddy
like that, the kid said so there are a whole bunch of you living
here together, you sure are lucky, so who's this Yinn character, a yoga guru or something, he seems like some kind of
supreme master, his eyes pull you in like magnets, wouldn't
mind spending a night with him either, hey I gotta go, my
parents are waiting at the hotel, I was supposed to be back
by midnight, they must be wondering where I am, Robbie you
sure are lucky to live your own life, don't know if I could do
it, disappoint my parents, besides I'm engaged to a girl so
there's no way out, it'd have to be a double life, hmmm said
Robbie, maybe, you never know, so there you go with one of
my innocent late nights at home, snug and cozy, father and
son, first lay for beginners, Christ you need to take out the
piercings one by one just to kiss the silly things, when all they
really want is to nap beside some Puerto Rican big brother,
still it's also comforting to the sugar daddies who go and break
your heart, Robbie quipped to Petites Cendres still huddled
beneath the sheets. Fleur remembered the sheet music and
parts left over from the composition contest and still at his
mother's, how had she persuaded him not to enter when it
was the thing he most wanted in the world, he could have
proved he still had it, that he was as good a musician as ever,
but no, she wanted him to play piano or cello in a Cajun trio
during the Captains and Boats Festival, it was a tradition that
paid well, no need for a special outfit either, he could just
show up barefoot, his friends Seamus and Lizzie would be
there too, all of them out under the stars, musicians, ballads,
and songs, plus the show would benefit her favourite cause
and help protect illegals from persecution, so forget about
composing all right, this *New Symphony* was just one of those
long hair pieces anyway, recycling the sounds of sirens in the
city, no, forget it and sign up with the Cajun trio, now wouldn't

that be fun to see him back with the two of them, so gifted, and Fleur hadn't seen Seamus and Lizzie for such a long time, didn't he care for them anymore now he'd taken to living in the streets, today in music any sound can be created, he wrote back to her, the cries and all, what on earth do you mean she wrote back, what do you mean all the cries, son, it's too late anyhow, too late for everything, little by little he realized he had been the root of their divorce, for his father approved of his leaving to study music abroad, he'd gradually come under the influence of Fleur's well-meaning grandfather, so he said yes to the Russia trip, yes, but his mother had resorted to divorce, he was constantly surrounded by their bickering about a future that was his and his alone, yes mine he raged from underneath his hoodie and snatched up his flute but played the sonata once again mechanically, with no concern for its beauty, and it hurt to feel this way, with Kim and her dog and drumming a few feet away, both the dogs, Damien and Max, growling at one another while Kim yelled at them to stop, a few weeks ago she had combed his hair and now it was all tangled again, his mother had said yes too late, but he thought to himself why, why is it too late, it's too late, the age of geniuses is past, but what did she know about him, thought Fleur, to speak to him this way, she'd always done this when a composition is entered in a contest, there's a chairman and members of a music committee, you could never stand up to that, son, these are serious educated folks, they're not going to give the prize to some street kid, believe me it isn't for you, all you'll do is scare them with your life-style, they'll jump on every flaw or mistake like that, you'll throw them off balance and they'll make fun of you, there's nothing you can do about it Garçon Fleur, that's simply the way it is, I'm not the same person I was up on the stage, whatever, the tavern, pub or sidewalk restaurant, I'm not the same despicable fake Garçon Fleur, nossir, living in the street has taught me my own brand of wildness and I know I could make the music committee respect me for being who I am, he wrote back to her, and not on any laptop like the ultra-rich Rainbow Kids that Kim despises, my music is completely me too and shows life as it truly is, harsh and real, and I live in the middle of it, I've never lost hope in my music, others, like Kim for example, don't have anything, and lots of others too, less than nothing, that's the pity I hang on to, he wrote when he took the time to write at all, stretched out hungry on the beach and glad at least that Damien was well fed and watered, no creature in all the world was as dear to him, the same as Max was to Kim, he couldn't do without the love of this dog, he couldn't explain to his mother why when all she said was that he cost her son too much and made him go without, her unspoken reproach was that Fleur preferred Damien to her, son you must be blind, he is after all only an animal, isn't he, but Fleur's reply was that without Damien and his sympathetic gaze he would feel even more worthless and depressed, she couldn't possibly see inside his cloud of defeat and bitterness, how could Martha know her son was always thinking of her, Clara, the only ray of hope left to him, she thought he dwelt too much on his reading about the lives of musicians and their work, never mind that he only had a grade-school education, still he read too much and that's where all his dreams and ambitions sprang from, it was too late and yet still he dreamed of going back to his music she said, but Fleur kept on thinking others are busy writing what I want to write, composing my music, conducting my orchestras, they're creating while all I do is run downhill, both inside and out, and all the while he played his flute but heard other people's music with a stab of sorrow, they had to hear his *New Symphony*, or else call it the Symphony of Disappointment or maybe Defeat, with its cock-crows, lung-wrenching in the hot air like the strident cry of sirens for a robber caught in the act, or of an ambulance, the patient inside in pain, cock-crows for how he hadn't eaten in days, some concrete carnal music like Péter Eötvös's *The*

Seven, written for the astronauts aboard *Columbia,* performed any number of times by now in memory of what all had seen for themselves on their screens, a space helmet atop a pile of the little debris to be found, space being a source of silence, nothing more, and not everything immolated in its wild race would come back to us, the silence of eternity perhaps, wrote Fleur to his mother, yes that one lonely helmet, so solitary and silent, this was the image that inspired the musician, this and seven more like it all reduced to nothingness and silence in a single astral spark, and television took countless people on its arrow aimed straight at heaven, then the sudden freeze and destruction, seven almost audible heartbeats from the astronauts, Fleur wrote to his mother, now that, wasn't that the true power of music after all, pinning down an instant of reality, describing it suspended between life and death, never to be forgotten? The violin concerto gave voice to the slipping of seven lives into the beyond, the exchanges in a mixed choir split the night, the violin refracted a spectrum of screams from seven broken bodies projected by a spray of fire and fused together in a wheat-like sheaf, and yet the musician had given each his or her own voice too, a last cry with an explosion of repressed joy through the choked rasp and shudders of the violin, a solo violin with six others scattered through the hall to reflect the last torment of each individual in this astral tragedy, the space between was the tomb that enveloped all its victims, human or animal and from whatever nation of the universe, one by one, perhaps a mere moment to drain them of life, these seven souls still drifting dismembered and scattered, drifting perhaps forever like so many other satellites, their exploration never ever ending, indeed their true mission in space, so sang the unseen violins as Fleur conceived them, an evocation of all that refused to die, that is what he intended, he told his mother, that is the power of music, she wrote back that he must, must come back home, even if he had to drag Damien along since they were really so inseparable, Fleur could help her out when she was too busy at the pub, she'd cook for him too and he'd get to see Lizzie and Seamus, his friends in the Cajun music group, sure, they could use him on piano or cello, why waste any more time, just come on back, and as he played his flute in the street he thought about what his mother had said to him over and over, too late, it was too late. As he swung in his hammock and smelled the summer fragrances, Petites Cendres recalled the wave of images and scenes as though in a theatre, he could smell jasmine on Yinn and in his black hair when he stood close enough in the bar or the Saloon, in summertime, when Mabel left him alone to his wafting perfumed memories, he swung in his hammock, what day was it again when those young New York models showed up and the boy with straight blonde hair and creamy skin smiled at him as he entered the Saloon, wonder if his designer was still playing chaperone back there and would he ever see him again, wait, there was another blonde kid, closer, more accessible, he was Yinn's new discovery for Decadent Fridays, an angel who never seemed to wear anything more than tight underpants or swimsuits day and night with money peeking out of them whenever he did table dances, this pre-pubescent Cupid or Eros, according to Yinn, had a yen for wild loose loving, though it sometimes ended very badly, pure affection, irresistible childlike embraces he offered to one and all by flinging his arms around someone's neck, when he used to go out every night how many times had Petites Cendres felt the brush of those airborne kisses from little Cupid with his short blonde locks and virginal pink chest like the New York model's, the one Petites Cendres still called his boy, he'd even yelled it out in the street when they wanted to arrest him for stealing a motorcycle, don't you lay a hand on my boy, he was just kidding anyway and they let him go right away, or his designer paid the bail and got his bewitching little punk back, it was a joke, just a stunt to get your attention, gentlemen, always doing dumb stuff like that when

I'm bored, anyway who knows where Petites Cendres' boy
was now, smiling the way he did as he entered the Saloon
back when Petites Cendres still stayed out all night every night
and could get a whiff of the jasmine in Yinn's black hair if he
dared get close enough. If today's the day to go to the vet's
thought Kim, Bryan's going to be upset if he still can't take his
dog for their usual bike ride around the island, how Misha
loved to run happily along beside him, but every time Bryan
showed up the vet said, we'll have to wait a bit, Misha's not
ready to be taken in hand, see, look how he's trembling, I'm
concerned he might not even recognize his master, so Bryan
would kneel down before the dog, saying it's me, Brilliant,
don't you remember me, they lifted us both up to the helicopter in a net, right up over the putrid water and branches, my
half-brother Victor beneath us, not moving, not getting up,
drowned, with his face dragging in the palm leaves and the
scum, seawater swelling out his overalls, we got saved Misha,
he didn't, if my friend were still with us I wouldn't be the way
I am Misha, please stop trembling when I try to hold you, the
Third Great Devastation is long over and there won't be
another one, I promise, Misha had been in the clinic since that
deadly hurricane along with other victims, he was every bit
as nervous as Bryan was but at least he'd get better, they said
taking such patient care of him, oh if only it could be visiting
day at the vet's, Brilliant cried all night long, saying his name
over and over again, poor Misha got struck down too and
now he doesn't even recognize me; Kim hated when people
let their emotions take over and she had no idea how she
would act towards a sobbing Bryan, if it were visiting day he
wouldn't be waiting tables at the Café Español, which means
he wouldn't have any fancy goodies to bring home, one more
night without anything to eat, and Bryan sure knew how to
serve up breakfast or midnight supper on the beach when no
one was looking, he'd pour some wine or champagne in
glasses that were also a gift from the café he said, what a

wonder life is, but for Misha, and where are they, his dear Misha and Victor, Nanny's own son, Nanny who couldn't stand hitting my white mother's son, nope, I wouldn't be the way I am if they were still here, things would be different, my books would get published, so Kim told him why don't you write a book about Misha, but Brilliant sobbed and said no, I can't, I feel guilty about everything, well there's nothing you could do about thunder and insane winds coming out of the sky, Kim said, if God exists the way my mother thinks, he answered, Victor and my dog would be here, Kim also knew Brilliant was the best cyclist in town and second in the final, and why not first said Kim, next time you will be, she placed a hand on his narrow shoulder, you've got to, then you'll get some respect, at this Brilliant felt a surge of confidence that maybe somehow tomorrow might be better and he told her, you're right Kim, I will come in first and it'll be in your honour, yep, that's what I want, to honour you and Misha. And while Robbie struggled to rouse him out of bed, Petites Cendres noticed Robbie's scorpion tattoo passionately signed "Robbie Belongs to Daddy", now that was passion or maybe overblown romanticism, feelings of one man for another that made Petites Cendres hunger for the nightlife he'd left behind so he could just sleep and daydream, he never used to like dawdling in bed here at Mabel's boarding house, total denial of all that ailed him he thought, both inside and out, a sclerotic passivity he was fully conscious of, the least memory played on his nerves and stabbed him like the indelible scorpion on Robbie's shoulder come to life and rubbing Petites Cendres' cheek as they fought over the covers, the tattoo reminding him of his entrenchment while others went on with their lives, loving, singing, dancing, showing off they way they did at the Cabaret or the Porte du Baiser Saloon, like nighttime transfigurations they all gained in age, whether in beauty or ugliness, for months that turned into years, Petites Cendres forever in his room or out on the veranda in his hammock where he could see the sky and the ocean, the flight of the ibis and turtledoves, as Robbie said, the times are changing my friend, and now it's my turn to wear the crown, no offence to Yinn, no, on the contrary, and that's why you've got to come to the coronation tonight brother, it'll be Yinn's thirty-third birthday soon he murmured, the pain of those words pierced Petites Cendres so that he suddenly panicked, what if his life ended today, before the sunset over the sea, just a murmured goodnight, his little spark going out like that, but here was Robbie laughing in his ear and that got a rise out of Petites Cendres who started laughing too, still staring at that scorpion tattoo on his friend's shoulder, the world doesn't stop turning because you're in bed asleep, look at Yinn's success in Asia, and now he's back and he's designing theatre costumes, running to and from his studio to our rehearsals, doing us up in oriental silks every night, then to the architect's with plans of the future home for young retirees, writing plays when he's got the time, but his thirty-third is about to sound, and he did say that would be his personal revolution, oh yes things have changed since you took to your bed my friend, Robbie whispered in his ear that any siren call to the valley of the shadow of death and that enticing eternity beyond was really not a good thing, Petites Cendres should stay far away from that temptation and cling to what mattered, love and life, exactly as Dr. Dieudonné said before leaving, Petites Cendres was on the road back to health he said, and he needed space to heal his wounds, injuries that hurt worse than any malady as Robbie said with humour, Dieudonné was too busy to deal with broken hearts, such trivia didn't concern him, he was driven to action, and that's why he'd volunteered to work in countries rocked by the cholera epidemic and not enough doctors, Robbie said broken hearts were not only pointless but ridiculous if you think about it, yeah ridiculous, things are changing, they already have he whispered again in Petites Cendres' ear, and I'm not as svelte as I used to be, ladylike ankles and all, Yinn says I've gotta lose some weight in fact it's kind of crazy how things change, I mean the Next One has already turned into Number One, or will soon, Yinn uses his first name Cheng now and says you should be proud of being Chinese, you're the most perfect and delicate dancer I've got, oh Petites Cendres you've just got to see him onstage, Robbie said, and so humble in a black lace blouse that shows off his long neck, yet you barely notice it beneath his black silk jacket, he doesn't really like putting himself on display, his face and slow, measured movements are the most moving, I can't explain how he does it, it's dance enchantment, a subtle magnetism that Yinn taught him, not even a hint of the old awkwardness, you wouldn't even know him from before, uh-uh, I'm not going anywhere said Petites Cendres, I don't care what's happening with the nightlife he lied, or the Next One, Robbie remarked in Petites Cendres' ear, who used to be so gawky and is now the Prince of the Cabaret though you'd think he was totally unaware of men's desires, even if he has turned into sort of a Yinn clone, that mask sometimes without a hint of movement or a smile, artfully hiding his feelings and the underground surge of desire, that's the common denominator Yinn's trying to build into the new ones, a kind of grandeur that people don't like or even get in our work, especially that kind of spare, straightforward look, but he cut himself short and switched to the subject of Fatalité, gone of course, and only to be seen haunting him, larger than life, day and night on his video screen, and Désirée, riotous as ever, eyes shining with malice, whose hip-slinking at Robbie seemed to say you're starting to forget me aren't you, that's only for the dead you know, they should be forgotten, but not me, I'm still here, see my lips move, my eyes glint, remember our supper on the beach in Mexico, well our suppers everywhere, wherever you go at night lately I'm there with you Robbie, it's only for the dead, Petites Cendres cried suddenly, you've got to forget them, but Robbie brushed him aside and reached for his phone with the red glow of a message, look, it's the kid sending me his picture Robbie said, let's see what he says, dear, dear Robbie with such sweet and sad eyes sometimes, here's a photo of me with my fiancée, thanks for putting me up that night in the big house with you and your friends, you all seem so happy together, Robbie went on, Junior and his fiancée, she's every bit as much fun as he is with her face piercings, see they even look alike don't they, how cute, he says they're getting married, postmodern punks, let's wish them lots of happiness and a ton of kids, so there you go, that's life, as Yinn would say, the imperfect cycle of eternal beginnings-again, but Petites Cendres said nothing, he was fixing a disturbed stare at the scorpion tattoo that adorned Robbie's shoulder. Daniel, having plenty of time to kill as he waited at the airport, thought back to the friends he'd known when he was young who had been addicted to cocaine, what relief that his kids weren't dissipated the way he was then, back in those erratic days he'd met the master choreographer Arnie Graal, who would end up teaching his son Samuel, this was the Arnie, he said, who wanted to free dance and chore-ography from barriers of sex and race, and he'd managed just that in *A Survivor's Morning*, a fusion of various arts and boundaries, Arnie the scandal-rouser who had dared put on the stage bodies that no one wanted to see anymore and which were dangerously close to leaving for their ultimate destination, in Arnie's care they were rocked gently to sleep by other dancers and then embarked on a transition that seemed only too real and implicated the audience unabash-edly for the full three days, each man, woman, and child's last breath, whoever they were, whatever colour, all underwent a mortification that Arnie countered with a cadence that accom-panied their leaving, African sounds that contracted them for a last outburst of joy, where, wondered Daniel, was this friend Arnie now who loved and desired the very boundaries his dance sought to abolish, provocation in beauty reducing them to dust, oh so fragile all of a sudden, he said it himself, a leaf wafted out over the ocean where everything disappears, and all that returned for Daniel was that provocation in beauty, Arnie's outrageous beauty and the words that escaped from his dance, I'll go beyond what is forbidden he said in *A Survivor's Morning* as I stave off age with the shine of my teeth, charismatic dancer of the darkness, pushing back frontiers then doing away with them, disappearing with them, Arnie the excessive and exceptional friend no more, but recollected by Daniel as though he were right beside him, face and body challenging him, suddenly there, smiling with almost insulting irony, he'd say, listen Daniel, this is me, Arnie, how the hell did you get through all those New York escapades so unscathed when I couldn't make it, it's like you once said, black artists and sports figures don't live long, must be the burden of our ancestors wearing thin the thread of our lives, then *pop* it's gone, sure I tempted fate by reaching too far and doing too much so the heart and nerves got torn, I wasn't only a dance genius to them, I was also Snow Queen of the sauna dance, and critics said I shamelessly encouraged the culture of Me, why not, this whole era is narcissistic anyway, but you were going to learn wisdom and moderation with a wife and children, weren't you, whilst I was like an animal with its throat cut, I fell into a black hole before I turned thirty, there, hear that saxophone and alto voice, they were for my choreography, a pas de deux, because of my excesses they wanted me to fail, fade away, but there I was like a dancing flame consumed by its own heat, then one day your son Samuel showed up saying you and I were like brothers, one damned for his commitment, and you my brother, on the straight and narrow, the clear path, which of us was right, neither one maybe, both of us driven by higher powers that would not brook our best and least selfish hopes, what do you think? Life's a mix, we get tossed into it and spun around hopelessly with an obsession that takes us to where I am now, and when

I think of your son and you, I dream of a world maybe where everything's comfy, yes ecological and comfortable, go my friend, follow that dream of yours whilst I go down with Nijinsky, dancing beneath the waves of that ocean you see through this airport window, adieu my friend, a voice insinuated itself into Daniel's deepest reflections, it was Laure saying are you okay, you sure nothing's wrong, no nothing Daniel said, I was just thinking about my daughter, what a pity if I don't get to see her photo exhibit at college, yes that would be a shame she murmured, but they've just announced we'll be flying soon, though they didn't say when, Laure replied, they really don't give a damn about us, do they, smoker, non-smoker, whatever, there's also a friend I was thinking about, Daniel said, I guess we've got too much time on our hands, we start thinking about lost friends, though the last part he kept to himself, unheard by Laure as her trembling fingers fumbled in her purse for cigarettes, even if she wasn't allowed to smoke it was still comforting to touch the coloured packet longingly and know it was still there, yearning for the smell and taste of every one she'd smoke by the hotel pool tonight once her life was back on track and her vacation had finally begun, too bad this guy Daniel, kind of nice, was so wrapped up in himself, she'd've liked to chat with him a bit, that's what the married ones are like she thought, so content with their lives, yeah a chat would be nice, but only with cigarette in hand or hanging from her lips, otherwise there was no point talking to anyone. I really don't want to sleep in the shelter tonight, Kim thought as she languidly tapped the drum with her sticks, her laid-back manner was bound to irritate Fleur as he played flute for the passersby who stopped to listen for a while then drop some coins at his feet, but the way he played, Kim thought, it was like he saw them through a mist, or maybe not at all because his eyes were closed, the shelter, that was for widows, loafers, nagging wives, old folks, or mothers with babies and no place to sleep, they lie around town in filthy sweaty swimsuits all day, or when they're cleaned up they'll steal my stuff and sell it for crack or beer, they get chased out of everywhere, specially the tourist spots, and they're always tailing me asking for something, hey kid you got a sweater I can wear tonight, anything, yeah I know it's supposed to be curfew for women, otherwise no supper and no bed, they close the doors and only keep the homeless mothers with babies, and if they leave the shelter the social worker takes away their kids, so either that or they're always there with their snotty kids crying day and night, they're not as bad as the ones that steal and chisel from you, in fact some of them are good mothers, but they're out of work and homeless till maybe someone finds them a job one day, and if I lend my sweater to one of those widows, thieves or light-fingers, even an old one, you know I'll never get it back, Kim thought, suppose I get some sandwiches out of the garbage, they'll steal them too, gotta keep an eye on them, chase them down, they're always alone with no dog and out after shelter curfew, no alcohol inside, they keep a strict watch, drugs too, if they're out late it's often so they don't smell of booze and they'll just go on thieving all night instead, lifting what they can, money, coke, anything, bitches, old women with no pride at all, they scare me, broken-down sneaks, they're sick-ening, no way I'll end up like them, no uh-uh, me and Fleur we'll get a house and never ever be back on the streets, all clean and well dressed, hey there's a hen calling her chicks, now where is she, oh hey up in the tree again, clucking away so high up her chicks will never get to her no matter how much racket she makes, it goes on and on and drives me crazy, 'cause I'm so hungry but I don't want to go to the shel-ter with all those swollen-faced old women, slick thieves, they oughta go sleep in jail, they often do, better than the street they say, three squares a day, a place to sleep, not out on the street, nope, they give you clothes in there, shower every day, you get to learn stuff too if you want, not like the street they say, slimy robbers, I can't stand them, old and ugly, hey kid, they say, in jail they respect us, treat us good, not like you and your delinquent friends, rainbow punks, all you do is look down on us, go on admit it girl, that's how it is, and let me tell you it ain't Christian what you're doing, hating us like that, not Christian at all, why even in jail we old women, the oldest most worn down before our time, even we get respect, sure we do, so why don't they get organized the way the men do, they're often more disciplined, get together for meals around tables in the parks under the palms by the sea, they grumble together, share bread, but they don't stand apart the way women do, bunch of hypocrites and robbers who've hit rock bottom, some bums look like monks, meditative, living in harmony with nature and all, but not those bitches, no, they don't get along with anything or anyone, just too crude, too low down to see, yeah they scare me, living in harmony with nature's what I need most, when it's this nice out that your heart could near burst with delight, the peaceful hoboes are just sitting there peacefully at the platform or table, they seem like they've been blessed, that's how free they feel, nothing to worry about but look out at the Atlantic, hundreds of birds on the beach, pelicans shaking their wings before they take off sliding over the waves, Fleur has a platform all to himself, and he doesn't want me following him but I do, I go up the steps behind him so close to the sea, and he works, he composes his music, that's what he always says, he wants to be alone, no Kim to bother him, oh he may talk rough to me, maybe even angry, but the wind just carries it away so I don't hear, all that comes to me are the waves and the birds, turtle-doves, gulls, doves, so beautiful, everything just so, as it should be, but Fleur stays hidden under his hood and goes on writing, he doesn't want me there, but I just lie down on the bench so he doesn't notice me, I don't think I have parents or anything anymore, I don't know what happened to them, Fleur is all I have, maybe they're off drifting somewhere, they must have given up their kids to the authorities who massacred them the way they tried to massacre me till I ran away, all I've got are Fleur and Brilliant and Jérôme the African, the ones I see every day on the street or on the jetty where the boats lie with sails all folded up, and empty chairs for swimmers and beach-walkers, Fleur says he writes some holiday nights and there's a jazz band on one of the nearby platforms, when he finally breaks down and talks to me, Fleur says all these spaces should be filled with music, this is where I first heard Benjamin Britten's *War Requiem*, some old conductor with crazy hair, yeah, that's what they need on all these platforms by the sea, so they know music is for everyone, it was a requiem for the people who are really down-and-out like us, that was back when he still spoke to me kindly, he didn't chew me out so much, it was real nice then and your heart would near burst with delight, then he looked out for me and the light-fingers and nasties and broken-down women stopped trying to rob me, they left my stuff alone. Daniel looked out at the sea, the calm, almost silent sea, and thought if the critic Adrien, a friend of his father's, were to pan his book *Strange Years* now it would have to be from sheer contrariness, it was a first novel by a young and inexperienced writer he'd be putting down, sure thought Daniel, Adrien's as sharp a critic as he always was, thinking Daniel had written it after a line of coke, that must account for how slow it was, elastic and apparently not knowing how to stop, not Adrien's exact words, of course, for the book's soporific and numbing effect on the reader, the events in play were troubling enough, Daniel hadn't actually lived them but had found out about them in his drug addiction, maybe that route to revelation via cocaine was not for an old man like Adrien, as caustic as ever, but now perhaps vulnerable and capable of being seduced by a devious young woman like Charly, and who knows, despite his acerbic leanings Adrien could have been partly right, without the solace of cocaine Daniel might not have been able to unleash those images of the past that everyone kept from him, his parents especially had always led him to feel he was born into a fairy tale wherein flipping back through the pages to the past revealed a horror story, and drugs had helped him see every bit, all of the hidden truths buried deep in time, cousins in Poland who hadn't managed to flee Lukow in Lublin, among them the uncle shot in the snow that winter of 1942, whose name was borne by Daniel's own son, Great-Uncle Samuel prostrate with all the other rabbis, here and there a hand raised to beg in vain, kneeling in the snow before their murderers and the final surrender, how many times Daniel would see them in his mind's eye, aligned and kneeling incapable of flight, Daniel, with the restraint that happens between friends, had never shared his burden with Arnie, who had nevertheless guessed it and treated him like a treasured brother of his own choosing, respecting the crushing unspoken weight he bore, a weight that seemed to have spared most of his and Mélanie's children and fallen only on Augustino as a heritage, thus tormenting him as well, as appeared in every book his son ever wrote, and in words his father might have used with the same precision in his first book *Letter to Young People Without a Future*, in his last second of life what did the Angel of Death, as they called him, feel, his real name forgotten at Auschwitz where he treated and dissected thousands of shattered bodies, thus wrote Augustino, what did he feel believing himself immune to all judgement for so many years, when his heart stopped in a private pool or a river where he practised the breaststroke daily, was he reliving all of it in that petrifying instant as though back in his abject lab in Auschwitz while the water turned the colour of his murders, why do this, why kick and thrust alternately with legs and arms amid this surfacing wreckage of bloody victims that threatened to bury him then and there in the filthy water, as his own inquisition settled in around him, this calculating and demonic creature thought there might still be a way out, he could escape them all, all he had to do was stop his heart from beating and they were all foiled one more time, he felt the splitting in his chest like a tree felled from inside and thought of escape yet again as barely audible voices called him towards the bottom, the tortured cries of women and children he had erased from memory, Doctor, Doctor Death, have pity, have pity on us for we are here though you swim away. That's it, Kim thought, I'll be seeing Bryan tonight, he'll come up to me with the usual hop in his step, holding a cardboard box with our supper in it, another freebie from the Café Español he'll say, it's for our midnight supper on the beach, really good too, freshly caught fish with veg, and he'll tell me all over again the story of his victory over people from seven countries in the marathon last year, he tells it a lot, South Africa, Germany, France, Canada, everywhere, he'll say, they started at dawn in the first shivers of sunrise over the ocean, one was a four-legged runner and no it wasn't Misha, he was still getting over his injuries, he used to love running with us before the Second and Third Great Devastations, this time it was Holé, they wanted to give him a first-place medal, nope, Holé was the only dog signed up, instead of Misha who was at the vet's and didn't know his master anymore, yes they eat together on the beach in the sound of the waves and free of persecution, this box lunch wasn't stolen, it was a gift as Bryan would say, and if it was Sunday, Fleur would put aside his flute and listen to the hymns sung by a baritone in the Episcopalian church, along with the midday bells when all was calm and quiet with only the music from temples and churches till noon and a piano echoed and drowned out the baritone hymn-singer, I wanted to ask Fleur during that peaceful oasis in the town what's going to become of the two of us Fleur, you and me, can you tell me, but he would've just turned away and grumbled you and your questions, if you want to know the future why not get Rafael Sánchez, the Mexican, to read the tarot for you, don't ask me

Kim 'cause I don't think we have a future the two of us, as my mother Martha would say, it's too late, way too late, our stars aren't aligned, then I'd be so sad and lonely in that silence, the bells and the baritone gone quiet in the noonday streets, it was times like that I'd think Fleur's in love with someone else, not me, even if he hasn't said it or in a way he has, I know who it is, Clara the musician, not me. There would be posters all over town thought Fleur, the Master Concert, winner of the Moscow International Prize, Clara would be the guest of honour in all the concert halls, and in the picture her face would be inclined towards her violin, "Hear the masterful violinist play works by Haydn and Liszt," and my heart would beat to bursting at catching up with her again, but what would she say when she saw me with no shoes and my hair a mess, would her agent or the conductor say it's Garçon Fleur, once as much a prodigy as our virtuoso Clara, she was the one who made it through, look how sweet her face is when she's playing the violin, transported by ecstatic gentleness, there isn't a concert hall that won't be at her feet, rigid rules, parents and teachers have wrought her youth to perfection with ruthless discipline, never letting go or having fun like other children her age, as sure as raps across the knuckles if she let her bow drift, back straight as a steel rod, but Fleur, well, no discipline at all there, just sliding down and down, knowing nothing at all about Haydn or Liszt, what was it his mother Martha said, she'd never let her son be treated like that, stiff, rough discipline, what, for music, never, she loved her son too much for that, though his father and grandfather said such a phenomenally gifted child was not his family's property, he should be allowed to go and fulfill his destiny, not be snatched away by motherly love, awakened to the blinding truth that Fleur must not belong to any one person but only to music, they begged her to let him leave the island and study far away so he could truly blossom on his own, but she clutched him to her and maintained her domination until the day he found Clara again, and when he saw her posters on the walls around town, her head bowed towards her violin, near once again, then oh yes then he'd enter his *New Symphony* in the Young Composers' Competition, oh yes he thought, the time would come when he was no longer the fallen man, a poor begging street musician. No, Tammy told her brother, oh no, you're not going out in black leather pants, shiny black shoes and beaded white gloves, no way you're going out like that, it's exam time and you're not going into Trinity College dressed like that Mick, uh-uh, why don't you just go listen to music in your room, you're not going anywhere on an exam day, it's nighttime for you she told him, the coolest look, the hottest dance steps, black hat pulled down low over black glasses, Mick checked it all out in the mirror in his room, nice eh, outrageous look, yeah Tammy said, but Trinity College is a conservative school, besides if Mama knew she'd never let you out, yeah but she isn't is she, today's her creative writing class and she won't be back till this evening, anyway I'm not scared of her, you're getting thin though, you've got to eat more Tammy, that's how they both get to push you around, you're too weak, they feel ashamed of having a feeble-looking kid in the house so they pay tons of money to those clinics, you're almost eighteen, we ought to run away, get yourself some lipstick and mascara, you just don't get what it is to be young and male and wanting to be on the magazine covers, I'm gonna make it, you'll see, I may not be that good-looking but I've got a wild imagination, and I'm gonna use my inspiration and uniqueness to go wherever they take me, are you on something, Tammy asked, putting her arms around his waist and holding him tight, it feels like you are, maybe you better not go to college for the exams today, they'll spot your weird behaviour straight off, they know about it, same as our parents, only they pretend they don't, if you want to go out, do it tonight, wait till dark, the uptight kids'll spot you for sure and they've got no use for you, well they'll see me and that'll be that, you think I'm afraid of them, Mick replied, they tried chasing me but I'm too fast for them, they're all a bunch of crude loudmouths, yeah the coolest look, the hottest dance moves, Mr. Sexy straight out of a magazine, you'll see, but Tammy was thinking about how little she heard from Mai on her cellphone now she was off at college, things like come back to us Tammy, please, back to earth Tammy, I haven't forgotten you, I'll see you soon, at Christmas vacation, oh it's exciting, so much going on, what a life when there's such a lot to do, my parents keep telling me to forget about Manuel and to stick to my courses, can't wait to see you Tammy of mine, but there's no way I can forget Manuel, he was my friend, for so many months Mai hadn't sent her a word from out there, nothing, it was a silence that left her hanging, where was she and what was she doing, Tammy wondered, she always had a lot going on in her life and here was Tammy with nothing, Mai was sociable, loved and admired by everyone, but Tammy was alone all because she was dumb and skinny as Mick would say, how stupid to get this thin on purpose, anyway he was off to Trinity College for his exams all tricked out like that, probably a bit high too, as usual, if he wasn't he'd certainly had a little something, thought Tammy, who could his pusher be now with Manuel's dad in jail, he hadn't known anyone else and it seemed pretty safe in Manuel's house, either that or the beach when they had their midnight dips, the doors were all padlocked now, same as the discos he owned in Lebanon, he'd stayed in many cities with his young son, taking care of his various businesses as he called them, all that and it still seemed like they were completely safe, no one watching us at night under the moon with only the waves to know, thought Tammy, yet all that time they were on our trail, outside the garden gates, people listening to us even when we went for a swim, always against us and thinking bad things, funny that Mick kept it up all the same, he wasn't worried about the eyes beyond the garden gate peeking into everything, even spying on our conversations and our games when we thought we were safe, that's how good we felt, fearless Mick my brother, did you forget that terrible story about Phoebe, she would say, kind of a new parable for all the teens bullied in school, she was just as carefree as you, charming too, and all the boys liked her, and the girls were jealous of the little Irish girl freshly arrived in the school and the neighbourhood, soon she made friends with a football player and the other girls were jealous and mean, so they started harassing her and being nasty, in the bookstore, everywhere she went, and they drew an X over her picture on the wall at school as well as bullying her on Facebook, then one day on the way back from school they threw a soft drink in her face and yelled Irish hooker, here take that, and they laughed at what they'd done, Phoebe's mother complained to the school and asked how many months this was supposed to go on, but they paid no attention, then guess what happened Mick, well, they went on that way for months, mean and jeering, yelling foreign Phoebe go back to Ireland, we don't want you here, Irish whore, you're here to steal our football players, go back where you came from, then after school one day the beautiful and proud Phoebe felt so put down and desperate that she hanged herself with the scarf her sister had given her for Christmas, hanged herself under the stairs to the bedroom they shared, same as you and me Mick, we share everything, so do you want me to see you bullied and persecuted, is that what you want Mick, she said to him, and Mick thought about his Prince, his brother from Neverland, where elephants and lions now wandered aimlessly in their Neverland limbo surrounded by kids every bit as bewildered as they are now the Prince has gone, the Prince, Mick's true brother and his father too, his real one, not this historian who never wrote about the present, Mick didn't want him and his out-of-date books on dusty revolutions in dusty centuries past, a great way to avoid what was going on in the real world, revolutions that would last, the less obvious but more passionate revolutions were being carried out by kids and their computers, not barricades thought Mick, my father doesn't get that it's about reforms without arms or agitators based on the art of a new way of living, outside their degeneracy, that's what the Prince had carried out on his Neverland ranch and around the globe, and now three elephants, tigers, and monkeys wandered disconsolate and abandoned in their jungle sanctuary, where was he now, the Prince of black outfits, at sundown you could hear him still being interviewed and telling the journalists, it's surprising but I'm one of the loneliest men on the planet, that's right lonely, the thought of it saddens me to tears, but look how beautiful my kids are, and I tell them you don't need to sing or dance, just be who you want to be but don't hurt anyone, then we all laugh, really, every day, oh they know I'm a per-fectionist and all I want is to throw open the doors to freedom, sure a pioneer and a perfectionist, opening doors can be a painful thing, still that's what he said, thought Mick, he gave everyone escape through the miracle of music, great music for all, the way he sang it in "Earth Song" — Mick listened to it over and over, suddenly throwing his arms wide the way it happened in the video, like embracing the whole Earth, then he held that position looking at Tammy, suddenly he said remember the Prince playing to an empty hall, totally empty and bathed in red light, and he sang "You Are Not Alone" as though he were everyone's brother or father, talking just to us, the children of a new planet, no you'll never be alone, remember Tammy, but all she said was I'd rather you didn't go to college today, skip the exam. I'll be right there behind the desk conducting, or a composer or a pianist, thought Fleur backed by the bells and the approaching sunset over the sea, I'd always be writing some new orchestral piece, and overseas travel is useful but exhausting, I wonder if I'd have the stam-ina for it, rehearsals, concerts, reaching the right public while

I'm still young, maybe tomorrow I'd be off to do some concerts in England, perhaps even meet Clara, some musicians do it all, conduct, compose, and I'd be one of them, with Clara by my side whenever possible, at first of course I'd be a pianist, but one with a delicate balance of virtuosity in other instruments, and instead of playing in the street or only when my mother takes a fancy, on the wharves and pub terraces for sailors and sailboat captains, I might have learned to conduct symphonic youth orchestras, conducting my music, my own music, along with other young composers, and we'd be feted all over the world and I'd get commissions the way Clara does, one day in Paris, the next in London, and we'd be married, so in the evening I'd go and get the kids from school, our kids, like that old composer with the wild hair on the platform by the sea with his Britten and Stravinsky, yes, I'd have my own requiem or my own sombre *New Symphony* on the stage by the sea, powerful voices for the resurrection, yes, a rising tide of voices, and what a worthy life I'd be living, my commissions would earn lots of money and eventually I could afford a synthesizer and a computer so I could write in a cabin all night long, Damien would always be there with me of course, *The Opera of Extinction*, that's what it would be with the very last sounds of the very last moments, I'd write it all, I am now as we hear the bells of the town, and Kim says she's hungry but what's she going to eat tonight, she says we have to get up at dawn tomorrow to clean the Old Salt's boat, the two of us, that's right the Old Salt, not a tooth left in his head, you and me, you remember him don't you Fleur, we do it for him every Saturday, I go right on pretending I can't hear Kim, hey anyways he'll give us a bike, Kim went on, a bit roughed up just like him with his black nails and no teeth, but it'll be good, a bike, hey we could go all over like Jérôme the African, but he never goes anywhere, just leans on his bike and lounges around the waterfront selling necklaces, no, he's meditating on the sea, Kim said, sells crack too, said Fleur in frosty bad temper, the whole day gawping out to sea, and he thought to himself this break is about over, now to pick up the flute even with sweat scalding his temples under that hood of his, Tammy turned to her brother and said, since Manuel's dad got arrested I've been thinking a whole lot, it's like that night was just bound to happen Mick, as usual when he was high he wasn't listening though, it was like everything fell all to pieces, that's what Mai said when I was dragging along behind as she skated along in the fog, it truly was a night that was waiting to happen, that's when I realized his dad never should have sold us those drugs, I wasn't ready for everything to come crashing down all at once like that, since they busted him I've been doing a lot of thinking, and when your life falls apart like that you can't get it back, hey Mick, are you even listening to me, nah you can always get over it Mick replied, if you eat normally that is, and do karate exercises and swim in the ocean all the time, when you're a young rockin' male like me, you can get past anything, even having deadbeat parents like ours, we decide what happens to us right from birth, for real Tammy, I mean our ancestors did, didn't they, what about the Prince, emerging from that mess of his own burning hair when they made that commercial in Los Angeles, pale face rising out of the flames, and what about that other star, the rock guitar player, staring down arrogantly from his easy chair, suede boots rolled up over his jeans, leaning back and volunteering nothing, like a devil of chaos being interviewed, and that cigarette hanging lazily from his dangled hand, Keith Richards might as well have said so you think I'm going to tell you my life story, the orgies and sexual games, yeah right, keep guessing, look I'm being honest, it would be lies anyway, I was a good soprano as a kid, I even sang for the Queen — like that, go ahead and believe it, right and everything after that would be lies too, lies like truth or truth like lies, half-assed, I really did love animals always, that you can believe, read the book, that's where I spit it out, anything that claims to be sincere isn't, I've always done things that way, never listened to anybody, not even friends who were like brothers to me, you know those scruffy faces from shady underground nights stoned and drunk in the wee hours on LSD, cocaine, heroin presided over by God himself, excess that's what gets me going, sure I did it all, and nothing ever really did anything for me the day I took a tumble, fell right out of a tree all covered in flowers, I'm surprised I'm still alive, Fiji it was, right out of a palm tree, okay so maybe that visit from the great god LSD and heroin was a little too close that time, I was just a guy that loved his addictions, always had to have more, I'd have a needle, you know a syringe, hidden in the folds of my hat and coke in my pockets, and I'd halluci-nate listening to the Ella Fitzgerald songs my mother used to sing, she still does he used to listen to Ella said Tammy's brother dancing on black patent-leather tiptoes, see that, Keith could get over a fall out of a palm tree, the other one was called Mick like me, scruffy, scuffed up, and stoned as him, and they made the Rolling Stones, see they made it Tammy, same as all the others before, you can get through anything said Mick tiptoeing in his shiny leather shoes. Still nothing on the flights, Laure said standing next to Daniel at the window facing out onto the shining sea, no telling how long we're going to be stuck in this departure lounge, god I hate this, I haven't had a smoke since this morning but it seems like days, she was getting frantic now, boy they just love putting the screws to us smokers and it keeps getting worse, you watch, one day they'll just kick us out of society altogether, arrest us for smoking on the street even, I'm not being paranoid either Daniel, believe me, too much, it's all too much, she was beginning to stammer now, and as though wanting to be par-doned for his preoccupation, he gave her a sympathetic look and said, you're right, I feel really bad for you, when in fact, seeing the plover scratching at the white sand with its feet, he'd been increasingly absorbed in thoughts not only about being the father of four children but also the fact that his grandson Rudolf would soon be six, he should be hearing the bells chiming, the clock measuring out the shrinking time for exaltation that still remained to him, or else give in and say it's late, time to go and sleep the guilty sleep of maturity, rest his dwindling strength — was it complacency, a habit that he and Mélanie both found deplorable, she who shared her husband's robust and active exuberance — no, this didn't seem real to them, nor had they ever been so much in love, surely part of the charm of being apart so often, yet as Mélanie became more radiant and youthful in the joy of her grandson and the pride of being a leader and fighter among women, Daniel took umbrage at it, ah the vanity of man, he thought, a grandson almost six years old while his own four skipped into adulthood together, that was already a lot, but a grandson who'd already learned to walk and talk like a grownup, already showing signs of independence, that truly consigned the bohemian daddy he used to be to the past, no longer what they called a young author and father surrounded by a cohort of youngsters as he wrote and read, the word *youth* that had clung to him would have to be peeled off, Mélanie though managed to keep hers with the arrival of Rudolf, Daniel was already two generations a father, God, Daniel had got here in so few years and now he'd have to ponder the unthinkable, that word he refused to say, soon it won't simply be maturity but old age, a grandfather's a man preparing to be old, waking up one day with a hundred wrinkles on his face, losing all his hair, as if robbed of his youthful looks by his children, now that was a sad thought, it seemed like only yesterday that Samuel was stroking the head of the infant hanging in front of him with little wool-clad legs sticking tenderly out of his baby carrier, he told Laure it was so touching, and he couldn't see a baby in its father's arms without wanting to go over and stroke its head and newborn hair, Laure was definitely not in the mood though, she grumpily rejoiced at the fact there was no such thing nearby, boy this one sure was sentimental, how could he go on about babies and newborns when she was miserable without her smokes, really miserable after all these hours of waiting, didn't he understand it was like losing a lover? What you need, Robbie told Petites Cendres, is a nice sprinkling of orchids and hibiscus in your hair, 'cause there's no way I'm combing that thick mess on your head, I need you looking good for my coronation tonight, well, at least we've finally got you dressed, look Robbie, said Petites Cendres, sitting on the bed in his shift and brushing with his lips the scorpion tattoo on his friend's shoulder, nope, uh-uh, no more going out at night for me, and as he said this Petites Cendres breathed in the enchanting perfumes of those January nights when the girls were showered with chilly-smelling artificial snow as they paraded out into the street in their fake furs a little before the last show, when the yellow chandelier shone at the foot of the wooden staircase in the Cabaret, Robbie's femininity didn't need enhancement though, splendid peasant that he was, and as he shifted to and fro to keep warm, his rubber breasts bobbed beneath the velvet neckline, which drew stares from everyone, he was also the one that women most liked to photograph, tall Cobra standing next to him sometimes and the two of them wafting out into the night that special brilliance and fragrant perfume of bodies ready to party, all this went through Petites Cendres' mind as Robbie reminded him of the sprinkling of flowers and grabbed his hair, which caused petals to fall from his own hair and stick to his friend's face, so bracing those January nights, as flow-ered and perfumed as they were glacial when Yinn suddenly appeared at midnight in a dark blue coat the colour of night sky, long enough to mask his legs right down to the high heels if he hadn't allowed for fine slits to reveal his sensuous thighs and penis under a black bikini, this of course was the hour when Petites Cendres would slide over to the red sofa hoping no one would notice him in the dark, the cloaked

Yinn certainly didn't, never thinking there was a silent observer in his presence, or if he did, then paying no heed, sweeping past in his vast coat, Yinn was too busy giving orders to the girls for the next show in that very authoritative masculine Artistic Director's voice, the panels of synthetic blue fur swept over Petites Cendres' knees and feet as he crouched there on the sofa, more like blows to him than caresses, as though in sweeping by in that sumptuous coat with such perfect indifference each time, Yinn were repeating over and over, you know, Petites Cendres, I don't even see you, that's right, to me you're invisible, I don't have time to care whether you're here or not, I have work to do, you know, work that Petites Cendres knew meant being the commander, the boss of the night ahead of them, hence impatient and driven by rigid fervour for theatrical perfection, dancers, singers, none of which the indolent Petites Cendres was part of, no, hoping in vain to cling to life and find a john, or else hoping nothing anymore after all these days of waiting for his cursed powder to bring him back to life, but no one was offering any, meanwhile all around couples abounded, sometimes three at the bar, kissing in sweet intoxication, young men starting out together, a symbiosis of three or four faces together he thought, whatever the range of colour, rose pink to flat black, but all with the same length of hair, the same little goatee around the lips, the same almond-shaped eyes beneath a large forehead frowning as though it were cold, same hats, yes, symbiosis like faces arranged for an icon, thus isolating Petites Cendres even more, these young energetic and polite people in threes or fours, all of them the picture of health, made him fade into the background as much as the sweeping panels of Yinn's coat, so little did he resemble them, Yinn like Petites Cendres belonged to nothing and to no one, and here he was tonight, despite the fragrances borne to him on the cool winter air and the bodies celebrating out in the street, he was but a shadow lurking behind and thinking of all this, of those January nights and the sweep of Yinn's coat, Petites Cendres said again to Robbie, nope, I'm never going back, ever, nightlife isn't for me, knowing how much he lied and how little Robbie believed him, still powdering his hair with bits of orchid, there, Robbie said patting his cheeks, it's nearly party time. Kim watched Jérôme the African prop his bicycle heavily loaded with water bottles and rags against the sidewalk, and he came towards her, taking away her drum, here you don't know how to play that thing, he said as he took the drumsticks too and started playing so hard that even with the street noise and five-o'clock traffic Fleur went and sat with his dog by the wall, that's what was weird about Jérôme the African, he was always stoned, and he smelt like a male beast who slept in parks, way less hygienic than being by the sea and showers Fleur didn't tell Jérôme the African this was his special spot, thinking how hungry he was and wondering if Kim had brought him some dinner from Brilliant, then he wouldn't have to go and see his mother for a few more days, he thought of hunger as an insect that chewed away at his stomach and his liver, the way music devoured his soul, so he was never at peace for a moment, and he was sleeping with his hood up when the howling voice of Jérôme the African woke him, saying or chanting or humming or howling who-knows-what and pounding his fist into the drum, in Côte d'Ivoire he said, I've seen rape and pillage and child-soldiers reared for killing, they got me too and I sang long live the fighters and militias, complete free-dom to recruiters, oh we got drunk so we could pillage and massacre and rape and murder, long life and freedom to the unpunished ones who round up kids to fight, no they'll never be put on trial, no International Criminal Court for them, nos-sir, they'll just go right on getting more seven- and eight-year-olds to kill and vandalize, long life and freedom to those who shanghai for rape and murder, they will go free and unpun-ished forever these kings of hell, so sang Jérôme the African and howl as he might he was barely audible above the

strident noise of sirens and the street, thought Fleur, piercing
sounds, the gut-wrenching cries of Jérôme the African, still
soon maybe they'd hear the song of the grasshoppers and
this, this would be what Fleur, with his ears buzzing, would
write into his *New Symphony* or *Opera of Extinction*, of course,
oh but how good it would be to sleep he thought as he curled
up with his dog, just go to sleep in Damien's warmth. And
what have I got to offer my grandson Rudolf, thought Daniel,
what feast does life hold in store for him when he's already
got everything, when so many others born into the same times
haven't survived abandonment, starvation, want, and any
number of conflagrations, was there any way at all that Rudolf
had not been spoiled from birth, for love of one's child has
now become love of oneself, an unconscious form of narcissism that is part of being a select social class and parentage
with its own special laws and privileges, from a baby's first
smile we know that admiring attachment to ourselves, or
maybe it's a mark of our morbid astonishment at being able
to survive in such a fragile world, some of us born dying and
others living long and comfortable lives, of course Rudolf
would be one of those, though Samuel had never felt a strong
paternal drive in him, more taken up with his art as a dancer
and choreographer, in fact he reproached himself with being
a bumbling father, not maternal like his own, though Mélanie
was an exquisite mother, nevertheless Daniel was the maternal figure in their home, he loved playing with them, always
kissing and cajoling them and fetching them from school in
his Jeep, it was as though all Mélanie's mothering was lav-
ished on her one daughter Mai, and for the others she was a
militant first and a mother second, raising awareness was her
preoccupation thought Daniel, and now poor clumsy Samuel
had almost drowned the infant trying to teach him to swim in
the family pool too soon, hmmm, a floating cradle bobbed on
the green-tinted water as the tiny hands and feet shivered and
stretched out towards the night as though already expressing

Rudolf's fearlessness, not the rippling water or the night or the song of the toads disturbed him, already a small man, thought Daniel, and in mere months would he even be needing any of us, such concentration of power and such an anarchic and scattershot will to live even when he was nursing, as if to say mine, everything is mine, such was the unfairness of it all, Rudolf was born for abundance and joy in living, Augustino was right when he ironically teased his innocent father as he often did, wait and see Papa, you'll do just as you did with my brothers and Mai, you'll tell Rudy to look around at all the beauty in the world before the bestial manipulators and dictators ruin it, you'll take him out to the archipelago same as us and say, look at those large birds with pink wings and hooked beaks, pink flamingos filtering the muddy lake and pond water through those beaks, and best of all, look at how they fly, even and majestic, then there's the iridescent bee digging its nest in the plant they call black root and of course the crocodile jaws, open and showing a thousand teeth out in an Everglades park, the grey-white eaglet that sometimes perches on garden fences, the scarlet hibiscus in bloom, not to mention all those birds that come to share our picnic on the table at noon, and the golden butterfly with them but not going far against the wind that forces its wings apart, then Rudy will ask how you did it said Augustino, why did the wind break its wings, and you'll say well the storm winds were so strong that the butterfly had to stop flying, like when it's too cold for them, they're not used to it around here, that's when iguanas die in the gardens, it's too chilly for them to survive, it's brutal, so we find them lying there in the garden in January, then Rudy'll say the same way I did, oh c'mon, tell me the truth now, you mean they're dead don't you, and when I felt disappointed you used to say the golden butterfly, like the iguanas, can't survive extreme temperatures or abnormalities that come about because of a distorted climate, that was how you dealt with everything, though you always prefaced it with words like *before the world falls apart or finishes falling apart, take a look at the beauty all around,* and on about the pink flamingos level and majestic in flight, you'd say we are near the end of the world Papa, and that's what you'll say to Rudy, that we're the golden butterflies and iguanas devastated generation upon generation by the glacial cold, there is little to look forward to, at this Daniel would take his own defence against his irascible son Augustino who always caught him off guard as unpredictably as he dressed, jeans worn through at the knee, hair standing upright, no Augustino came the answer, I don't share your dark pessimism, I'm not just going to tell nice fairy stories to Rudolf, I'll tell him about a world whose beauty is still very resilient, yes that's it, he said to his son Augustino, realizing he didn't know him well at all, perhaps he was totally unfamiliar with the anxiety that lay deep in his son, mysterious and so quick to flare into outrage, was it because he, along with his mother, had been the most afflicted by the death of his grandmother, never, never did he say the name Mère or Esther, to do so would have meant betraying the immense sadness he felt, like Mélanie, he'd learned to hold it in, though in quiet moments on his brief trips home when he thought no one noticed, it was as though his eyes were filled with tears thought Daniel, did he feel the consoling hand on his shoulder as he fled towards the beach abandoned by night or went out running till dawn then threw himself down on his solitary bed? It was Saturday and the Old Salt told Kim, that kid who's always with you, what's-his-name, Fleur, he's a dreamer that one, doesn't know how to dock a boat or swab it, poor girl you wear yourself out dealing with the lines all alone and what does he do with his life anyway, he can't even use a water bucket, he doesn't want to get his hands dirty, Kim said he's a musician, well then let him wear gloves the way I do answered the Old Salt from a mouth unencumbered by teeth, hey now why doesn't he get up and out of the cabin and help you clean up girl, a bright blue sky like this is meant for being outside and breathing the wind, an easterly wind and I bet you my heron will come and land right on my gangplank at one o'clock, always does, we chat for a while and he takes off again, flies right out over the blue waves, he's a sailor too you know, but he prefers a good clean hull, likes it when everything on my boat's shiny, and what about you girl, do all those guys treat you with respect, Fleur and them, oh I wouldn't want to have a girl, boys is all I've got, long time since I saw them, a girl's too much fuss, and when are those parents of yours getting out of jail, that's no place for them when they've got kids, that's not a life, gotta be pretty dumb acting that way, not thinking about them, 'course haven't seen mine either for centuries, the centuries pass by and so do we, sometimes you wonder if you ever really had them at all, all I could think of was being a sailor forever out on the water, know what I mean? And Kim said, junkies, that's all they were, they'd've sold us if they needed a fix, one day, let them rot, I never want to see them again, I can get on fine without them, sure we'd've been sold for a fix, they're no parents said the Old Salt, no way, no parent would do that, nope, human garbage is all they are, Kim felt debased all of a sudden because of her parents and asked him, is it true the grey heron comes to see you every day on the gangplank, you gotta be patient he replied, he'll come see us, he likes a good easterly wind, he's travelled far and wide over the seas like me, sometimes as far as Baie Saint-Louis if it's bad weather and his feathers are ruffled and his wings are dishevelled, but he'll come, I promise, soon as the wind changes he comes to warn me it's going to rain and storm real bad, maybe hurricanes from July to September, then he swoops down to the boat all atremble under the darkening sky and tells me to let my brother mariners know, tie up your boats or it'll be like 1909, I still remember that one, the wind actually took out a cigar factory one morning in October, 'course I wasn't there naturally — I may be old but I'm not that old — they told me the whole thing

and it still sends shivers up and down my spine, folks got up
in the morning and found nothing there, no factories, no
cigars, no fancy hotels, just wooden wreckage everywhere, all
that was left of their houses, hey what's up girl, why you so
sad, it's that boy isn't it, Fleur is what's bothering you, so why
isn't he here cleaning the boat with us, he can't she said, he's
inside writing his music, he mustn't get his hands dirty, musician's hands, that's all rot said the Old Salt, it's plain he's not
the boy for you, look okay you can have my bike seeing I
can't use it anymore, friends tell me I'm gonna bust my skull
if I try getting through these streets at night, specially after the
pub, well I mean a man's gotta have a little fun doesn't he,
what do you think girl, do I look as old as they say those other
sailors look, jealous I'd say, and Kim told him he wasn't a
hundred so he wasn't that old, his skin was just tanned by the
sun and his blue eyes had that washed-out look from staring
at the horizon, while she said this she was really thinking that
Fleur could never love her because he loved another, Fleur
inside the cabin young and handsome, such a loss, her own
hurricane of 1909, hey look, yelled the old man suddenly,
there he is, the grey heron's come to greet us, always on time,
he so loves that easterly wind, see he's ruffled and all over the
place but here he comes, specially for you, and there he was,
a huge outline against the blue, maybe the Old Salt was right,
who knows if he'd come back all this way for her, and she so
wanted to yell to Fleur, hey look at how wonderful everything
is today, balance and harmony, just look will you it was past
five now and Jérôme the African in his multicoloured hat
folded his shades and casually climbed on his bike with a
clink of water bottles in string bags, then took off to the
wharves to sell his necklaces, at least that's what he said, but
Kim figured it was more about coke, anyway off he went, but
not before spraying his face with water and laughing loudly
as though making fun of Kim and of Fleur who was now
packing his flute reluctantly, well actually come to think of it,

there was nothing and no one he didn't make fun of, and as she listened to his sharp footsteps on the pavement and his bike overloaded with rags and bottles, a languid clicking, the soundscape of their misery, Kim then realized it had been a long sad and painful day after all, with nothing but Fleur's music to alleviate the desolation, and tomorrow they'd be on board the Old Salt's boat again, forever on the sea and so close to the sky, maybe he was the father she never had, the right one for her, not some junkie, he was so hospitable to her, too bad he didn't like Fleur and figured he was lazy, she tried to explain it wasn't like that, he was unique, like no one on Earth, and even while he played on and on listlessly he knew he had to write that opera or the *New Symphony* or whatever weird mission he might conceive of, being a great-grandchild of Doctor Death, incapable of warding off that heritage, was it some sort of secret punishment to be part of a family that heralded in Age of Crime in which the science of a physician-poet suddenly made killing a perfectly normal part of life, a modern-day Prometheus, one that Fleur carried as part of his burden, Oppenheimer, writing and reciting the finest poems as the bomb was about to go off and sharing this ambiguity amid evil with Fleur, never hurting a fly but for this one poisonous idea, first and foremost the soul of innocence baptized in blood and in the name of science, a kind of cool delirium that chilled Fleur to the bone despite his hoodie, yes a Prometheus for these cursed times, stealing the gods' fire to consume cities and humans, like him Oppenheimer was also a well-meaning man of science with the delusion that he could create mortals not with clay but with a radioactive atom that would immortalize him, he however had no restraints imposed on his madness, not chained to a mountaintop or devoured by eagles, his chemical assemblage had gone unchecked, for it was not his alone, backed by the approval of his colleagues and all around him, this Prometheus of the nuclear age held in his feverish hands the plutonium pellet he would hurl into mythology, hallelujah, and life on Earth would be destroyed as surely as the project at Los Alamos succeeded, the bomb even had a cute little nickname, the Gadget, and when he went home to his wife at night they would discuss it, she being the only one perhaps to feel a gust of terror separating them, the plutonium ball, the Gadget, might part them forever like a veil even in their most intimate moments, so loving to his wife yet raised for life among men, this American Prometheus distressed his wife by yielding nothing to her feminine intuition or apprehension which alerted her to some monstrous but dimly perceived danger, but listening to her would mean giving up his mission and his duty lying right there before them in the magnificent landscape of Los Alamos soon to be irradiated with the very first bomb blasts later to be repeated in Japan, and what came after was precisely what Fleur would write, after the sin, almost his own, and perhaps it was that too, the *Opera of Extinction* or the *New Symphony* would be that rise of the last breath of ashen powder, then a hand lifts itself, flowers spring forth once more, the desert explodes in the rich colour of blood petals, and the tears of regret or remorse of the doctor of such promise would flow like a river of blood, no longer able to kiss his wife for fear of staining her face, no sooner washing his hands in the lab than seeing them stained with the deathly froth once more, consumed by the fire stolen from Heaven to vapourize humans, the dazzling man of science, still so young, will sleep no more, neither alone nor with his wife, and she tormented by the weight of his sin, no more sleep, indeed barely lying down only to hear there's the target, Hiroshima, straight on target, on target, don't be afraid, just the explosion of so many suns, the thudding rise of blinding suns, and that question too haunts him, those, those below this lightfall, what is to be done with them in this cloud of light, you can't see them can you Doctor, but it will happen, horrible and stupefying, unimaginable he thinks, then reassures himself that it's a rational scientific experiment and nothing more, but that's the confusion of insomnia talking, to seek ways of targeting the enemy and wiping him out, of course, a wartime exercise that's all, General Groves did say to aim at all, all, the toxic radioactive plutonium would spare no one, nothing, in other words the entire city, and one day history will salute me and I'll write a poem about how to face the desert alone, he thought of John Donne's sonnets, oh how he wishes he had written them, and even in the throes of troubled, uncontrollable insomnia, the poet's lines rock him gently, sometimes like a sleepwalker he approaches the room where his little girl sleeps, other little girls like her in the city of Hiroshima, yes there too are little girls like his, yet different, not the same race, no it's not the same, he must banish the thought, he heads back to his room, wraps his arms around his wife and goes back to sleep, or will he, will he forever be deprived of sleep, after the first explosions you will see nothing anymore, after the nebulous night of the atom, day will turn into night and you, like the heavens, will hear the tearing of stone, the voices of all the little girls in the skies, thousands of them, not unlike your own, crying Doctor Death, Doctor Death, don't you wish you hadn't Doctor Death, this Fleur's opera will allow us to hear, the stifled sobbing to Heaven of little girls hanging from the spattered trees, then the macabre voice of the orchestra in a desperate clamour welling up from the fissured earth, next in the distance a soprano female voice still crying desperately, no, don't do it, think of our daughter, you mustn't do it, but the clamour of comets reversing trajectories drowns out the frail voice which he would have rejected anyway, in love with his wife or not, reciting lofty spiritual poems for her to the end, sometimes accompanying her as though praying by her side, yet he knows he will not listen to her, will not give in to her charms or human pity, to nothing and to no one will he bend, from the first flames lighting up the sky over Alamogordo, New Mexico, that very first test against a stormy pink sky, the mantle of his divinity wrapped her tight in its grandeur, for surely his wife knew she had espoused a god, a god of radioactivity, and why this panic all around him with a sky of such vivid pink that one needed thick glasses for protection, what a pity for such a silent and beauteous night to be spoiled by a tempest so violent, by his wife's side later on he suddenly said yes, children, children hanging in the trees just carried away, a solitary three-legged dog cinder-blackened, limping and alone under a sky the colour of ink, was this an August day, he said, and what funeral-draped year beneath soot-bathed clouds was this, and these little girls, were they asleep or awake with their books ready for school, and how many of them were there Doctor Death, for our records you understand, but then perhaps I'd be better off losing all memory, without this atrocious burden of divinity conferred by a gift for science, will it eventually grind me down, and here, here the soprano voice would come in singing, sleep my love, you can sleep, yes sleep, for in this atrophied godliness a man would nevertheless be reborn from his own ashes thought Fleur, yes, a woman's voice, and then the orchestra, Kim remembered what the Old Salt had said, when men make wars, and I know a thing or two about that, the first to go are children and animals, oh you should have seen us, me and the others, exterminating first sharks, then whales in the Pacific, a shameful vision that stops me even now from fishing like the rest of them, my time, the criminal time, may be past but shame still wakes me at night, we lobbed grenades at them for fun, oh and I can't tell you everything we did girl, you're too young, you'd never understand why we did those things, then we moved on to children in their mothers' arms, but I'm not going into that, young as you are, you couldn't begin to plumb the depths of our villainy, and yet here I am out on the water begging forgiveness of the fish but surely not deserving of it, but that heron, he comes every day on the dot at one, and I know it's his way of saying all right, think of it no more, you are made as you are, then he'll open wide those wings and off he'll fly without another word, this is how it is when he comes to my gangplank each day, a wondrous good thing from Heaven, I truly believe it is a favour, said the Old Salt to Kim. The siren shrieks reached Kim and Fleur as two ambulances with their separate victims passed one another on opposite sides of the street, fun with coke, thought Fleur, boys and girls overdoing it and going under or almost, and now for the white sheet and a medic pressing down on their heart, saying breathe, breathe, it's oxygen, breathe, and wondering where they were headed, betrayed by some glitch in their circulation, irregular pulses at the temples syncopating with the rhythm of the metal buckets that Jérôme the African was playing on the sidewalk, long, hollow sounds, come on breathe, and Jérôme responded with feet and hands within earshot of the patient laid out on the gurney, yet somehow Fleur felt more in tune with that other one, Doctor Death, the doctor of death to all those little girls in Hiroshima and per- haps to himself as well, for how could one survive God the Father's own original sin, even after denying his existence, *God* being merely the name we give to our reason for living, yet that too is really a matter of physics, not some completely disconnected god, perfectly impersonal if anything, so pro- claimed the twisted mouth and mortified body of the other physicist, thought Fleur, the humbled Stephen of supreme dignity in a wheelchair, now his indeed was the truth, whereas Doctor Death served a personal god of distinct traits, and in doing so set himself up as the atomic divinity, though still a man, husband and father of a little daughter, unlike Hawking who challenges no earthly deity but that impersonality, that absence which ironically perhaps condemns us to love one another, so went Fleur's reflection, even if the physicist was not as preoccupied with human feelings as he, a mind bent merely on the pitiless laws of physics, beneath that mop of hair almost a child in some respects, his eyes blinking with pain behind the glasses along with his twitches and creases, appearing to say these were just individual body parts afflicted by an illness that still left the rest of him a happy man, fortunate enough to enjoy a life shot through with the beauty of the universe, fortunate enough to work on the theories of physics, a rare domain my handicap leaves open to me, fortunate enough for my books to be read and even reprinted in paperback, who would have thought I could reach so many readers, so many living beings, but also unfortunately they bring me so many questions I can't answer, I have very few solutions to life's problems, those are enigmas I can't solve, physics and math can teach us a lot, naturally, like how the world began, but human beings and our behaviour are beyond their reach, the way the impersonal God, thought Fleur, leaves us to our own devices, and Stephen in all modesty knew this full well, imagine your mind is a computer and your consciousness its program, well that will go on working even when the computer itself doesn't anymore, theoretically it's possible, isn't it, no it isn't thought Fleur, it can't be because even if the computer, life, comes apart, what happens to a consciousness cut adrift from its body, what still active regions of memory does it go to, where does its eternal activity lead it, to say, inhabit new bodies freshly born, since it alone hungers after eternity, transcendent and permanent, surely that was it, for the physicist who looked like a kid has said the end of our world does not exist since all worlds are continually expanding and will do so until they reach emptiness and night, increasingly desert-like and darker like the inexorable darkness and void beneath the South Pole, far beyond our worlds both known and unknown, but the kid-like physicist wasn't born with all these theories, so full was his brain that he was also a poet just as Oppenheimer had been, and though he couldn't be certain, he asserted that if we survived long enough we'd be able to control the entire solar system, even colonize it like Earth, though nothing could ever be as hospitable to us, and if our own planet proved hostile and uninhabitable there was no certainty we could survive any-where else, our long-term future depended on reaching far more distant stars, and that required a great deal of time, perhaps more than we had, what differentiated the scientist of the nuclear age from his predecessor was that Doctor Death had been sure we could colonize the solar system and that all stars were within our grasp, but before we could colonize other worlds and planets our experiments would have to reach the stage where they wiped us all out, the little Hiroshima girls being merely the first and quickly forgotten like so many falling angels or falling snowflakes, never thought of again, this was the direction Fleur's mind was taking as the begin-nings of his symphony or opera emerged in grating sounds from his flute, heavy clouds hung over the beach, it didn't really make sense to write on an empty stomach, besides who could ever unscramble the scribbles and cabalistic symbols in the feckless and unbridled manuscripts of the uncouth man who loved Clara, no more than a child prodigy turned into hideous oaf who made crushed and frayed sounds with his flute, for what else could he offer a woman who was a prod-igy herself, though an uninterrupted one of superior intelli-gence that had never been allowed to wither in trivialities, servitude, or warding off hunger and thirst, not Clara, no, she ate well each day without care, a care that was constantly his along with his humiliation and subjugation to a welter of needs, such as feeding on garbage or nothing at all or slipping into drunken sloth or ceasing to think and exist altogether, yet live he did, and as proof there was his ability to love her despite his numbing misfortune. Enough of these damn sirens thought Kim, where had Brilliant got to, would he even be here tonight, though it was often after the midnight service that he came, either on foot across the beach or in his boss's convertible, then he'd suddenly say to her, sleep for a few hours, I have to go out for a while, and he was gone but a

few hours, but where to, wondered Kim, probably out drinking, though in the light of dawn his face was tanned and
serene, there was no way to know what he'd been up to,
nothing about him, not even the places he hung out at night,
what if one day he just never came back from who-knows-
where, not that he was a liar, but he always showed up laughing and gave nothing away, and said here we are in time for
breakfast at the Café Español, I swiped a croissant for your
coffee Kim, his gaze fixed far away, who knows where, Kim
noticed the hair growing long over his ears, a bit like a dog,
one he'd switched identities with out of a sense of loss, Misha,
Misha, he lamented, when am I going to get him back, and
he looked at Kim with the same welling up of fury that he
saved for panhandlers in the street who got their dogs to do
all the work for them, lazy buggers he'd yell, dress their dogs
up like clowns to beg for them while they loaf in the sun all
day with sunglasses and a hat, lazy buggers, poor dogs, such
dignity and such degradation, if the vet hadn't saved Misha
after the Third Great Devastation, it's those unscrupulous panhandlers who'd treat him that way, slaves to their indolence,
but when Brilliant blew up like this, she thought, it was probably a sign of the increasing ups and downs in his life, a life
in the disaster zone, a derailment he'd say, just one great
devastation on top of another, if he'd been one of those spoken poets holding forth to foggy clients in a bar, his misad-
ventures in the supposed safe haven of New Orleans would
be getting foggier too, covering his tracks so no one would
know he was Bryan, just Brilliant, the poet winning them over
in droves with his charm, but in private, well, these explosions of anger, even fury, Kim worried that they might be
symptoms of some more serious disorder that stemmed from
his alcoholic childhood, the tremors and agitation and para-
noia about the theft of his as yet unwritten writings might
mean he was having the DTs, in fact hallucination seemed to
be his main trait, for lately he'd taken to telling her he saw

them everywhere, in the bathroom mirror, on the floor tiles, and that was the reason he stayed away from the room his sister had rented for him in town, pursued as he was by all the deluges of New Orleans and even by words on mirrors, walls, and floors wherever he went, in fact in his calmer moments he actually took delight in reading them, but then when he lost it he claimed they'd been stolen from him and put there by someone else, that was when the delirium struck him especially hard, lasting for several days, and Kim would apply ice to his forehead and remind him he'd gone off the rails, remember that, now wake up will you Brilliant, you have to be at the café by eight, used to these constant battles with his ghosts, he'd reply, sure Kim, now where are my white socks and my good Bermudas and my shirt, they're waiting for me and I have to look neat and tidy or they'll throw me out and jobs are hard to find, what am I thinking, hey what if they made off with it when they took the giant palm leaves, the acacia, the beam, the beam it was in the crash, then he felt Kim's hand on his head and ice cubes melting onto his scalp, ah my head, it's there after all said Brilliant, must be if you're holding it in your hands Kim, whew, yes I have it back again, now all I need is to get to work, it's there, all of it. From under his hoodie, Fleur opened his eyes surprised to see Jérôme the African running down the street nearly naked, no sandals, nothing but those tight black underpants clinging to his black skin, running at an easy relaxed pace with a triumphant air, though Fleur could see the whites of his half-closed eyes looking almost as though he'd come through a fever and exulted in racing his body with renewed pride, running free and naked as a man of the wild thought Fleur, to the beat of his music it seemed, or was he just wildlife on the gallop never to be caught, not like those habitual city joggers, his sprint was of one pursued and expecting a hand on his shoulder, or was it the strident noise of sirens and the street that made him quiver sensually thought Fleur, prey to a kind of ecstasy as the pink hues of sunset began to sink beneath the sea, it was past five and the town was at its rowdiest, hard to believe that through all this din you could still make out the murmuring doves, their sweet songs almost sighed, this was something he could reproduce and amplify on the flute, hard as it often is for art to imitate nature or glorify it in some way by amazing sound inventions, murmurs, and rustles from all kinds of instruments, he should jot this down right now while the solitary cooing stood out against the woven backdrop of sound, its barely breathed song of love, perhaps to be totally devastated by human madness but still audible for now, then thinning into a hopeless lament, Petites Cendres emerged from Mabel's boarding house with Robbie clutching his arm as though afraid to see him crumple onto the sidewalk with the shock of being outside after so long, okay at least he's standing Robbie said, he's coming to my coronation tonight and it was your music that finally got him up and out, honest I don't know what I'd do without you Fleur, the latter just smiled without answering though he wanted to say he was hungry, never thinking of anything else at this late time of day, and there was Jérôme the African still running through the sticky heat, would Fleur end up going to his mother for food or would Brilliant show up with his cardboard box of the day's goodies, what was it that made Kim dog his steps like that, still, forgetting his resentment, Fleur introduced her to Petites Cendres, this is Kim, we hang out in the same spot, immediately losing himself in his flute music, something he'd once written for harpsichord he said before retreating inside his hoodie, and Robbie said how beautiful it was, in fact though Mabel was a pious woman she'd say it almost makes you think you're in the Community Church or the Temple, Robbie of course went to neither one, not his calling he said, no way, he was still holding Petites Cendres upright as though he'd stumble at any moment, geez here I am getting a spare tire and you're practically swimming in your clothes, Kim too noticed Petites Cendres' skinny body, jeans and tank top both too big for him, less hair too and that was the last trace of his flamboyance, now one sickly apparition, something like Brilliant, what's the point in caring about these guys, thought Kim, if they're too out of it to go anywhere, besides goodwill and charity were kind of pathetic so she wasn't crazy about them, okay there's still time before the coronation said Robbie pointing to the gold paper crown on his head, Petites Cendres, you and I are going for a cocktail by the ocean before you start going all self-pity on me, hey taxi, taxi, quick, my buddy here can't walk much he said as they jumped into a cab, holding Petites Cendres with a firm grip close to his own belly burgeoning under a green dress that was too tight over muscular brown legs, that was when he realized how much Petites Cendres' relatively short stay in bed had weakened him, geez he should have chased him out of there sooner, he regretted, you just don't go on letting someone sleep forever like that, it's really unhealthy, and he recalled all those taxi rides with Fatalité, including the one by the sea back when things were really getting bad though they never actually talked about it, then once they were out on the terrace Fatalité would quickly get drunk on champagne, he laughed too loud and Robbie told him so, not realizing that these were his only diversions, satin dresses, stiletto heels, and Cuban cigars, sure Fatalité laughed and laughed, whatsamatter aren't you glad I'm having a good time, eyes starting to tear up under the creamy lashes, well you see we're not on stage right now Robbie replied, this is a classy establishment, chic in fact, you used to know how to behave before, didn't you, who me never, Fatalité shot back, besides when did you get all hoity-toity Robbie, must be your latest daddy kicking in, there was something else on Robbie's mind he wasn't saying, although Yinn still loved his hubby Jason he seemed to be irresistibly attracted to My Captain, and Jason was the jealous type, well no daddy will ever own me again Robbie said vaguely, not a one, believe me Fatalité, Jason, Yinn, even Yinn's mother, Cobra, Geisha, and the whole bunch have had lovers but that didn't prevent them from being family to Robbie, and Yinn's philandering or longing for someone else would have upset the stability and balance in his life, though it was already shaky, for Robbie himself had taken off with numerous manipulative sugar daddies and got tired of them fast, a stormy month or two would do it, in the push and pull of one's drives one gives a lot to a man one doesn't know, then one gets over it, that's why Yinn told Robbie not to trust strangers when they dazzle with talk of fortune and glory, it's all just pretense, they only want your body for a night, that's when Fatalité's loud tense laughter exploded somewhere deep inside Robbie, whether it was cocktails by the sea, stretched out on the beach or wherever, Fatalité's spirit would escape in laughter, never defeatist though, Fatalité was just taking his leave gradually, without making a thing of it, in a cascade of laughter as though he were still singing and dancing onstage in all kinds of burlesque contortions, those were the times when an uneasiness came between them, if they shared a beach towel Robbie might get up all of a sudden filled with a frail kind of pity for Fatalité's body in the sun's glare as though cursed in its nudity in every way, you're recoiling from me aren't you Robbie, you're afraid you'll hear my vertebrae clicking or maybe they show too much in the sunlight eh, look honey, go take a swim and leave us corpses to ourselves, I won't mind, Fatalité laughed again as he pulled the towel his way, it was only now, here in the street as he helped Petites Cendres keep from falling down on the sidewalk, that Robbie wished he hadn't left Fatalité alone on the beach, Fatalité who was weak and couldn't go into the water himself, he could still see Fatalité that day lying helpless there on his beach towel, hurt but still laughing, go on honey, take a swim while you can, it's okay, you're athletic, hey it wasn't long ago you used to sit behind me on the motorbike, remember, whizzing through the countryside, nothing was too much for us, California, Mexico, and you hanging on to my back with your hand on my thigh, I was a man's man then and boy were you impressed, male by day and female by night in the clubs, the whole jig-saw of sexes, a perfect physical performer as Herman would say, yeah go on, don't hang back Robbie, just leave this old thing lying here on its beach towel letting the sun shine through with no shame at all, you're young, healthy, and handsome Robbie, just leave me here, then stricken with remorse while he was bathing, Robbie ran back to Fatalité and sat next to him on the towel that got all wet from the pressure of his body and the rain of drops he shook from his hair, look you're young and beautiful too he said, you get crazy with all your grandiose ideas and your absurd laugh, yeah I get that from my mother Fatalité said, everything in fact, a nutty woman and larger than life, a high-class hooker, let me tell you, not just any slut, she brought me up and fed me, every-thing sublime I get from her, he repeated, no easy job bringing up a kid in those circumstances, well you did do some time when you were eighteen didn't you Robbie replied, that's not the best way to get brought up, it was no big thing Fatalité said, Yinn had to come and get me out, prisoner, outlaw, oh my mother sure liked her heroin, didn't you Mama dear, that's what killed her, I'd started dealing a bit like her but I was saved by a fairy godmother with a big heart who decided to adopt me, sort of her son or brother, and that was Yinn, it was a dirty needle that got me sick, just that, it doesn't take much, hardly anything at all and you're suddenly a leper among lep-ers, surprise, surprise, who'd've thought, oh invincible Fatalité, yeah right, son of a high-class hooker, nope, never saw that one coming, Fatalité no longer laughing talked a lot about his mother to Robbie that day on the beach, she had me when she was only fifteen, kind of like a big sister, but who wants a fifteen-year-old with a bastard, so he had to strike out on his own, and I had to go everywhere with her, even in the arms of her men, nobody wanted me except her and she held on to me, she was the love that underlay all the hate and humiliation from other people, two shipwrecked delinquents, but who feels sorry for fifteen-year-old mothers and their sons, we were inseparable, one as pale and blonde as the other, we both had so much to forget and we shared a liking for all kinds of intoxication and addiction, let's see, first we needed to forget about my birth, then being poor we felt entitled to do what we liked, so we learned to steal, but for the longest time she was my dearest companion, no one cares about people like her, and sex was sort of a pathology for her, a kind of melancholy separate from her other scattered senses, she was in a constant state of crisis, never knowing if we'd eat anything that night or if we'd find a place to sleep, who would care for her or ease her suffering body even when she saw no quick way out but suicide, reality having become a distended version of everything around her after she'd taken something toxic because there was no shrink to help her, this was the abyss of the marginalized and largely invisible, perilously unsettling whether mentally affected or not, no one to answer for her at fifteen, certainly not me or her, poor thing and her offspring sighed Fatalité, well let's get some sun and forget about all that, and he started laughing once more. Fleur was still thinking about the music they heard in town and all around them, in the open-air bars and hotel gardens, on the wharves, his friends in the group Cool Springs would be playing there and getting paid well, from seven to midnight jazz and blues groups would show up in the cabarets and theatres set up for concerts, all of them in black suits and white ties, getting paid to play, they had poured their souls into it every bit as much as Fleur, though he had nothing else to invest, they had wives, homes, cars, and people came to sip margaritas as they listened to Cool Springs and some rockers Fleur thought were too noisy and didn't mix with, though his mother held it against him, for Martha herself had an evening pub overlooking the ocean, refugees and immigrants would bring their families, even young children, and dance on the terrace, now what was to stop Fleur playing for them, she'd long sheltered the stateless and displaced waiting for papers that never came, she knew their life, she'd been influenced by Alphonso, a nutty priest and bold philanthropist, he'd self-lessly hidden Haitians and Cubans in his church far out on the Archipelago, he relentlessly turned in priests who were sexu-ally abusing children, and that was why they kept sending him farther and farther away, not that it stopped him, as he wrote to Martha, the political hypocrite in the Vatican still protected those criminals, so he just denounced them more vehemently, I'll never shut up he said, sure my mother has right in her heart thought Fleur, she loves humanity, too bad she had to be his mother just the same, a family of twelve would have done her just fine, but her overabundance of love got dumped on only one son and it was too much for him, he wasn't the one for her he thought, no really not, the Cool Springs were into their jazz and blues now and it was nearly time for the acrobats, charmers wearing snakes coiled like collars, peddlers of roses and jewellery, and then there was a shout in their midst, it was Mabel, whose parrot Merlin had fallen off her shoulder onto the planks, followed by the cry of a painter concentrating on the sunset, it's him, it's the Shooter, it's him Mabel, he fired the shot, I just had time to spot him before he covered his face, we all know it's him, the young killer who shoots all the animals, the one they've been looking for, Mabel, the painter by his easel seemingly didn't hear Mabel's cry over the noise of the waves, the lamenting and terrified clamour, for Mabel had actually felt the pellet whistle past her head, but what had happened and where were those tiny balls, many of them fired with great precision all around her head, oh no, there on her shoulder Merlin's orange breast and blue-and-gold wings were bloodstained as the Shooter's precise aim dropped him from her shoulder and

Jerry the other parrot said in his strident begging voice Mama, Mama, look, let's go Mama, let's go yelled Mabel, but who among the art sellers and animal trainers had heard, or even the magician who bragged about his cats dancing through hoops of fire, and the painter busy turning his canvas purple with the setting sun, the Shooter, it's him the Shooter attacking the innocent, Mabel looked at her feet incredulous, her Merlin was dead, such a beautiful bird too, look at his head thrown back, he's not moving said a man next to her, he'd shown birds before and sold roses now, look at all that blood on his wings, who did this, who did it, we didn't see or hear a thing, it was like a party, fireworks and all, fun is all, those little bursts held tiny pellets, so small we can't even get them out of his body, no I'll do it wailed Mabel, my Merlin's not going to any pet cemetery with pellets still in him, and there she stayed a long time crying and carrying on with the bird in her lap, but it was her Sunday best and she was going to wear it when she visited her daughter in Indiana, so she mustn't get it stained, Reverend Ézéchielle had given her a plane ticket to go and see her third grandchild, but this didn't augur well, Merlin being, being, but she couldn't get herself to say the final word that would seal his going forever, as if into a drawer open before her with all the dead jumbled together, no Merlin, no, she'd keep him with her till she took him to the pet cemetery beneath the shade of Australian pines among white dunes by the sea, no this didn't bode well, Merlin so chatty and suddenly silent, looking as though he were asleep, well now maybe he was resting so he could last to eighty and outlive any of his owners, longer than Mabel herself, no, he wasn't, that's all, he wasn't, asleep was all, but the twinkle in his eyes slowly went out and a veil was gently drawn over them, yes, like being asleep she thought, no don't cry, you mustn't stain that dress, you bought it specially for the trip, no, it's to see your daughter in, even if Mabel could go on without Merlin, what about Jerry who kept on saying let's go

Mama, I love you, let's go, and she replied gotta be patient Jerry, gotta be patient, we'll have to get on the bike and go to the pet cemetery, be patient now, your brother's gone poor thing, what are we going to do now you and me, eh, and her mind went back to Herman's lace cape, torn in the motorcycle parade as he rode along on his multicoloured tricycle yelling there's a sniper in the crowd, it was as though a kid's penknife had been tossed into the air, said Herman, or firecrackers, Mabel thought also of Marcus who was in prison because of him, because he'd got sedatives to help Herman with his cancer, risked his life, given it up in a way, while Herman was still roaming around free, and Marcus would never get to be a nurse because he was in prison for him, Herman no longer a convalescent, was out singing and dancing at the Cabaret every night, in fact the Shooter had sworn he'd get vengeance during a celebration or show of some kind, vengeance maybe but why Merlin, why on earth him wondered Mabel, the motionless bird in her arms, Merlin never hurt anyone, totally random, that's what it was she thought, shooting blindly everywhere, out under the Australian pines she'd place some flowers and spend a long time stroking Merlin's breast and riddled wings, a long time, so Jerry, now you'll be the only one on my shoulder eh, that's how it will be tonight, your brother's gone, let's go, let's go Mama Jerry replied, okay, but first I've got to pry these pellets out of his wings, you know no matter what the Reverend says, it was cruel of God to take my Merlin from me, that's right, he did take what was mine didn't he, down there on the beach silken tents had been set up for a wedding, and oh what fun they were having thought Mabel, women in low-cut dresses and men feeling awkward and sweaty in their suits, wine flowing into glasses, hearty laughter, a stuffy-looking wedding thought Mabel, and here I am unhappy and adrift, you hear that Jerry, nobody cares about us, my oh my, look at those bouquets of yellow roses on the tables, they're gonna drink and eat till midnight, totally unaware of us, I wonder what Petites Cendres will say when he sees you're not out on the veranda anymore, what'll he say, huh, that the world just keeps on bleeding beauty, pouring it out, that's right Merlin, and there's not a thing we can do about it, look now they're lighting the torches for evening, the painter said still working on the sunset, there are perverse kids doing perverse things, I think it was a kid, no mask, just vanished, he said he was sorry for her loss and she smiled back at his elderly face despite her tears and suddenly felt old and tired, it's like he got me through the heart instead, and she pointed to her ample bust, you gotta call the cops so they can look for him, you gotta call them said the sunset-painter, yeah sure I will said Mabel without conviction, I can go with you, I'm a witness he said, sure okay we'll go tomorrow said Mabel again, feeling even older and uglier than before, I've got a boarder at my place who isn't doing too well, a depressed boarder she emphasized, and he isn't right, and this boarder of mine, he's gonna be awful sad when he finds out about Merlin, that he, but she stopped short and went on to talk about her daughter expecting her in Indiana, and I'm gonna be a grandmother for the third time she told the painter, but he was wasn't listening, absorbed in portraying an ocean had suddenly turned ferocious and melted into the night with lots of blues, two kinds, navy on top and pale beneath split by an imperceptible sliver of gold, though he was still thinking what a pity it was about the dead bird, why did fate seem to have it in for this poor black woman, now why is that, didn't she have enough to worry about, tonight she hadn't sold a thing, no ginger brew or roses, I bet they'll end up on Merlin's grave, even with blood on them, no it was real sad he thought, he was luckier though, no sooner had he finished a painting than he sold it, not for much of course, but he could really churn them out, and here he was each evening, same sunset dissolving as night came on, must be a misunderstood artist, a real one who knew exactly how to render the fluidity of blues one on top of another, one darker navy and one lighter, that's it he thought, it needed to be structured like a Bonnard, the colours intense and dominant, it might have been one of his watercolour seascapes such as *Paysage de Saint-Tropez*, he had wandered through Spain and Morocco enchanted by the warm even torrid colours of the street artists, yet he managed to sell a lot, and this wasn't lost on the other painters, who envied his success, though still misunderstood, too subtle for them his burning hot tones, too subtle he mused, an undiscovered Bonnard, still he'd become rich, not them, and as for poor Mabel, well it was a pity wasn't it, the parrots were her bread and butter, too bad about the roses too, the straw-hatted painter carried on with the sun angling down into the fierce colours of the sea, he wished he could include the wedding party, almost a hundred of them on the neighbouring beach, late-afternoon bathers too, black dots against the waves or arms moving lithely over the deep blue water, on another pier almost deserted there were white umbrellas all folded up as though ready for the night silence creeping across the entire ocean, he wanted to paint and keep it, the blue day so very blue, almost green with the line that bounded it all, like Bonnard he'd done his share of bumming around, and he did like his pictures well structured, bold colours, hot, but in his case nothing would be exactly the same, probably always to be unknown, just a hot-seller, nothing more, oh how he'd love to seize the eternity of this day, the sky, the wedding party, the white umbrellas, the voices in the waves, and if that woman Mabel had been easier to deal with, he'd've liked to paint her too with the parrot on her arm, sure, all of it, everything, this ran through the painter's mind under the straw hat, such a delicate touch thought Mabel, even eating from his bowl, elegant movements from his legs to the tips of his claws as he lifted the rice to his curved beak, oh Merlin, she thought, my royal bird from Brazil, you could pronounce so well, Mama let's go ordered Jerry to hurry her up, it'll be evening soon, let's go, let's go Mama, I love you, what time is it, beddie-byes Merlin, beddie-byes Merlin, what time is it, Merlin you were such a good mimic, what a recital she murmured to the bird still motionless in her arms, the other, Jerry was white as snow and clung to her shoulder, yes okay we're going she said, we've got a way to bike over to the white dunes at the pet cemetery, that's where your brother will sleep Jerry, right, let's go, we've got to be strong, God was cruel to take you away from me, I'm gonna say that to the Reverend, wait and see, what made him take my Merlin eh, why, I'll say to her, and Fleur's mind went back to that day the concert was announced on a poster, the picture of Clara, his own Clara, he'd need a suit and shoes, first the shoes, boy what a lot to get done, it wore him out but he'd be there, then guess what, the concert season was cancelled, there it was in the morning newspaper, nothing before winter because the musicians were on strike, some backer had not paid them, ticket holders would be reimbursed, what a disappointment, they'd been waiting for this, okay everybody take it easy, the season will begin again in January, just a little financial adjustment to make that's all, no need to crowd around the concert hall, Fleur did though, I've got to get in, I've got to see her, she's a great virtuoso he said to the hostile man at the door, look you don't get it do you, there's no concert before winter, and even then who knows, do you have any idea of the times we're living in young man, me for instance, I haven't been paid one red cent, I was supposed to listen to the music free and sell tickets to latecomers, that's all, not even a tip a lot of the time, yep, that's how it is nowadays my young friend, I wouldn't have let you in anyway, not barefoot, never ever heard of that before, bare feet in a concert hall, no swimsuits neither, nor cellphones, you can bet on that, and certainly no dogs, no way you'd've got in, so that was it thought Fleur, only mediocre music got rewarded, same thing with musicians, rockers like Cool Springs and their noise, while devoted musicians like the symphony got cut to the bone, no choice but to go on strike, boy that's humiliating, revolting thought Fleur, forever playing his flute out in the street while he literally shook with hunger, and what made it even harder to stand was smelling all those heady aromas from the restaurants as the doors opened, striking musicians, what a blow to Clara, everyone, soloists, trained musicians, fervent artistes on the receiving end of such contempt, such downright lazy cowardice, no using their instruments for months and Clara's name stripped from the poster like a slap in the face, he thought of the striking musicians as absent spirits onstage, like in a dream he often had during those uncomfortable nights on the beach near the edge of a wood where no one would see them, him and Damien in their cardboard kennel on the sand, the dream went back to before Fleur was born, and he was the guest pianist in an opera, either Mozart or Beethoven, at a festival in Vienna a little after the Second World War, the musicians kept everyone waiting a long time, where were they, beneath which pile of rubble, this was supposed to be a time for renewal and rebuilding yet no one knew what had become of the celebrated artists invited there after all those years, but they were expected for the performance to be given by the surviving musicians and singers, Fleur positioned his fingers on the keyboard and looked around, but for hours, even days, no one showed, yet there he was in his tux when suddenly a wave of red light washed over them and, as out of a grave, the actors and musicians emerged, all of them skeletons, some still with tatters of skin clinging to them, now the conductor was at his lectern and nodding to Fleur, saying when they killed my orchestra they killed their music, I am conducting because I alone survived those unimaginable catastrophes, the silence of the dead is what you will hear for this is the time of postwar silence when reconstruction begins, not one musician from my orchestra is left alive, not one, then Fleur would wake up under the stars alone with no one but

Damien, who was fast asleep, no music, nothing he thought, there would be no performer in Fleur's opera, nothing but the sound of waves, and no one to play any music, for I too will have disappeared like those in my dream, only shreds of consciousness and life remaining, as he touched his chest he knew he'd been dreaming, a regularly occurring nightmare, he felt the warmth of Damien's head next to him, he stroked his ears, running his fingers through the fur and thinking I'm alive, I'm breathing, oh smell that morning ocean air, sure it was a dream, nothing more, that vision of the missing and disappeared haunts me every night, out there as he played his flute, he pictured Clara's face gone from the poster, white paint barring her name, maybe he'd never see her again, no concert before winter and then some doorman said nope, Clara's gone, young people were emerging from a pizza place gulping it down two or three slices at a time, some kind of idiotic contest they thought was a riot, thought Fleur, must be students on vacation, the sticky dough hit him with its vulgar smell of tomatoes, anchovies, and olives that set him off in all directions at once, somewhere over their greedy mouths and perfectly tended teeth, god it's revolting he said to himself, the street pressing in on him, in so close it never relented, and the smells gave him a headache, and as if to put him off even more Kim said, see that, everything's wasted with them, even food, if they don't finish those pizzas I sure will, this time he felt sorry for her and didn't bother telling her to shut up, she'd never known what a home was, parents collapsing their veins didn't count, the street was all she'd ever known, why put her down, though he'd often been prompted by his habitual irritability, Brilliant would be here any time now yelling and twitching, hey here's the catch of the day, fresh veg too, look, asparagus, potatoes, a real feast for once, so Fleur wouldn't be going to his mother's, no ma'am, still some nice brown beer with Martha would be nice, it was time he got cleaned up too, top to bottom he thought, still the smell of the anchovies and tomatoes didn't seem so bad now, he was certain Brilliant was on his way with something hailing a taxi and climbing in with Petites Cendres the way he used to with Fatalité, Robbie thought about the eternity of marriage ahead for Yinn and Jason, even if Yinn had been pure in his love at first sight and his marriage to Captain Thomas years before, My Captain he called him when he came calling at the bar in the Porte du Baiser Saloon in his checked sleeveless halter-tops and his captain's cap tilted over one eye, oh too much, too much, Robbie thought to himself trying not to tumble in head over heels, so where was Yinn's sense of balance now, flipped over and upside down perhaps unlike everything else in the house, which was so well ordered and harmonious, Yinn with Jason for a husband plus a stoic mother who respected everyone's whims and fancies except when they disrupted the orderliness of things in the house, whims sure, unruliness no, especially now when everyone seemed to be walking on eggshells, all thoughts were on Fatalité and his unlikely future, certainly Robbie could think of nothing else, save him, save him and keep him from those dark thoughts, rekindle his hope for the present, which for him could only be a source of rejoicing, whimsicality, and poignancy, though Robbie would have hoped for something a little calmer and wiser, hell no he thought, that isn't going to happen is it, I mean this is Fatalité we're talking about, a case of excess if ever there was one, more excess, excessive excess, the coma-tose nights on coke, and to top it off Yinn, as though needing a counterweight to all this, was leaning on the bar in a white tank top, sandals, and denim cargo Bermudas, hair brushed back from his prominent forehead and over his shoulders, a cigarette dangling from his lips, and a little distant, perhaps with a coolness that served only to heighten desire, waiting for Captain Thomas to come in from the street with his mind elsewhere as Robbie recalled, possibly the ocean depths he had been visiting day and night right into the wee hours of

the morning, I got to swim among the sharks quite confi-
dently, he told Yinn, the clearest water, branches of coral, and
he was off soaring to mystical heights in the depths of the
ocean, real peace of mind he said, it's so amazingly beautiful
you don't ever want to come back Yinn, you know the deeper
you go and the less often you breathe the more you become
that plant in the coral we once were, or the fish resting on a
sandbank, practically nothing at all, it's so inexpressibly
ecstatic and sweet, there are no words for it, Yinn was listening to all this with impatience at not being noticed enough
himself and, with a certain nonchalance that seemed unconscious but wasn't, Yinn, being neither indecent nor tasteless
but more like a nice but naughty boy, slipped down his denim
Bermudas, under which he wore nothing, to just below the
waist, but all Captain Thomas got to see was a constellation
of tattoos on his hip, oh and I forgot, he went on, it was the
full moon and those satyrs of ours were out and about in total
freedom, all blonde manes and torsos, but you Yinn with your
pants down like that, your torso, your silky underarms, fresh-
shaved legs, you're better than any hairy boy, and that skin of
yours has to be velvet, uh-huh you're coming on my boat
Yinn, bring Jason and Robbie with you, my friends get a sailboat ride and champagne, plus breakfast with strawberries
and lime cocktails you'll never forget, what else are you offering asked Yinn, standing with his hip to one side, tell me what
else, well anything your heart desires the captain answered
still dreaming of oceans and heedless of Yinn's erotic little
game however minor it was or however languid his staged
offering, the captain went on unaware, we'll see the dolphins
at play, so I'll expect you and your friends on board tomorrow
morning, and this captain was the one Yinn would soon be
calling My Captain, somehow cancelling out the infidelity to
his husband, yeah that was back before Yinn turned thirty-
three but it's so right now thought Robbie, the lavish times of
his glorious immaturity when Fatalité was still alive, a time

that seemed so far away though it was barely yesterday he thought, yes, really long ago. Fleur had another dream that was balm to his soul, often on dry nights in November or else when the jasmine was in flower as summer approached, the ocean waves brought him its enchanting perfume just before he lay down to sleep on the sand with Damien, barely were his eyes closed when it took him back to his grandfather's fields in Atlanta, away from the city itself, and these had taken on huge proportions in his early youth, as though he and the plantations had grown up together and as though the harvested fields had never had the grass burned off or put forth only what was unproductive, Fleur had walked among grasses that seemed to reach the sky and it was like meandering through the bright colours of a painting, beet and wheat fields, and beyond that a second garden made up solely of luscious fruits, a luxuriant orchard where fruit trees also reached skyward and there were peaches and wild apricots to be eaten while ambling through it, but what most struck Fleur was the amazing height of the grasses unchanging in their greenness, then all of a sudden as he picked his way through them, more than head-high even for his grandfather, who was tall in his prime, there he was, Grandfather himself, saying to his beloved grandson for whom he'd wished a magnificent musical career, Fleur do you hear that, every blade of grass is the voice of a man or woman singing the opera *Fidelio*, there do you hear them, and once more the boy heard the harmony of voices when he woke, it's the wind Grandfather had said, the wind sighing through the grass in the fields and the fruit on the trees, it's the wind that makes them sing in unison like a choir, can you hear it Fleur, and there it was as he and Damien woke in their cardboard shelter on the beach, the wind with its salty smell and taste, like soprano and bass voices or their inflections repeating themselves as they sang in the waves, quick thought Fleur, I must write this down while it's still fresh or I'll forget, no I mustn't do that, it felt like happiness or was it just a sensation, well anyway he might have to change the title of his opera to include the word *joy*, hmmm yes, he thought, I'd sure like to know what they're going to do with us, Laure said to Daniel, it'll be nightfall soon and here we are still locked up in this terminal, humph, what are they going to do with us anyhow, no way they're gonna let me smoke this whole time, yes indeed, an instrument of repression, that's what it is, what else can you call it, the airlines are all against us, must be something serious to keep us hanging around all this time, said Daniel calmly or pretending to be calm, but the sky is perfectly clear and there was no apparent reason to keep all the planes grounded, really clear, there must be some reason they're not telling us, but if he'd been really honest he'd've told Laure she was pigheadedly selfish, after all she wasn't the only one stuck in this situation, there were more than a hundred others piled in here with them and most were waiting in silence, busying themselves with reading or electronic games or cellphones or portable computers, while Laure on the other hand was idle and stuck to Daniel like his shadow when he wanted to be alone like everyone else with his computer open to the picture of his daughter's face, Mai came first with her inquisitive eyes, pierced ears, and straight-line brow, then her brothers and Mélanie on the next page like a map of the planets, comets, and worlds he would navigate, as though master of the universe, able to stop just an instant in his aerial voyage at the campus in Ireland where he was to speak tomorrow to many pairs of inquisitive eyes through which Mai's own would shine, her face was more adult-shaped of late and resembled Mélanie's during their early days in New York, when he'd fallen in love at the same tender age and she'd told him that drugs would only dull his writing edge, not liberate it, and there she was again in Mai's inquiring eyes with the same relentless intransigence he thought, pensive and seeming to voyage with Daniel when he read or wrote on the computer, a technological miracle of almost supernatural dimensions, Mai, however inaccessible, was somehow always there by his side like an image he could never shake, just as she had been when, very young, she'd played among his books and manuscripts while he worked, cooing to herself as she turned the pages of heavy books or scribbling away on the scrap paper he'd tossed away, and like a squirrel or cat or some other curious little animal in the garden, he always knew where she was, yet here he was in this terminal, too considerate of Laure to dare open his computer to her picture, for his fellow voyager stuck to him like glue, saying you see Daniel we're all held down, held in, and there's no getting out unless they decide to let us, not even a stroll in the hallways with those stupid glass doors everywhere, what's going to happen to us, tell me Daniel, what, I've never gone this long without a smoke, it's repression by the company and everyone, but I'm not giving in, oh no, she's right thought Daniel as he listened to her, it's true she was repressed, going this long without smoking was like depriving an alcoholic of drink, yes he owed it to her to listen and understand, even if he did feel distracted by what Mai had written to him the day before, my profs are going to inform you Papa that four of us, Karine, Christy, Vita, and me, might get bursaries in art and photography next year, still it isn't fair because the others have to keep working to pay their fees, and the first two are African Americans from families so poor they had to go to foster homes, so you have to understand Papa that it would be unfair for me to take the money, and if you look at the picture you'll see each of us has a red and blue ribbon of honour, in it we're having dinner with our profs, it's a real treat because the three of them really deserve it, Karine wants to study medicine and become a surgeon and she needs every boost she can get Papa, I already have you and Mama and I don't need to work while I'm a student, besides you know how I am, not particularly ambitious and I won't need to study long-term like my brother Vincent, in fact

I'm probably just as lazy as Samuel in school, the best thing
is to go dancing after class with my friends, like when I used
to go to the beach with Manuel, Tammy, and the other girls
late at night in our bikinis, there's no beach here so we go to
the disco instead, Papa do you know if Manuel's dad is out
on parole yet, do you ever see Manuel these days, I've got to
go sweet Papa, it's time for class, kisses to my one and only
Papa, I do love you so, Mai, words that Daniel loved to watch
flow down his screen, waves of them rippling and singing,
then slowing to a bashful trickle as Mai realized it wasn't a
good idea to mention Manuel and his dad, especially when
Daniel reproached himself for knowing next to nothing about
that part of her life except that he had a premonition of danger
when she hung out with the boy, afraid he might be losing
her, or perhaps it had already happened unknown to him, that
mysterious and disturbing period in her life, oh how secretive
our children can be, like so many other parents he and Mélanie
had sent her away to college, far from those threatening sur-
roundings, what if they'd been wrong he wondered, though
she did sound so confident when she wrote to him, her words
flowing naturally as a brook, could it be they actually hid
something in their depths, perhaps a veiled homesickness she
was feeling far from the one she loved, Manuel, a name to be
avoided like his father, perhaps she was really giving voice to
her ennui there among strangers in a strange place, the
thought of it saddened him as he revisited the trips abroad
that were meant to nourish his writing yet produced nothing,
the writers' colony provided none of the solitude he needed
but surprised him with how different he was from the others,
a sort of asocial originality, alone among a talented cohort,
self-isolating, rarely spoken to and rarely speaking, so why
shut yourself up in a Spanish monastery with other artists and
writers he was asked, it was to write his novel *Strange Years*,
still not finished even now, write and rewrite it as he might
every day, Daniel was first and foremost an ecologist, and

writers and novelists couldn't work without a sense of eternity before them, they wrote in a present that folded the future into it as they said I'll redo this tomorrow, not right now but later, or so it was for Daniel, who couldn't help thinking more about his children than his writing, one day he'd be old and able to work with no fear that the Earth was about to blow up, indeed that's who he'd be, an older but wiser writer somersaulting into indifference, indifference to everything, living by his pen alone in his room, though that room would need an opening onto the sea and the birds, for he'd be impervious to humans and their torments, though not to nature, but he longed to be proof against the anxiety that took him by the throat on his walks through the orchards and fields in Spain, outside while the others were inside their cells writing or painting or sending up discordant new sounds from the music studios, the tamed anarchy of art, while he, Daniel, created absolutely nothing, produced absolutely nothing in the nothingness of his blocked and aimless soul, sinking deeper every day into listlessness, only to be wakened from it by a pain that was greater than his own, a little girl crying in the scorching silence of the afternoon, crying in immense sadness while her mother pleaded, no Grazie, don't cry, you'll see what a fine dinner it will make, all those artists need something good for their dinner Grazie, but the little girl continued crying, my rabbit, he was mine and you cut my rabbit's head off, she murmured, he was mine, he ran around in the forest with me, my very own rabbit Mama, there were no distinct words to it, but two old men Daniel had met playing bocce when he was out for a walk were beneath the trees, grumbling about the foreigners up there in the monastery, artists, writers, what are they doing here, or so Daniel imagined them saying, of course maybe they were simply too wrapped up in the game to do anything but grumble out there under the trees like that on such a devilish hot day, but after he'd heard the little girl asking for her pet and the farmwife who wouldn't give it to her, a piercing soul-sickness afflicted his throat, double-pronged, as he heard her weeping, for this surely was only the first, he thought, a precursor of many more devastating losses to come, and there's nothing I can do for this poor child's heart, not a thing, for tonight I'll be one of them, one of the visiting artists, writers, and musicians in the monastery gorging bare-fanged on Grazie's pet rabbit at the refectory table, what shame I feel for all of us, what sadness, yet Daniel, far from being an ascetic, knew he wouldn't refuse it when Grazie's mother served the rabbit to them that evening, no, in fact he'd be drawn to it as surely as the others, warming to the farmwife and her culinary abilities, ah can you smell that he'd say, and more such idiocy, apparently forgetting the afternoon tears of a little girl's very first grieving in the delightful smell of such a well prepared meal, the stubborn uneasiness would give way to carnivorous delight as he raised his glass of red wine to the health of one and all, addressing them not as refined creators but as gross feeding-machines such as he was himself, while feigning to be as they were, conscientiously plying their arts in their cells, fully he knew how false and frivolous was his façade, having written absolutely nothing since he'd got there, and tomorrow would be no different, the tears of a little girl in the scorching silence of afternoon in an austere landscape, a leaden angst piercing your flesh, the burning sadness of knowing your own mortality, nevertheless tearing through dinner, not a thing, no, Daniel said nothing, he felt how completely alone he was. On party nights, thought Fleur, as fevered streets began to eclipse the fading day, onstage at her pub and the life of the party, cheeks afire, occasionally accompanied by a singer on electric guitar, Martha managed to look opulent yet graceful in her Indian tunic, and Fleur recalled these words in the night, the ballad sung by the woman who accompanied my mother, blessed be you who wander with no roof or place to sleep tonight, you without country, souls forever wandering yes, blessed be you, thus it went as Martha's protégés, Jamaican, Haitian, and Cuban refugees, gathered on the terrace till Martha swept them up in the dance right out there under the stars, Fleur showed up briefly while she was getting them into the throbbing beat, oh son, there you are, you came after all, your musician friends Seamus and Lizzie are waiting for you son, come and dance with us, all your old friends are here, the ones who'd been to the concerts Fleur played as a child now held him in contempt, no matter if they hugged him and made nice, none of it was true thought Fleur, not one little bit, he recalled their jealous gossip when they saw him at the piano, only five years old, you watch the little prodigy, he'll be down in flames before he's a grownup, Garçon Fleur, sure, right, Garçon Fleur, watch when he's twenty and can't play a single note, he'd had to ditch those phony friends who gave him the overwhelming urge to head straight back to the street, oh no, don't go, his mother said, you're not leaving already, come into the house tonight and let's talk, he worried about her taking in all these people, Mama you can't look after all of them and they'll get deported, then what about you, you're likely to get arrested like Father Alphonso, but she replied do you think I'm scared of the law, besides Alphonso wasn't arrested, his superiors sent him to a parish in New England, and do you think that's going to shut him up, no way, he still goes on exposing the Church's crimes against children like those orphans in their seminaries, they are never going to silence him, besides, do you really think I need to be afraid of the law when the law's unjust, Alphonso hid refugees in the Archipelago because he had the courage and so can I, but Mama you're not Alphonso, you're only a woman and a woman alone, I'm all you have, ah well now, she said, having a son uprooted and footloose here in my very own town only a few steps from home helps me to understand a whole lot of things, and she took his hands in hers, then fell silent, her eyes moist, at least take a blanket with you for the nights, she said, thanks Mama, I'll use it for Damien, thanks, and he was gone, for how long she couldn't know, Kim wondered as she looked at Fleur forever playing his flute with his face buried in his hoodie, he's got a terrific mother and a divorced father who still writes though he never knows exactly where to find him, all I've got is a couple of junkies rotting in prison for ten or twelve years, not that they deserve any better, too bad the courts didn't do it sooner when it would have done us kids some good, all three of us, my mother let the youngest die of hunger, skinny little boy in his cradle, premature and sick, he wasn't going to make it past thirteen months, who could afford the operations and medication anyway, my mother said they robbed apartments and cars only so they could pay for their crack and coke, none to waste on the littlest one so why bother feeding him, bird's gotta fly by itself they said, he isn't made right anyway, a reject, he'll fly away on his own, I mean before they had us they were just boho nomads till they got the criminal seed sowed in them, then turned into delinquents and brought us up in this mess, I saw everything that happened to my brother, I was right there, I knew if he didn't get care he'd die, I watched the whole thing, everything they did, no courts to step in then and if I told someone they wouldn't believe me anyway, nobody would've taken me seriously, that scrawny baby just lying there, they'd never believe me, I was still pretty small myself, besides I was afraid of them, yes really afraid, they'd tell everyone how much they loved us, even show off their tattooed legs: "We hold you forever in our hearts," we weren't kids, we were ghosts, three bony ghosts swirling around them, barely there at all, then one day my thirteen-month-old brother stopped breathing, gone, disappeared, dead from lack of care, weightless body, little bird flown away, ten or twelve years in the pen isn't enough for them, no way, thought Kim on this dirty febrile day, painful and unending, geez where was Brilliant anyway, probably drunk again, takes good care of himself when he's working at the

Café Español, but where on earth was he, by now the cocks and hens were fluttering into their shelters among the bougainvilleas, cooing and cackling over their newborn yellow ones, brown ones, they all came darting for their mothers across the streets and down the sidewalks, hordes looking for their mothers across from them, clucking with distress and calling out to their little ones from among the evening onslaught of cars, some stopping to let them by, others barging straight through, with mother waiting patiently on the other side and maybe a huge colourful rooster looking like he was directing traffic in the middle of the road, the entire tiny choreography of slow-moving birds along the street or sidewalk or boulevard till their mothers finally herded the bewildered chicks under their feathered wings, Kim felt moved as she followed the procession of tiny creatures, hardly more protected than she was yet still struggling against hope to survive, come what may tonight or tomorrow, she'd still be there to fight off the young thugs preying on the hens and chicks on Bahama, wounded maybe, but Brilliant would patch her up the next evening in his boss's car, saying the one to really watch for is the Shooter, there, a little sea salt and you'll be right as rain, now you need to sleep while I go see some friends who want me to read them my novel, I'm up to chapter two, it's the story of my running away by train for two days and nights, that's the best part, they even talked about it in the New Orleans paper, "Mayor's Son Disappears," that was before my mother converted to the Children of God, what a disaster that was, her God didn't love runaways like me, so neither could she, so the fourth chapter is dedicated to my nanny, the one Mum told to whip me till I bled, and she did, but not because she liked it, poor Nanny couldn't stand to hurt anyone, y'know, people love it when I tell them about my ass burning from the whip, they want me to show them the marks and scars, I tell you I'm a living book Brilliant said, stigmata and souvenirs that's me, and it's all bursting with truth the minute I get up and tell it, what more could you want from a poet, and that was how he kept on thought Kim, but where was he right now and when would he get here, if only it weren't this late, but at this hour Mai wasn't at her boarding house, out every evening with her friends instead of being at home studying the way her father wanted, she simply didn't feel all that studious, too bad really thought Daniel, though he remembered his own escapades at that age, not quite the exemplary student he wanted his daughter to be, especially when the writer in him roared more like a rebel, out of keeping with the routine a student needs, and he played it to the hilt, now she shared the same taste for excess that could have destroyed him, yet here he was, the preaching parent like so many others who make the mistake of forgetting they were once young, he thought to himself if it weren't so late I'd love to hear Mai's voice on the cellphone, he could reassure her about the three eaglets they found dehydrated on the golf course, now being cared for by young people from the Wild Bird Centre, Daniel even had a photo he could send her right away of one of the birds in a girl's arms, its muscles needed healing after a long time immobilized, who knows how long they'd been unable to fly in that state or how it came about, yes that would get him Mai's approval, a brief moment of common accord magically linking them through space, nothing tangible could erase that distance of course, oh Papa, that's great, but those cages aren't big enough for them, they're growing fast and they'll have huge wings soon, oh it'll be all right, you'll see, Daniel would reassure her as always, as soon as they're better, they'll go free, ah that's good Papa, that's great, do keep me up on them and how they're coming along, won't you, of course Mai I'll tell you, hugs and kisses sweetheart, then her voice went away as if Daniel had dreamed it all, one click that's all, nothing more than a clear echo in his ear, don't forget to phone me when you get to Ireland, Papa, it doesn't matter if it's late, and late it was, for he was still in the airport awaiting his flight along with all the others, he knew she'd be worried if he told her it was delayed almost five hours, that was her, impatient like her mother, this was serious, but her father always took it with such calm, even if he might be in danger and too naive to realize it, waiting without knowing what would happen was really at the heart of all major tragedies and catastrophes in Mai's view, the sequence of hurricanes, tornados, wars, and all that, she was given to panic he thought, believing he knew his daughter so well, this huge accumulation of fears that is now the fabric of our lives afflicts our children as much as us, surely even more given their sensitivity, like animals sensing a cyclone or an earthquake from far off, and what good were all those antennae and radars when most disasters were man-made, the annihilation of children and animals is essentially ours, not nature's, and that was a theme in his book *Strange Years,* of which she had read some bits that most related to her, so how about a taxi ride along the seashore, Robbie asked Petites Cendres, seeing the disappointment on his friend's face, the same exasperation he'd seen in Fatalité during outings like this, look, Petites Cendres said, when you're having serious stomach trouble you stay home, besides you know I hate going out lately, why don't we get one of those ice creams you love said Robbie, three scoops, vanilla, chocolate, and caramel, how about that, see I remembered, besides you're wrong he laughed, if you stay in bed you'll get pins and needles in your belly and god knows what else, boy I bet the lizards love you the way you vegetate like a palm tree baked in the sun, but Robbie wasn't pleased by the forced smile he got back, too much like Fatalité's resigned look when he'd said Robbie, take my motorbike, I won't be needing it anymore, I feel better sitting on the back and I can put my hand on your thigh for a change, oh yeah, I can see you now parading in your lavish dresses after the show with me hanging on behind, such a charming couple we are, and no helmets, your hair trailing in the winter wind, my bike is your bike Robbie, but we won't be going to California or Mexico anymore, you by yourself maybe, okay lay off the predictions will you, Robbie yelled, now here with Petites Cendres, not wanting to see or hear this repeat performance by Petites Cendres, no more than an interlude between one sad epoch and another, but I don't like ice cream the way I used to Petites Cendres was saying as he thought of Mabel and her parrot show out by the wharves, strange, he went on, Mabel didn't come home early tonight as she always does, Petites Cendres went on to explain how Community Aid would be looking after him before long, Yinn of course had set it all up for him so he'd be more at ease, and in a few months he'd find himself in a big new apartment freshly painted white, by then Acacia Gardens would be finished, and you'll live in comfort, even luxury, brother, with doctors and nurses and orderlies won't you, but Petites Cendres said, oh no, I already owe a lot to whoever it is who pays for me to live at Mabel's, where I can sleep all day, but that's the problem Robbie replied, we're moving you out of there so you can break the habit of sleeping your life away surrounded by all those doves and parrots, no more of this dumb self-induced coma of yours, you're a man and you've got to live like one, Mabel agrees, no more knocking yourself out and wasting away for no good reason, you were meant to live your life Petites Cendres, when the time comes we're all going to get together and move you into those nice white freshly painted apartments with marble walls and the sea at the end of the walk, Petites Cendres wanted to say exactly, you know what it means when they park us there too, but he didn't say anything, though one could read the dark thoughts behind his eyes, he again gave the tight smile that wounded Robbie to the soul, look it's all right, Petites Cendres said, it's better that I stay at Mabel's, it can be my job to help her look after the doves and parrots, it's a sweet job and it can be mine, from the veranda they could hear Fleur playing, it's as beautiful as paradise said Petites Cendres, she's a saintly woman, irritable but saintly, protested Robbie, okay, okay, replied Petites Cendres, let's not talk any more about the apartments by the sea, Acacia Gardens and all that, no, no more, Petites Cendres was determined as he reassured Robbie, though what he thought to himself was, enough of all this organization and building Yinn goes on about, no more about Yinn, okay, no more. Still thinking about his grandson Rudolf and how much of a future he might have, he had to imagine Rudy holding the latest mortgaged iPod, to which the child would consign his tactile ability like some kind of mirror reflecting his indifferent image back to him, then he'd consign it to his pocket until something even better and more magical was conferred in its place, such were the rungs of progress, material acquisition and nothing more, the increasing subtlety of virtual soulless objects and nothing more, to become so skillful and blasé, yet perhaps without an Earth or a universe or a world, possibly lost through his parents' and grandparents' fault, sitting between what little remained of a pair of glaciers, most of the ice gone with the wolves and polar bears in rivers of mud, with only those objects to keep him company, still thinking of Rudolf, Daniel seemed to glimpse his grandson in the airport waiting room, it was a couple with a very small child bearing the finer traits of both his African father and his Swedish mother, his looks and her finely outlined mouth, forgetting Laure who had stuck to him like glue, Daniel began speaking to the two strangers as if they were old friends, and he learned that the father was a writer and the mother a translator, both spoke a multitude of languages, if so maybe the world could find its way to understanding after all, what an amazing prolongation they could make, even walled up in an airport there seemed to be almost limitless space, a world that never stopped surprising him with its breadth and riches, the child that caught his eye didn't seem at all like Rudolf anymore with his dark skin and deep black eyes, yet this was Rudolf in the arms of first his mother then his father, the white shirt and tiny jeans his mother started removing to change him, yes, this was him only yesterday, that smile and new teeth, a bit cranky already though, of course he was hungry and thirsty, still he pushed away the bottle, which had cooled, how long had they all been stuck in this terminal anyway, yes that was a smile of recognition, capricious perhaps but recognition just the same, the child was torn between sleep on his mother's breast and the bottle however lukewarm and flavourless, his temper was starting to show as it would in later life, as it did in Rudolf already, imposing his every wish on his parents, the winning smile got his father to take him from his mother, kiss him on the cheeks and hair, as wavy as his mother's, the pout made its way to Daniel, who suddenly felt the world open wide to infinity as if the Earth would by saved by this child from its probable and ultimate calcination, if ever, if ever this fruit of evolution projected itself into the future, perhaps born out of difference but not foreignness, as if the human race had decided to unite rather than divide, disparate bloodlines becoming one vital channel, was this vainly utopian Daniel wondered, was he dreaming again as Augustino often chided him, incapable of thinking, despite himself, that the world could become better than it was, transformed into something benevolent though unrealistic, a mirage possibly, self-delusion, it was still true nevertheless that this child's smile, barely hinted at and glimpsed in an airport waiting room to which he was about to feel captive, swept Daniel up in a wave of hope for a future not pillaged and miserable, and why not hope rather than be morose like Augustino, there could be no life without hope after all, and Kim recalled those nighttime rambles when she went looking for Bryan, where could he be, what was he up to, and there he'd be many times in a pub or a tavern, clouded by smoke on the sidewalk, so not like him, not the same person she knew by day, with his shaved head and the long sideburns that made his cheeks older and his face longer and bonier, here he was surrounded by elderly society ladies down on their luck and wearing their white hair in headbands, Kim heard him in the throes of telling his story, ah Lucia, my dear admirable Lucia, so you're from New Orleans too, well let me tell you all about the Second Great Devastation, but only after a few glasses of wine, they were bored with his anecdotes and preferred to hold him tight and pat him, saying you could almost be my son, of course I wouldn't make as free with him as I do with you, don't you think you've had a bit too much to drink my boy, but Bryan just laughed and said he was having too much fun, the most he'd ever had, oh yes they really had to hear the novel he was going to write, all about his black nanny whipping him with his mother's approval, in fact Lucia reminded him of this mother, a nicer version though, a little drunk maybe, indulging her prodigal son more, and the two of them shared a laugh at the salacious turn of events, Lucia and a woman of piety converted to the Children of God, standoffish, a picture that he could never erase no matter how far away he was, Kim wondered why's he avoiding me for these people, Lucia today, another tomorrow, they're old and decrepit, that must be what he likes, but what about death lurking just behind them, crazy, he's crazy, that's all, lifting a glass of rum with people just as crazy as he is till they finally throw him out for acting up, Kim felt her loneliness like a chill, though her body was burning up and starved, that was where the heat came from, the dry fire of hunger, Fleur avoided her too but not always, still at certain hours of the night she'd feel the absence of anyone to be with, no Bryan or Fleur, at least there was her dog to protect her from mugging and rape, maybe that Lucia wasn't so broken down anyway, perhaps she was just sick or something and it slowed her down, drained her memory, prematurely aged her, perhaps she no longer remembered that her sisters were keeping a lookout for her as she wound her way home, or even that she'd seen Bryan in the bar, not certifiable yet, possibly someone was watching over her closely as she went around feeding her cats and forgetting about her dogs at home, wondering how come she had so many, the truth was she simply couldn't leave them stranded and homeless, her sisters might say Lucia you've forgotten to buy food for them all, look at the state their coats are in, and she'd yell back at them to leave her alone, they all wanted to lock her away because she was a little short on memory, now is that so serious, then the laughing face of Bryan etched itself in her crumbling memory and she told her sisters I have a son, a very nice boy who lets me touch him, oh he so loves stroking and kissing, not a good-for-nothing like my own boy, never comes to see his mother, he's like you sisters of mine, he wishes I'd go away, my dogs and cats too, send me off to some black hole, a black hole where they can keep close watch on me, and what do you know Kim thought, with those doggy sideburns Bryan does look kind of like Misha, his strident laugh and hippity-hop manner weren't the most comforting to a woman with no memory who remembered him well all the same, Bryan was the light of her life though, as he was for Kim, not always but definitely at times, he showed Lucia his stigmata, the scars and whatnot on his arms and back, whipped, he said, really, look Lucia my dear, and as she placed her hands on him and felt his old wounds, she said dear boy how sorry I am, you'll get only words of love and tender caresses from me, what sort of mother could treat her son so, no don't even say her name, it's a curse to me now, a Child of God, that's her religion Bryan said, well it's a barbarous one, I must pardon her though, no you must never do that, no person in his right mind can do that, well you see my mother may be very high and mighty but she's also beautiful like you, Lucia, yes white hair and as beautiful and dignified as you are, one day he, Bryan, would be the one to walk Lucia's dogs and even get Misha's vet to come and take a look at them, and he too would be the one to look after Lucia's unwatered gardens, she forgot everything, always active and useful, though always a bit drunk too, Bryan would make Lucia's house worth living in, her cats and dogs fed, she'd be able to say to her sisters, I have a protector now and you can't hurt me anymore, I know you're itching to have me locked up in some hospice and take away all my money, that's what you want, nasty girls, you want what I have from the store where I made and sold all the jewellery myself, well the bank took the store and the jewellery, all of a lifetime's work, but I have Bryan now and he'll defend me, yes he will, I believe in him and that's the way it will be thought Kim, but would he get here tonight, the sun's setting over the sea, will he make it with today's meal, I pray he will and he almost always does with that hippity-hop step of his as he gets closer, besides Fleur would likely go to his mother's and play the piano as he used to when he was a kid, his mother always venerated that piano, refusing to sell it so he could come back home, if he came only once a month it was for that, the piano in his old room, all his scores and compositions would be there, he knew that, and possibly without even seeing her, like a blind man he'd walk straight over to the piano seeing nothing and hearing nothing but his *New Symphony*, sure thought Kim, he'd even neglect the meal his mother had ready for him and the clean clothes she'd hold out, saying you can't go on for- ever living in those dirty old things, even in the street, son do you hear what I'm saying, then she'd add, you do know the music sounds off, don't you, oh you used to play so well, and he longed to scream, so perhaps, knowing her as he did and wanting to avoid this, he might not even go there at all, it was late and here he was still in the street playing his flute amid the noise of the traffic. The last light of day lingered brilliant out on the lawn of the tennis court thought Adrien, the last of the rain had left tiny pearls on the grass like morning dew, he knew this from rising at dawn to write or translate in the lamplit room with blinds closed before the sun could force its way in, as it did while he set out walking slowly towards the sea and from there to the lush grass set aside as a tennis court, in the silver-shrub path lined with gilded palms, now he saw Charly's car pull up as if to wait for him at the court while the sun set on the ocean in bursts of orange flame, yes that black car was hers, well, well, my chauffeur's here just like she used to be for Caroline, careful now, because towards the end of her life Caroline warned me to beware of this girl, she's cruel and diabolical, I'll always be sorry I chose hers in Jamaica for my collection of faces in the spirit of the Caribbean, oh how wrong I was, and look what it's got me Adrien, despite my reputation as a photographer I'm all alone, maybe even the laughingstock of the friends I ignored when they warned me, well why wouldn't I, forever independent, that's me, this time though I'd've done better to heed you all when you advised me, not make fun of you, for I had to be drugged and robbed before I'd realize what had happened to me, this might be how Caroline gave voice to regrets that her employee Charly had abused her and her hospitality when she was no longer able to drive herself, her friends cursing a young mixed-blood girl named Charlotte, now the age of his own sweet daughter Karin, for slandering Charly, after all, literary circles were just as liable to curse and calumniate as any others he thought, and they denied that Charly had abused Caroline, oh if only Adrien had some sort of proof, what he did know was that he could not live without his adored wife, Suzanne, he sorely needed something to occupy and settle his perturbed spirit, he lived in frequent dread that she would no longer be there with him after so many years together, often glorious ones, the most admired writing couple, or rather the most envied, it was said without jealousy that they had everything in their favour, Adrien going so far as to envy the wife he esteemed above himself, marrying her writing talent with altruism and philanthropy as she did, bringing up children that were not her own, scooping them up from foster homes for young offenders, an exemplary woman from every viewpoint, and one whose poetry was noteworthy for its strength and clarity of vision, though sometimes criticized for its Hindu spiritual influences, of course Adrien himself was an altruist and humanist, though one who thought little of those outside his small circle of family and friends before meeting her, and paid little attention to this, being a poet much absorbed by his own writing and his translation of other authors, many of those other books piled up on his table and eliciting a scowl from him pending his critical verdict, it might be pitiless or generous, cynical or implacable, depending on his mood that day, we'll see, he thought, if only Suzanne had left him alone in his complacent egotism, reinforced by the intellectual habits of a reclusive writer not to be disturbed and with less and less free time, Blake, he had to concentrate on Blake, listening to Charles recite the author as he used to with Frédéric supplying musical accompaniment at their place in Greece, visited by the wise and the scholarly like some ancient temple, all this was far from his mind at the moment, yet the instant he lay down to rest, early to bed as he was, the memory of Charles and Blake came flooding back as if from the beyond, Charles's spirit saying time to sleep my friend, though I might ask you if you were not a little severe in this morning's review, me severe, said Adrien in the dream, you can never be hard enough on young pedants who don't know how to write he told Charles, you and Frédéric used to commune with the dead, remember those spiritualist sessions in Greece, please tell Suzanne not to distract me would you, she keeps telling me she never had enough time to write and it's my fault she published so little, at this point Charles's ghost was fading away on tiptoe, as he did in life Adrien thought, he could go back to sleep and when he woke up perhaps see the outline of Charly in her black car, gleaming in the sunlight after his game of tennis, and perhaps she'd lower the roof and say get in Adrien, I'll take you home if you like, then we can go shopping, or I can come back later if you'd rather, he was getting a little too attached to this routine, seeing her black car stop for him in the alley lined with silvery bushes and palms and the young woman in a cap waving to him from afar as though she'd been waiting for him, dreamily entertaining those barely formed proposals, he recalled poem fragments on yellowing scraps of paper that he still liked to fondle sometimes in the inside pocket of his blazer or in his white trousers as a reminder that he still liked writing love poems, this was somewhat artificial and quite new to him, and he knew it was rather odd in the twilight of his life, he set himself the challenge of never letting Charly know these vain feelings that could be so easily wounded, and gradually he supposed these poems would cross the forbidding threshold of the guilt he felt towards Suzanne, having turned his back on her and her demise, her deliberate choice and one that had forever isolated them from one another, so was it craven to believe he could live without her, she, not he, being the one with galloping leukemia who had opted for a swift end to it all at a clinic in Zurich, that supreme vanity of refusing to decline and suffer had been hers not his, hers and hers alone the choice to die in joy she said, and to go where, my poor Suzanne, to what sunlit landscape, oh she'd probably read too much of the Hindu spiritual masters he thought, not proper reading, childish words had convinced her she belonged in another world, one that did not really exist, when just like everyone she'd simply fall into a void from which there was no return, no restoration, no rehabilitation, no wiping clean of the slate, like a palm leaf, a pebble kicked accidentally, that's all, nothing, she would be nothing, the beautiful body of her youth, her hair, everything Adrien had desired and so loved in her, she'd said to him, recite one of your poems Adrien, that way I'll hear your voice while I . . . while I . . . and he hanging on to his existence had refused to take part in it with her, even letting go of her hand, for she'd be cold before the poem was over, listen my sweet he said, there's none I know by heart, but you used to Suzanne replied, no, now I can't, I've come this far with you and I must go, I'll miss my flight, I must . . . must . . . the words stumbled but were hardly compassionate he knew, others would be present at her provocative act, the ones offering the mortal remedy and the counter-remedy to ensure that the first was not rejected by her stomach, the steps in this ritual march were well prepared and sure-footed, Adrien though would not be a party to it, he'd leave first, yes leave, he was overwhelmed, disgusted by that sort of thing, and his own chest seemed to echo Suzanne's last heartbeats, the rhythm of her last steps into the night, the despicable night of a God he knew nothing about, a little music please, Suzanne said, what kind he asked, irritated, the piece that Frédéric played at the recital in Los Angeles a few years ago, I brought it with me, but Adrien was angry and wouldn't listen to Frédéric or anyone else, this wasn't the time, he blamed his wife and said so, you haven't thought about how hard this is going to be on Karin, have you, no, Suzanne replied, I've talked to the girls about this and we understand each other, in fact my dear Adrien, it was Karin's idea in the first place, well they're criminals too then, he shouted, wanting their own mother dead, no, Suzanne replied, luminous in her woman-hood and strong-willed as ever, they understand my right to dignity and always have, they were part of it, we decided long ago when I still had full control of my life and health that this is how it would be, no long, pointless, and torturous stay in hospital for me, watching myself fall apart, I wanted to go before that happened, while I was still whole, at first Karin and Tania said no Mama, we'll look after you if it comes to that and very good care too until . . . until . . . and I thought oh my poor girls, what am I getting them into, no, I've decided, this is how it will be, my dear Adrien look after our children, and once again at this final hour as she prepared to leave him and take the deadly medicine with the overzealous help of her self-effacing executioners, Adrien saw two nurses and a doctor, or was this his dream of the final step, and at that instant his irritation exploded and he said to her, my children, our children are adults, I beg you don't talk about them Suzanne my sweet, it's you I worry about, are you really sure this is what you want, there's still time to say no and we can get back on the plane together . . . we can . . . suddenly it terrified him that his wife was saying goodbye, letting go of him, of them, at least let her not pile their children, adult children, on him, for he had none, no family but her, Suzanne whom he'd always loved more than all, even his children, she was his love, his desire, the root of his being, all that he could not lose, she with whom he had always worked and written while she did the same on the other side of the Chinese screen, at times like one spirit in one body, so he might cry out all of a sudden in an anguished outburst, Suzanne you are there aren't you, then hear her laugh, so clear and calming that even now as she held the poison in her hand, helped along, yes definitely, by these effaced executioners, oh was he dreaming or insane or, she wouldn't be taking it just yet she was waiting till no one had anything more to say, then at that instant that same laugh tinged with irony, come now she said to her husband, be reasonable, you must go, it's almost time for your flight to Zurich and perhaps time I was alone, tomorrow you can kiss Karin and Tania for me and tell them I'm in a country of light, and tell them . . . Adrien shouted out no, no, I'll tell them nothing except that what you're doing is a scandal, oh yes that's what it is you know, not a thought for us and the horror we feel at this, oh yes a scandal, and upon that Adrien left the chamber where death was to be rendered, given, absorbed, and consented to, whether legal or not, whether he wished it or not, he felt guilty and repudiated by the one he had loved so very much, he wiped away tears, ridiculous, that's what it was, Suzanne was right, he wasn't being reasonable, he'd just march ahead and grab a taxi, she'd been far too enthralled and led astray by her spiritual masters, how had he managed to miss the risks she was lured into by these forces, well, well, as he arrived at the airport the following morning, tired and harried in his crumpled white suit and blazer with pockets full of used tissues, who should be waiting for him but Charly and her black car, it was her idea to draw closer to him, or was this just another wild dream of his, actually there was no one waiting, no one to help with his bag, reminiscent of Jean-Mathieu coming home downcast perhaps, but at least Caroline wasn't long in getting there complete with hat and gloves of course, counterpoint to Jean-Mathieu's perennial red scarf, more alone in life than Adrien, who wasn't dreaming after all as he scented the corn smell of Charly's delicious perfume from the black car that pulled up beside him, c'mon Adrien, please, you've had a rough trip, I'll take care of your bag for you, but at the same instant from the parking lot emerged his entire flock of children, sons and daughters, their hair flying, nervously badgering him with questions, dearest Mama, how did it go Papa, poor widowed Papa, let's take you home, oh how awful for you, for us all dear Papa, and while they vied with one another in their sympathy for his formless yet inconsolable sadness, Charly's car slid away into the city as she gradually disappeared beneath the shade of her cap through tinted windows, so this is the farce they call life thought Adrien, oh he'd've sold his soul to see Charly once more, how often he'd closely examined and written about each new book on the Faust character, damnable and immoral certainly, but not without a lingering attraction for a man like him, Faust having sold his soul not for the return of his youth but to satisfy his thirst for knowledge and pleasure, all pleasure being forbidden it seems, but he could identify with the character's insatiable thirsting after knowledge, including the occult sciences and the devil-given ability to accomplish miracles, now who wouldn't be tempted by that, by metamorphosis into a young man in search of every delight, the ability to be intimate with Charly and savour some of his more unwholesome penchants, yet here again came the voice of Caroline, please remember, my friend, how this girl ruined and devastated me, I must tell you this, one day she beat me up in my own house because I wouldn't give her a piece of jewellery that belonged to my mother, so violently that I fell, injured my face, and even lost a tooth, I was so humiliated and hurt that I didn't go outside for days, and when I did, how could I tell my dentist what had happened, beaten up like that, no, I stayed at home and didn't go to see any of you, so wounded in my pride I dared not ask for help, though I knew all of you, Adrien, Suzanne, Charles, Frédéric, and Jean-Mathieu, would have come to my aid, but you know how I am don't you Adrien, I hadn't the courage to ask for anything, so do beware of this girl, Adrien, he remembered now the silent Caroline shut up in a house to which only Charly held the key, Caroline, so very sociable when called upon, always on the arm of Jean-Mathieu, Caroline with her hats and gloves, inaccessible now, sick perhaps, and Jean-Mathieu enquiring of his friends what on earth is happening with our dear friend, I've written but got no answer, I've phoned and left messages, the same thing, I even left a letter in her box telling her how worried I was, tell me friends, what's going on, tell me, and after that he stopped writing or phoning and the drama she was undergoing in isolation lost the attention of her friends, perhaps that was what she wanted, to be alone as she so rapidly aged, or was she held hostage, and who was this young Caribbean woman they saw out walking her dogs anyway, Jean-Mathieu had seen Caroline alone with them late at night, occasionally going around the same block several times as though unsure of her way, and when the dogs tugged her towards her flower-decked house under the elms, she'd repeat vaguely oh yes of course, that's where I live, this is the street, as she rang the doorbell and the fleeting shadow of a young woman took hold of her and pulled her inside, come here, come on, imagine going out with your dogs, aren't you afraid someone will see you like that, Jean-Mathieu heard those words and felt shot through with sorrow, thinking oh dear Caroline have I really lost you then, yet here she was repeating in his ear words he had no desire to hear, don't trust her dear Adrien, I sensed far too late that she was capable of beating me, of stealing my money and jewels, so mightn't she also tear up letters from my friends and erase phone messages, of course, simply burn and destroy it all, mercilessly lay waste to my life perhaps, my entire life, but Adrien thought okay now, let's not get carried away, we can't let ourselves be utterly destroyed without agreeing in some way, and I'm sure, Caroline, that you had a hand in it, maybe even an unconscious wish to be loved or to relive your youth, sold your soul to the devil in exchange for affection perhaps, Charly's presence in the house charmed you and possibly postponed the hour of your death, as it would for me, Caroline, nothing was broken off or destroyed without your consent, don't overdo it now, still her words haunted him, crushing and heavy, beware of Charly, that's all, but maybe it was already too late. Bryan strolled through the streets carrying the cardboard box tied up with string so nothing would fall out, this was Kim's dinner, in fact when he stopped at the usual bars and cafés along the way, a thin stream of the lemon sauce on the fish flowed down his wrist as he chatted excitedly with his friends, no one listened as he told them it was possible to go to hell and get out again the same day, or that he'd loaned his room to Marcus's brothers who'd stolen his books, his furniture, and even the pictures painted by his sister in New York, all of it simply loaded into a truck, yup, to hell and back in a day he said smacking himself on the chest, without some higher power he couldn't put a name to grabbing him by the neck and saving him each time, he wouldn't be here anymore, okay, Maria listened, okay, she clinked her glass of St. Croix rum to his, you sure don't lead a boring life Bryan, you've got too many things going wrong for that, it's true, I'm not lying he said, this morning everything was gone, my room was empty, the only thing left is my bed and the nails in the walls, Marcus's brother robbed me to buy coke for the week, and all I have is the waiter's outfit I'm wearing right now, good thing it's still clean and white, and the shoes too, I tell you, without the higher power to guide me, really friends, I wouldn't be here with you he yelled, today in fact they caught the guy and he's spending the night in prison, along with his brother Marcus, they're up for the same thing, but of course no one knows where my stuff is, it's not that I'm glad he got caught, believe me, he was a good guy, that's why I lent him my room, but that's some weird family, him and his brother and his sister Louisa, some weird family, this morning I sent flowers to my mother in New Orleans and do you know what, she sent them back, Happy birthday Mama, your loving son Bryan and she sent 'em right back, honest, you can go to hell and back in one day really, and this Force that always came to his rescue at the last second, this unnamed, unknown Force suddenly spread itself out before him as he set off to find Kim, and she'd never forget that night, after his shift at the Café Español he might have forgotten Kim waiting for her dinner in the cardboard box, in any event there were so many tempting detours on his way through the streets at day's end, friends calling out from here and there, hey Bryan, where you off to, how's it going, what's up with the box and the string, no more dripping from the edge by now and he didn't want to get his uniform dirty, so he walked calmly gazing out at the sea as he passed a Catholic church filled with adults and children all dressed up, either a funeral or a wedding this afternoon he thought, the bells were tolling slowly, ah there you are it's a funeral, hmmph that bitch sent my flowers back, boy doesn't that just hit you where it hurts thought Bryan, and she has the guts to get down on her knees and pray, that's hard to picture, snob that she is, hey Bryan, c'mon over and join us said a voice, and Bryan thought I've really got to tell them you can go to hell and back in a single day, today Marcus's brother steals me blind and he's already in jail poor guy, it's not fair, I never sleep at my place, I didn't need the bed or the furniture or the bookshelves, I can live without all that stuff, okay not my sister's paintings, I do want those, but the guy shouldn't have gone to some stinking prison cell for it, he was thinking all this and waving his hands, his mother had said he spun like a top, yeah but the flowers, he thought, they'd come back with a card that said Dear Son, remember He said He'd come like a thief in the night, so are you ready my son, ready to see those Horsemen in the sky, are you ready my disowned one living in depravity, He will come as a thief murmured Bryan, yeah and you can go to hell and back in one single day, right, and the proof is my boss telling me off this morning, if you're late for the breakfast service I'll have to fire you the same way I did Vladimir, no problem with your clothes, they're fine, but you're late and your hands shake when you serve the first cups of coffee, you look hungover and we can't have that here, same as Vladimir, Pete, or anyone else, so I said to him, thought Bryan, Vladimir wasn't honest like me, he got fired from three restaurants, same thing with Pete, both of them illegals, these immigrants get everything we do, then they take our jobs, they're just liars and thieves, so why don't they go back where they came from, probably 'cause they're no good there either, no-good swindlers and hoods, they get Medicare but I don't, how's that, they get the whole thing but not me, oh now don't be racist the boss says, but it's true said Bryan, worked up, then he noticed night creeping gradually over the turquoise water, boy what a day this has been, he heard the cries of gulls, hens, and cocks, they'd soon be climbing into their hiding places in the trees and the branches would weep reddish petals, it was true about Vladimir and Pete, hoods, that's what they were, but no one believed it, he was the honest one, okay, just one short stop for a pal who hailed him and he'd be off to rejoin Kim and Fleur, there in the bar he had a stroke of inspiration and he started drawing with his finger, no chalk, no pen, no pencil, nothing but his finger on the marbled bar, it was good, everyone said so, large birds, no matter if they all laughed and called him the Madman of Bahama Street or maybe he was playing the fool for fun, they considered him to be bright, and he went right on drawing and contemplated the cardboard box on the counter beside him, soon he'd be there with Kim, well Kim and Fleur plus their dogs, and he couldn't take too long because he so needed to get some sleep, in fact right there with his head on the bar would do, he'd already drawn on it, maybe even written a chapter of his novel at the same time, and Maria laughed some more, the others too, oh how they laughed when he said yeah it's probably Virgil, Marcus's brother who took everything in my room, I mean I wrote on all the walls, even on the bathroom tiles, words jumping all over the place like fish, honest, I saw them, okay all those words and pictures would be invisible to you but I could see them and they were going to eat me all up, so maybe it's time I moved out of there, while I'm still in one piece, skin, bone, all of me might be gone soon, no my friends, it's time, I mean it, every single word of this is true, Virgil and Marcus, both of them caught with drugs after they sold all my stuff, up against the wall and the cops handcuffed him, of course you can go to hell and not come back in a day as well, I Brilliant hereby swear that every word of what I've seen today is true, oh boy do I feel tired, sleepy, then before slipping into a drunken sleep he remembered Kim waiting there for him same as every evening, he spotted the box on the marble counter, mustn't forget that he thought, no mustn't forget Kim and Fleur, though Fleur didn't like either of them, no one in fact, thought Bryan, he was obsessed with music and nothing else, he disliked everyone, but Kim, thought Bryan, I mustn't forget her. On this bizarre and unusual taxi ride with Robbie, Petites Cendres reflected that this wasn't the only weird thing he'd encountered since being dragged out from under his bedcovers, why was he up anyway he wondered, and where was Mabel with the parrots Jerry and Merlin, how could Petites Cendres forget the scene when some nasty fan of Yinn's, no doubt a junkie with white powder still on his nostrils from a recent line, and Petites Cendres still in withdrawal, headed straight over to Yinn in the street, grabbed his sexy leg, then his foot while Yinn was relaxing with Jason between shows at the Saloon, so relaxed in fact that one leg peeked out from under his blue satin dress, he hadn't really noticed until an incongruous admirer took off his shoe and began greedily nibbling his foot, quite detached, Yinn asked what was going on, while the other, still holding the foot in both hands, said you're such a great dancer, yeah well I won't be tonight if you don't stop biting and licking my toes like that, totally uninterested thought Petites Cendres, or did he not realize exactly how libidinous, more than lascivious the young man's actions were, and why on earth was Yinn so complacent, even nonchalant about it, was he just weary or bored by the lubriciousness this late at night, did Yinn really like fooling with sordid arrivals like this wondered Petites Cendres, jealous once more, fiercely jealous that night, with Robbie beside him so calm and wrapped up in his thoughts of coronation and all the partying he was chatting about with the driver, with not a thought for Petites Cendres and his inflamed memories, maybe love was vain if it meant feeling this kind of mean jealousy, jealousy killed love, didn't it, but the sting of jealousy Petites Cendres felt could easily come back with raging ferocity he thought and go on living practically forever, Robbie, in all the innocence of his coronation daydreams and his determination to get Petites Cendres within sight of the sea where he could smell the salt air, then of course drag him off to said coronation later in the evening, and the other girls, especially Yinn, queen sublime for a decade, would be there of course, Robbie was fully expecting Petites Cendres to make this comeback, it would take more courage though because living was more than merely getting by Robbie said, and this lofty courage was the kind shown by Fatalité, right, but it didn't keep him alive did it thought Petites Cendres, not in the least, someone in a green plastic bag was all he had become, sure he was beautiful onstage with those long legs that went on forever and that snarky smile, then *poof,* all gone, the shadow cast by a light bulb, the one they left on in her apartment, see she's still with us, her shade having somehow woven its way through the harsh white rays splayed against the dark, there's no other way it can end thought Petites Cendres, even for the ones who manage to draw things out at Acacia Gardens, unaware in their whitewashed places that they're still being discriminated against, all conveniently gathered under one roof, one banner, even the ones who no longer dare to go out at night or walk in their own gardens by day, yet giving way a little at a time to the disintegration within as they endure, high up on their balconies gently rocked by the sea breeze, limbo is theirs already, clammy skins, unseeing eyes, and in need of canes if ever they dare to go out on the town, young yet skin and bones nevertheless, Petites Cendres thought no, this is not for me as he took Robbie's hand overloaded with rings, then with more assurance he said out loud, so Robbie you're taking me out for cocktails by the sea like you used to with Fatalité, daytime too, my brother and my ally Robbie said somewhat absently, brother most of all. Martha had made a museum of Fleur's bedroom and now she was its curator and here time stood still, he reflected, there was a dust cover on his piano, newspaper clippings, pictures and articles all about him as a child still on the wall, even a poster of him with Clara at a music camp in Europe for an improvised concert they gave on piano and violin, this poster marked the cutoff point in his life he mused, after two faces joined in their passion for music came nothing, a dreary and unhappy existence in his case, the sordidness of the streets one could never wash off, the young boy playing piano barefoot in the fringed vest his mother had made, hair straight down to his waist and combed repeatedly till it shone, how was it that the boy willing to tackle such a demanding sonata hadn't foreseen this, what careless folly had led him to squander his gifts, so indolent and joyous in these pictures, the boy was like a canary or a dove or the nightingale he used to imitate, fingers to the keyboard, so full of imagination, how had he become this sad thing in which, however diminished, the tiny flame still flickered, but tomorrow sitting at the piano would he hear his mother say no that's off-key, you really need to practise more often, you don't work the way you used to, living as a beggar, really, whatever did I do to deserve such a son, what indeed, and her brow would furrow into such wrinkles, did he put them there, lines of bitterness, first you're getting a bath, she said bustling around him, patient and charitable despite it all, she did love this disgusting boy as only a mother could, mothers do understand everything, or they should, otherwise who else can she added, mother and son both humiliated he thought to himself, and he pictured those others he met performing in taverns and bars at night, so much like him, ambling slowly back to his spot on the beach with his imposing dog Damien leading the way and weary of it all, tired of the filth and the hunger his mother chided him about, condemned to keep moving through the dust of the town, alone but for his dog, sometimes bumping into some other musician, one of his future selves playing on the terraces, very young with a baby face and playing his electric guitar and stepping all over the wires on the wooden floor with his bare feet, he took requests and wore a fringed vest just like Garçon Fleur when he was small, his long hair flattened under a misshapen hat, the song was a sad one about a friend killed by a demonic gang in the middle of the desert for having double-crossed some cocaine- or heroin-pushers, poor errant knight, or perhaps he'd been unable to pay them off in time, *poor errant knight my friend*, so went the song of the boy who looked like Fleur, his moving sincerity got its share of applause, and if only it had been Fleur singing about his yearning for Clara, but this wasn't for him, no, he was a concert musician, not the clown musician his mother wanted him to be, no more idiotic harlequinades, no, the pathetic days of Garçon Fleur the buffoon child prodigy dished up to a ravenous audience were over, this was the object of Fleur's daily murders, begging in the street and still playing his flute so well, he was his own parent and thus far above this miserable condition, and the murder of Garçon Fleur consumed him, tormented with its spectre, yes, yes, this very murder consumed him day and night. Faust was interpreted by each writer in his own way, thought Adrien resting in the park surrounded by the silvery bushes after his round of tennis, he wasn't quite young enough for such vigorous exercise anymore, losing a match now and then hardly mattered either, but health and exercise and taxing his muscles, these made Adrien the man of health he'd always been, then why these headaches and this insomnia now that Suzanne was gone, last night she'd been easier on him and he'd slept better, though he saw her in a dream wearing a white summer dress and she said hello dearest friend in all my life, surely you can see better days coming to you, but perplexed, he'd asked her if she wasn't putting him on, making fun of him just a bit, are you sure, he asked, that I really was the friend of a lifetime, was and still am, I sense some resentment in you, I really do, but Suzanne hugged him, laughing her bright clear laugh, oh here they were together and embracing in that very same park beneath the silvered palms open to the summer like parasols, and they'd sit there on the same stone bench where Adrien sat before heading home from tennis, talking and touching hands, I'm telling you again, Suzanne said, you have been the friend of a lifetime, for so many years we were lovers, remember how we met when we were twenty, all set to be published at the same time by the same editor, but you'd be the one with the success and all those prizes and I'd be so proud of you, no, Adrien said, no I don't, I don't remember anything, what I do remember about being twenty was what a vain, obnoxious young man I was, I didn't deserve you at all, what could be worse than a conceited writer, emboldened by his arrogance, the thing I hate most in young writers, ah that's why you hounded poor young Augustino, no, no Adrien said, you can't really call Augustino vain, though he does bother me a great deal, and at this point the conversation took a nastier turn, with Suzanne yet again accusing her husband of such awful negligence and other flaws, but this time the dream was not tarnished by her reproaches to him, she tenderly raised her eyes to him and appeared to forgive every last bit of his nonsense, she simply asked him how the work was coming on Marlowe's *Doctor Faustus* and how far along it was, you were the man of my life she concluded as she prepared to leave him, leave where he asked, he tried to grasp the edge of her white summer dress and caress with his fingertips the sparkle of life and laughter beneath it, but she was already gone, nowhere in sight. Bryan hippity-hopped his way to Kim, still holding the cardboard box by its string, leaning a little as though tottering through the last crowd of cocks not yet flown up into the bougainvilleas, with horns honking at them the cocks and hens and day-old chicks panicked, boy what a racket Bryan thought to himself, go on and go to sleep all my angels, quick up into the trees you cocky cocks, boy, sending those flowers back was some insult, especially his mother's note on the card, banished son, will you be ready when the cocks crow neither at evening nor at dawn, when the moon is a dark circle in the sky and the evening's cup is filled with blood, will you be ready, son, to see the stars fall to earth from the sky, will you Bryan, and the woman's great fear pierced Brilliant's heart through and through, even at this distance, too many rum drinks with the affectionate Lucia, that must be it, delirium as Kim would say, transmitted from mother to son, more of her religious ramblings, each word resonating within him, yeah him and his hurricanes, she'd sowed the Fear in him alright, it beat inside him like a heart, but the Force would come to save him was his reply to her, look over there, it's luminous in front of you, and there too, this I would wonder with the brush of Fear's wings inside me, maybe it was only Lucia's voice reasoning him back to calm, her hand or Kim's on his cheek, they'd be the ones to save him when he untracked like this, but it might also be that these were really terrifying predictions written in the sky and he wasn't going to be spared after all, true he did see them written everywhere, on the bathroom tiles and the marble countertop and on the bar, all messages from the Fear or from life or from some unfathomable and inaccessible design, everywhere too was Victor, Nanny's real-life son, his black brother, since Nanny was a mother more real than his own, she'd been the one to teach him his very first prayers, and even then her jazzy voice rose in him against the deadly waters rising all around him, ballooning Victor's coveralls and drowning him, drowning him and him only among all those whites who knew how to swim or paddled by, and Nanny's voice calling out to Victor in the deluge, the sound of her prayers and supplications accompanied Victor's swollen coveralls as they carried Victor away, now no longer trembling and thrashing and, thought Brilliant, it was Victor too who had given him the Fear, finally just too many calamities, Adrien wondered, why was I really so indifferent to Jean-Mathieu's departure for his last Venetian summer, every day he wrote to me from his boarding house yet I hardly ever replied, okay sure I was busy working on my piece, I always am despite constant interruptions, but Jean-Mathieu, such a venerable friend, how could I forget him and the letter he meant for Caroline that she never got, Caroline the manipulated, Caroline the prisoner, no she never did see that letter of his, manipulated and held prisoner by Charly or so they said, but perhaps it wasn't true, just a nasty piece of gossip, you can't believe everything you hear can you, sometimes the most alluring people are victims of the worst envy and petty viciousness, and who doesn't envy youth, today I'm visiting the Doge's Palace Jean-Mathieu had written in that calligraphic hand, there I'll see the works of Veronese once again, when I was on the third bridge over the canal I thought about the Titians I'd see again too, oh what happiness my dear Adrien, all I lack now is Caroline by my side, please drop me a line to say how she is, I'd really like that dear Adrien, without her I tend to forget my scarf, that's how I caught cold this damp summer, Adrien smiled, he was so wrapped up in his art and his Venice walks that he forgot everything else, and what do you bet that all the time he's looking at the Veroneses and Titians he's really thinking about Caroline, they never travelled apart, and the more my old friend thought about her, the heavier it weighed on his heart, I'm sure it was like that when I failed to answer his letters in my icy indifference, so worried I was about finishing before autumn, Adrien, as you know, I'm an agnostic, and for us art is not the ultimate consolation, even this his last letter sounded like a call for help, and Adrien had not taken the time to reply, though it did strike him as odd that Jean-Mathieu mentioned a painting he'd seen in the Louvre with Caroline, Antonello of Messina's *Christ at the Column*, she had hated it though for no reason Jean-Mathieu could find, the bareness of the face perhaps or the purposelessness of the painful contortions, what was it in Christianity, Jean-Mathieu wondered, that so repelled Caroline that they wound up quarrelling over it right there in the museum, something the peaceful Jean-Mathieu deplored, he so wished she'd understand that art related solely to the profane and universal soul, a choir of all voices, all impulses united, the absolute depth that precludes all division, and Jean-Mathieu, in his bed soaked with feverish sweat, shivered under his scarf that by now was also damp, thus died the aesthete in his Venetian boarding house, aesthete to the end, his Veroneses and Titians companions to hoist sail with him, as when he was a kid aboard his own boat in Halifax, where he'd learned his trade at the age of fifteen, master of the seas with fog drifting over his boat, and now in a modest Italian rooming house, while I, Adrien, was just as unresponsive as Caroline, though not manipulated and forcibly confined at home like her, never even receiving his letters she said, wandering the streets with her dogs when she was let out late at night so no one would see her, such is life thought Adrien, not enough time devoted to our friends, ah if only I'd known, if only, Jean-Mathieu, Caroline, and my dear Suzanne, if only I'd realized, of course I'd have done things differently, and alone on his stone bench Adrien watched the silvered palm leaves like umbrellas overhead, he was about to pull a notebook and pencil from the inner pocket of his blazer to record how the large leaves spread around him in the heat, especially seated at this spot in summer when their tropical growth is at its best, how these leaves seem like sharpened blades, no, that's not right, there was nothing aggressive in this part of nature apart from the violent winds that shook his house right down to the stilts, what was it then that made him think of knife blades, oh how he missed his wife, that must be it, no he could no longer write or even prepare his mind for it, no this is not how it is with such aggressively driven images and metaphor, the thinking, the writing is cock-eyed, Charly's black car showed up in the lane, its roof shining in the setting sun, that's it, he was untracked enough to think it was real, that she was there lurking behind the window shades, pure evil, the powerful venom he thirsted for. Daniel could hear Laure's sharp voice demanding the right to smoke, to smoke anywhere she liked, even in an airport, how many hours was it going to take before planes started taking off again, what was going on anyway, a bomb threat maybe, someone had something to hide, a plot against passengers held in waiting areas surrounded by screens showing nothing but sports as though nothing else was going on in the world, no, nothing to tell you, not a flight out since this morning, and what did Daniel think of that, there's nothing normal about this, nossir, wait and see Daniel, they'll find a way to pass a law forbidding us to smoke in our own apartments or even our cars and that's only the start of their intolerance, we smokers are outcasts, now what do you think of that, but Daniel had fallen asleep in a rather uncomfortable chair as he watched the plover do its sand-dance on the beach while the sky pinked over the waves, the day's nearly over he thought, she's right, this isn't normal, we get so used to delays and never knowing when we're coming and going, in limbo between two places and neither is a certainty, at least he can read, write, and phone his kids, so this is his office, yes of course he'll get there late, maybe never at all, and through the plate glass he saw a transparent sea beneath a pink sky, then briefly closing his eyes, he envisioned his grandson bathing there, yes Samuel was holding him by the hand and saying go for it, and as Samuel let go Rudolf's the eager little hand, he was off running, dazzled, through the transparent water of this calm sea, but not too far, okay, come back now Samuel called, Rudy come back here will you, all at once the slack water became turbulent and the sea began to roar, where was the boy, his father continued to call him, Rudy, Rudy, as the water rapidly changed colour, weighted with something acrid, black and grey, and Daniel saw the boy again, this time among the brown-coated pelicans, turtles and fish off the coast of Louisiana, all of them struggling against the waves, barely breathing under the oily film completely covering them like a sheet clinging to their bodies, the boy was among them, barely breathing and yelling Papa, Papa and struggling for the beach, but where was Rudy's body under all that, was he even alive now, all that could be seen was an eye shining through the encircling oil like a pelican's or tortoise's, the eye of children and animals judging us, and the voice, the searing voice of Laure desperate for cigarettes, pierced his dream and awoke Daniel, still haunted by what he'd seen as though his grandson's burial in oil had been all too real, yes too real indeed, it had come to this, our worst nightmares no longer had to be imagined, they were all around us, and with no one to blame but ourselves, you dropped off said Laure, I knew you weren't listening, we've got to clean off Rudolf, all of us, scrubbing till we see the white of their skin, the glint of their eyes beneath the sticky tears of black oil, let me clean them all up, all of them, Rudolf, the brown pelicans, the newborn turtles and their mothers, wash them all clean, but does that mean they can breathe, no matter what we do, will they still breathe, Samuel's striking choreography would open in New York this fall, that is what Daniel had fallen into as he drifted away from Laure, he'd watched rehearsal clips on his computer, yes of course that was it, like Augustino when he wrote, Samuel had translated implacable reality only too closely into symbolic dance, and though Daniel admired his son, this was truly unsettling and upsetting, yes that was the thing, both sons troubled him by constantly confronting their father with what they were thinking, rebellious demonstrations and testimonials, as though haranguing him in unison, yes Papa, you've got to be part of this mutation and revolution Papa, its about being or not being, why hesitate, why hold back eh, what exactly are you clinging to, but Daniel had no answer for them, except Mai, he still had Mai and her innocence and Rudolf as well, they had to be spared, and perhaps even his own ingenuousness too, possibly an inexplicable sort of candour, perhaps behind the times, even backward they might say, candour being to them a weakness, then maybe he wouldn't say anything, just listen to them in silence, and would that silence be a sign of victory for both Augustino and Samuel? Yes indeed, each writer had his own interpretation of the restless young Marlowe's Faustus, the short-lived playwright must have seen his own defiance of death in the devil's invitation to a feast of the immortal senses thought Adrien, pleasure being his own form of victory over death, rebel that he was, he struggled bitterly for justice and against the power of monarchs and the corruption of money, for Marlowe the devil was among us, at the core of kings and governments, leading us to ruin, the superstition and cruelty of the Middle Ages still so very close, his Faustus had to appear in the most vibrant colours, with blood flowing abundantly over the hanged and crucified, and finally Faustus, through the extravagant Marlowe, cast down and punished mercilessly for power-lust, not merely downfall but damnation, what disintegration, men abusing women, the poor Marguerites of this world abandoned with their children, yet neither overthrown nor punished, many men perverting the innocent, thought Adrien, then continuing on their way, the Mephistopheles of Goethe and Marlowe in all of us, dreaming of erupting in all his bestiality, caring little about being reduced to this sole part, thus ran Adrien's musing there on his stone bench beneath the silvered palms, and if he had been this Faust, such dubious morals held under the sway of Mephistopheles, he would have requested an hour's peace of mind so he could sleep one night alone without Suzanne, who was still too close while in her nirvana, yes, that's what the devil could grant him, one night of peace without conflict or bewitching presence, one night that didn't serve to sharpen his sense of her as before, that didn't bring back the sound of her laughter, no, perhaps he'd also negotiate a brief hour in the car with Charly in the twinkle of her lying look as she turned to face him under that cap of hers, the dark twinkle of those trickster eyes, no, this he knew, he'd ask only to have one glance, as though Charly were a statue, then he could manage to forget

Suzanne, well now maybe he should jot down these thoughts on Marlowe, if only to answer Suzanne's metaphysical question how's the Marlowe book coming my dear Adrien, as if he were an intellect and nothing more, a mind in search of words and phrases, or at least the mechanism of a mind, a precious thinking-machine, one that now seemed so empty, yes, one night without insomnia was all that he asked, or possibly one with some voluptuous phantasms, it was getting late and his dictionaries lay abandoned on the table as they did each evening, he'd take a long swim in the pool, bah he thought, pact with the devil or no, I'm happy to live my life, why not call old Isaac in his towers on The-Island-Nobody-Owns, still boyish-looking in his beige shorts, and tell him, tell the old architect, still developing plans for houses built high as always, so he could be close to the sea, surrounded by thousands of singing birds like some fresh-built paradise, say to him, well, immerse himself in the vigour of a man who seemed immortal, and what could be more comforting than that, Adrien thought, when one's heart can be so troubled about so little, whether Charly or the devil. He may have been feverishly excited and that was why as he walked Bryan imagined that every woman and man was walking along with him, racing along faster than usual, but where to, and the febrility increased as they all shed their skins as though they were clothes, till they were a crowd of skeletons running wearily and discarding their flesh like leprous coats on their way to some illusory community dinner they'd been promised at home, the apartment that was no longer theirs, only a few would get into this delusion of a home, thus it was that they ran faster and faster and their bones grated against one another, men, women, children all running in the heat of the sun, and the thought of it panicked Bryan, who was walking too fast and wearing himself out, the cardboard box still in hand, no, his mother had invented those messages from heaven, she lied about everything, and it was cruelty that prompted her to send those birthday flowers back to her son, especially when she liked to think of herself as a charitable person, why hadn't she taken pity on her son who was in the middle of this stampede of people running to their Friday community dinner and a place to spend Saturday night, he was taking a chance on losing his job at the Café Español to those sly ones Pete and Vladimir, oh no, he wasn't going to let that happen, sure he was the same as Fleur and Kim and all those others racing for the Friday meal the merchants offered the homeless, especially the young ones, all of them running, running even as the flesh melted from their bodies till they could not even recognize one another, Daniel realized that what Augustino wrote was probably true after all, older criminals were no longer the ones being punished, they had the time to wait, officials guilty of a million crimes, videos showing the killing fields of their victims' skulls and bones in Cambodia, sure these high officials of the Khmer Rouge were guilty of genocide but they'd never be sentenced for their crimes against humanity, no, old age was their way out and one was now Minister of Social Affairs, an idealistic member of parliament in the terror regime, impassive as the bones of the millions they'd killed unspooled before the court in unending videos, barely affording a sardonic and idiotic smile at the mountain of bones in a field, one, a woman, lowered her eyes behind her sunglasses, no, see nothing, not a thing, but as Augustino wrote, no one would be punished, not one of them, the fragility of age was their smokescreen, wilfully blind to their massacres, no feelings of shame, faces blank and showing no more than a sardonic wrinkle of a cruelty so infinite it would concede nothing, even hardening over time, petrifying into the idiotic stupidity of senility, little by little to be forgotten about, yes forget, that's what we do, we acquit those who commit the worst crimes, so wrote Augustino in his book *Letter to Young People Without a Future* Daniel thought, no, of course these things cannot be denied but why must Augustino constantly rehash the past, he grew up amid happiness and celebration, so why must he turn against the very privilege that saw him born, it's incomprehensible, it was the same for so many anarchistic minds, considered Daniel, touched by the revelation that reality is not what they thought, they became irate and complex like Augustino probably, pioneers against our well-being, yes he thought, that was probably it. Jerry, the fluffy white parrot, clung to Mabel's shoulder as she rode her bike, and he kept squawking and asking her where they were going over and over, we're going Mama, and she replied we're going with Merlin, yup to the pet cemetery to bury Merlin your brother under some roses, as she wept Jerry kissed her on the cheek, sliding his feathery head closer to hers and gently pecking at her temples just under the thickness of her hair, Mama, Mama he repeated, OK, OK, we're going, I managed to dig out the pellet the Shooter put in him, a tiny one really, that I got hold of with my fingers, it was in his wing and I got it out through his crest, boy one day I'm gonna get that Shooter and haul him over to the sheriff, you can bet on that Jerry, I will, I've got him here in the bicycle basket covered up with my shawl, the most beautiful bird in Brazil, they tore him apart on me, so cuddly, me cuddly Jerry picked up, yes under the red roses in my basket, Mabel answered, finding the ride a long one through traffic, feeling defeated, she pedalled slowly, so Jerry said, faster Mama, faster, but Mabel was feeling the heaviness of sadness and all she was wearing, so someone seeing her go by would take her for any poor black woman having a bad day, but they'd be wrong, for Mabel was the owner of a boarding house, in fact she was afraid they'd send Petites Cendres away for treatment when she really would like to keep him with her, especially now Merlin was gone, oh the most magnificent bird in all Brazil, a wonder, that's what he was, and if Petites Cendres goes too the house'll be empty, my Bahamian grandmother's house and my mother's, not all my guests are as nice as Petites

Cendres even if he is lazy, which okay is a sin but his benefactor pays me well, let's go Mama, let's go Jerry insisted on her shoulder, at least I sold all my homemade ginger drinks tonight, some artist bought them all, the house still has a mortgage on it and quite a few of my tenants steal things, which is a sin, and I have to tell them to go shoot up somewhere else but they keep coming back, plus some of them are all right, yes Mabel still has her family home but what's the use if Petites Cendres has to move out, his anonymous benefactor says there's a whole medical team waiting for him at Acacia Gardens, still I know him like he is my own son, he just needs some love that's all, Bryan was hippity-hopping drunk, recalled Lena, later a psychologist but now a student along with an army of volunteers who had opened the Lighthouse Centre for homeless kids, rainbow kids, and others like Fleur and Kim, not exactly kids anymore but she called them that anyway, Lena the exalted one gathered kids from Mexico, Peru, and wherever else she went and brought them to the Lighthouse Centre, that was their cause, all of them, but at eighteen Fleur and Kim were too old for this, you'll get hot water at our shelters, toothbrushes, even the Internet so you can contact your parents if you want to, but Kim and Fleur said they had no one and anyway they could sleep on the toothless Old Salt's boat, where the tattooed orphans helped him fish, teens with a history of violence who Kim and Fleur tried to stay away from, though the Old Salt had a way with them, as he said, they're better off fishing with me than rotting in prison, you see you've got no radar to guide you said the psychologist Lena, our shelters will be your beacons, we'll help get you back to your families, go back to school or find a job, no sermons, not from us, we only want to get you off of the streets, no one under eighteen sleeps in the dorms with the adults, we won't allow it, no legal record of you or food stamps, our Lighthouse Centre is for emergencies only, look, wouldn't you rather go to college and become an engineer or a biologist, adapt and fit in, the streets are dangerous for you my friends, think of those squatters in New Orleans this winter, burned alive in an abandoned house, eight of them wandering the streets and squatting together like ravenous wolves on the prowl and trying to keep warm on a freezing cold night, all of them burned, Lena was determined to save people like these homeless squatters, no child without a roof over his head, that's what we're about, they listened but they didn't get it, Kim and Fleur and Jérôme the African, they weren't going to be engineers or accountants or whatever, they'd just go on in the same old unwholesome way, brushing their teeth in the street or on the beach alongside their dogs or with their pet rats or mice perched on their heads or else snakes or iguanas clinging to them, no child without a roof over his head, such was Lena's mantra, that's all we want, as though she were talking about pets left out in the night by their owners, but there was a multitude of them and the charitable girl couldn't take them all in, she was only a student after all, Brilliant longed to buy her a drink but she didn't partake, only water she said, and what little she had on her was for the homeless, you know you are the lighthouse laughed Bryan, though he was put out that she refused his company, c'mon, one drink at the Café Español, still it did him good to remember her, maybe there were a few beacons in the night after all, not many mind you, I wonder where she is now, what city is she in or what alley or tin shack, no you didn't see them often but they existed, these beacons in the night, where was Lena, in Mexico or Peru, still pursuing her dream of no child without a roof over his head, Lena bent double under her backpack in the dirty alleyways of slums, wherever she pitched her tent and kids ran through the open sewers, a beacon, sure she was, Bryan thought, a beacon, and he remembered the festive nights, what parties, so many celebrations on the beach where he worked as a waiter, lighting their bamboo torches in a halo of smoke that made his eyes water, evenings after weddings or some holiday or other, a white sea of tents all around him and white tablecloths with all the settings and candles in place, then suddenly it was time for the gigantic feast as two servers in white carried in a stuffed piglet on a silver platter, Bryan could barely bring himself to look at the poor animal freshly killed that morning, its whole body with the eyes put out, he dared not think, here it was about to be carved up and eaten by all these people who were already too well-fed, stuffed too, he dared not think about it, barely turning to face it like some wounded child on a stretcher, pink-skinned from the oven, oh if only he hadn't seen this, was it his mother the mayoress who hosted these morbid banquets, the leftovers to be eaten downstairs by Victor and Nanny, now what was this, was it Vladimir and Pete pushing him to one side in their white outfit, yet looking like gravediggers, yes, something like Vladimir and Pete coming through, let us by they said, what's your problem boy, go back and take care of your parasols you beach clown, don't you know how dumb you look in those white shorts and socks, the sea beyond them was as blue as ever, luminous, and the bamboo torches threw their smoke into the sweet air, men and women laughing and singing, Bryan remembered those party nights, all that celebrating down by the beach when he didn't even know where he'd be spending tonight or tomorrow, maybe in his boss's car, for he couldn't go back to his room, too many phantoms of the deluge with the dead and drowned following behind as you climbed the steps, always, they were always there, and people would just laugh at him and say the young Madman of Bahama Street is staggering home, they say he was locked away but his mother felt sorry for him and sent him here instead, we'll take his place said the gravediggers Vladimir and Pete, sure, why not. Seeing the ocean and hearing the bird cries from his taxi window, Petites Cendres' mind wandered to Dr. Dieudonné who'd be back from his volunteer work in Haiti soon, bet he's a worn-out wreck, he got very little sleep as it was, sometimes he went three nights with none then fell into a chair at the clinic or the hospital, come back on Thursday he'd say to his patients, that's the day I don't charge, it was also Petites Cendres' day, Dieudonné ran two hospitals and hospices and he was soon to be honoured by the town, receiving a plaque from the long red–tipped hands of Eureka, directress of the Ancestral Choir, he'd be needing a tux for that after he managed to catch up with his wife and kids thought Petites Cendres, despite free Thursdays for his most dissolute and wracked patients as well as Sunday consults, Dieudonné still managed to take his girls to school each morning, Reverend Ézéchielle called him a saintly man who took the word of God seriously by living for the poor, while Petites Cendres was swarmed by dreams and images far less praiseworthy as he once again felt Yinn's fingers playing in his hair, it's so curly Yinn said in those dizzy hours at the Porte du Baiser Saloon, I just love your hair but you do need to untangle and comb it, why not come see me in my studio and I'll brush it for you, or would you rather have corn-rows, oh Yinn's fingers on his head, so vigorously insidious that Petites Cendres couldn't suppress a shiver as they travelled down the nape of his neck and ruffled him every which way, he recalled as well the scenes of Yinn undressing his boys, well, his men, and forever measuring, poking, and prodding, pins between his lips as his mother would hold them, and it was all necessary for his work, so it went on everywhere, even when he was relaxing at the bar and maybe pulling over a boy or a man to undress him solely to toy with him and say oh is that your thing you're covering with your hands, boy it doesn't take much to give you a swelled head does it, that kind of false modesty won't get you far in life, okay you can get dressed again, this'll be easy, you haven't even got underwear on, but what confused them about being undressed in this kind of sexual fantasy was that Yinn might be wearing sandals and his serious-looking boy outfit, or else a low-cut evening dress and stilettos, always surprising and captivating in his manner of abruptly grabbing everyone, even the least attractive, his male laughter infusing them with self-acceptance, even self-indulgence, or so his spontaneous abandon seemed to Petites Cendres when Yinn would take you into his arms, though they were really meant for Jason and perhaps also My Captain, you could never be sure, yes maybe Captain Thomas, though Petites Cendres preferred to avoid that avenue, the mystery of Yinn and My Captain, was it love or cocaine in exchange for a kiss or a sailboat ride before My Captain disappeared into the diamond depths in his rubber wetsuit to experience the ecstasy of disappearing like a merman rather than the young man Yinn liked so very much. What if Dieudonné were Petites Cendres' anonymous donor, the one who kept track of his addictions to sex and crack and cocaine, of late Petites Cendres had done without these delights, his sweet taboos, so maybe Dieudonné his patron had decided it was time he stopped degrading himself as a prostitute just scraping by with physical exploits, but what if he'd also made Petites Cendres apathetic and helpless, this celestial or spiritual chaperone may have gone against the grain and taken away his pride along with his living, prostitution was both, so who had made this decision for him, Petites Cendres wondered with Robbie's ringed hand weighing heavily on his own as the taxi sped along by the edge of the sea, the annoying thing about old Isaac, thought Adrien on his stone bench, is that he's always after me to sign those petitions of his, yesterday it was to protect the Florida panther and its cubs on his primitive island, and what'll it be tomorrow, why doesn't he think about something else, like women for instance, of course not, too old for that, and when he stoops to come into town he eats only with the very rich, then more petitions for everyone to sign so he can get back to his island as quickly as he can and sit there planning new tours, he says when I'm gone The-Island-Nobody-Owns will be my legacy to young scientists so they can come here and do research on the fauna, well why not a retreat for old writers like me thought Adrien, that sort of vast solitude would give incredible inspiration to a newly widowed poet with practically no friends, but then the thought of atrophy in solitude on old Isaac's deserted island laid him low, even with all its varieties of grasses and trees and birds, some of them very rare like blue and green hummingbirds, I've got to muster the courage to go and see him for a day, he thought, it mustn't be like Caroline and Jean-Mathieu, no, we must learn from our mistakes or suddenly find ourselves deserted and alone, life is so changeable after all, but what on earth was Robbie up to, veer off onto the main road he told the driver, so we can get a glimpse of the girls all ready for my crowning tonight, so they stopped right in front of the Porte du Baiser Saloon, and as Petites Cendres cringed in the back seat of the taxi Robbie said don't be afraid, no one can see through these tinted windows, hey look, it's Geisha and Triumphant Heart and Santa Fe, they're already strutting the street in the party show dresses made specially, wow the electric-bright flowers on their dresses, it's almost as though every petal was a neon light under the fabric, every one of them has a distinctive flower thought up for her by some gardening genius, Robbie cried out joyfully, oh this evening's gonna be such a hit, you wait and see Petites Cendres, but the latter panicked, thinking I can't see these night-people, Geisha, Triumphant Heart, Santa Fe, and Cheng the second prince of Asia in his scarlet-flowered dress, almost another Yinn, barely post-adolescent, Cheng had once been called the Next One, and the soft masterful hands of Yinn had modelled and formed him for these nocturnal feasts of the senses and other pure ceremonials such as Robbie's coronation, whether on an improvised stage, out on the street or down by the sea, community celebration even mothers could bring their little ones to, but this kingdom of the night was not for Petites Cendres any more, no, he thought, and now Rafael Sánchez was setting up his spot next to Kim, a folding chair with a table for his tarot cards and his jewels and necklaces, he was even decked out like a multicoloured work of art himself Kim thought, the Mexican was a good-looking guy, a Christ-like figure come among them, he had his own studio in a loft so he didn't need to sleep out on the street or the beach, the ornaments he was wearing, like the tunic he'd sewed with golden thread, made him look imposing she thought, as soon as he joined them there seemed to be more respect for her and Fleur, Rafael had customers for everything, tarot and jewels, a sort of oracle with his singsong voice calling out the Moon or Death, his impressive hands on the tarot deck, the Moon, Death, the Chariot, while Fleur derisively told Kim this Mexican will tell your future, you want to know everything, don't you Kim, but his mockery hurt Kim, you do know there's nothing in the cards for us, don't you, Fleur said bitterly, you know perfectly well he's fooling himself and he's fooling all the others who listen to his uplifting prophecies and predictions, though Fleur felt a twinge of guilt hearing himself talk to her the same way his mother would have talked to him, almost as though compelled to imitate her despite everything, Kim was so young and woebegone he thought, she really deserved a future, however short, it had begun badly, a misfire deep inside, yes, thwarted like his own life, it shook him that he always thought of her in terms of immense failure and sadness, a setback for him too indirectly, why such injustice, whatever his misfortune hers was worse, his parents weren't junkies like hers, and contradictory as it was, he had been loved and spoiled by his own parents and grandparents, he'd even studied music, maybe he was jealous of the Mexican newcomer who had joined them and set himself next to Kim so close his green-eyed hypnotic stare was almost in her face, I can read the cards, the enchanting Rafael told her as she listened innocently, that was the weakness of her youth thought Fleur, she was so young and open with men, and what would become of her without him, what indeed he thought, I see a boat threatened by a tornado said Rafael, and two young people, oh it's awful, you and Fleur mustn't get on that boat, don't go, I see a white heron in the night landing on black waters, so pale against the dark curtain of the storm at night Rafael told her, he was in a trance and speaking softly, almost a murmur, and Kim asked the seer, Fleur, what do you see in the cards for him, yes Fleur, see this boat, the one in the night, oh it gives me the shivers, may God or the gods that reign over the oceans and seas hear me, no I can't look at this, there are young people who . . . but remembering she was waiting in all her candid innocence for an answer about Fleur, Rafael replied immediately oh Fleur I'm not worried about him, no not worried at all, then closing his eyes upon the vision Rafael said, far, very far, he will travel the globe, what is this I hear he has written, a symphony of gigantic proportions, something grand and hybrid with a great deal of noise, yes very noisy, but in the dark of night the white heron will land on the waves and the boat will capsize in the wind, I see monsters, yes I do, no you mustn't get on that boat the two of you, he repeated, so he's going away and we won't be together, us and the dogs on the street anymore, he's thinking of going away murmured Kim, he's thinking of leaving me behind, there is a curse on the boat Rafael repeated, no, don't go there tomorrow or even tonight the two of you, he wants to leave me, go away on his own thought Kim, that's what I was most afraid of and he will, I know it, she tried to keep from crying. If the past is a manuscript one cannot go back and change, thought Adrien, then there's no point in thinking about corrections, it's irrevocable so why then do we keep revisiting it, and wouldn't going to see old Isaac on his island be just that, this time he'd be alone on the twin-hulled one-sail catamaran, no Suzanne or Caroline or Mélanie with Daniel and the kids, like that magnificent day they scattered Jean-Mathieu's ashes over the ocean, the day Adrien tried not to remember, there were so many of them together on board the catamaran that Isaac had rented for them, then waited for them in his horse-drawn cart on that island paradise, perhaps it had been let go a bit, but that too was the past and therefore not to be undone, a broad but imperfect canvas of Adrien's life that would gradually start to fall away, would he once again hear Caroline complaining that the wind was playing havoc with her hair and canvas hat when just that morning she'd been to the hairdresser, for she was still proud of her appearance back then even if her memory lapses were beginning, or possibly they were cultivated to sweeten her sadness, not knowing or pretending not to know that Jean-Mathieu had not come back from Italy alive, and adding in her distraction that he would soon be there and oh how this wind was annoying, yes, that was when it began, the forgetting, the erasures as Adrien considered them, and now perhaps he'd like to be the one to deny the memory of what he'd seen, yes, when Charly drove Caroline to the dock and said I'll come and pick you up tonight, he recalled Caroline's docile smile, thanks Charly my child, submitting herself to a disastrous fate that had taken Jean-Mathieu away from her, defenceless, and offered in his stead a creature as pernicious as Charly, an exchange she greeted by saying I don't know what I'd do without her, of course her mind was really on Jean-Mathieu, as if meaning to say what will I do without my lover and companion and friend, or had she really forgotten everything Adrien wondered as Charly's black car sped along under the brilliant sun, the same car he'd watched for a long while seated next to Suzanne in the big catamaran while the wind got on their nerves too and made them wonder how much worse it might get once they set sail, they'd be out on the sea for a full three hours before arriving at the island, he wished he could forget the touch of Suzanne's hand at that moment, why so pessimistic dear Adrien, she asked, why, because of Jean-Mathieu he brusquely replied, he really shouldn't have

put us through this, if only he'd worn his scarf we wouldn't
be here, it's all due to his absent-mindedness, what possessed
him to go out not dressed properly when he knew how damp
and cool it was, the evenings always are in Venice, what in
heaven's name was he thinking, just then Caroline raised her
sunglasses, asking what's happened, why isn't Jean-Mathieu
with us eh, why isn't he here, do you think the planks of this
boat are solid enough to get us there, Adrien groused to
Suzanne, still she tenderly took him by the hand, surely there
are too many of us for this old boat and I bet it'll be uncomfortable once we get there, so Adrien would also have to
forget the grouchy bad-tempered man sitting right beside the
sweetest of women, Suzanne was there by his side, he hadn't
been able to love her well, too wrapped up in his grumbling
melancholy on that funereal day, no regard for the passionate
woman right there with him, his own Suzanne, attractive,
seductive, yet he seemed oblivious to her, and now what he
wouldn't give to feel once again the warmth of this hand in
hers, yes, what he wouldn't give, he thought alone on his
stone bench, no point in going back over it, was there, the
past was a well of sadness and desolation, of regrets and
remorse, a page badly written, one that with all his skill and
ability he still could not fix, oh the translator and grammarian
felt horribly helpless, still perhaps he should take on the past
with Suzanne and Jean-Mathieu and Charles and Frédéric, for
it was his most prized possession, the one that gave him the
most joy, and what a blessing that his friends, all of them,
writers and poets and musicians had never been estranged
from him despite his disposition, which when he thought
about it he had to admit had often been scratchy and disagreeable, offensive even, when his life to this point had been
nothing short of a miracle, Robbie noticed the contrary look
on Petites Cendres' face and his slightly green-around-the-gills
pallor despite his dark skin, why are you all squished back
into your seat Robbie asked him, no one can see you, you

know that, besides Geisha, Triumphant Heart, Santa Fe, and Cheng are your friends, aren't they, and they'll all be here with us tonight, Yinn too, Yinn in a white dress in my honour he said, wanting to shake Petites Cendres out of his torpor and terror, what's this all about, you mean we can't have fun anymore, no singing or laughing, and as he said this to Petites Cendres he saw himself with Fatalité as they tooled around California and Mexico, his hands on Fatalité's thighs inside his jeans or his tight-fitting leather pants, this was their escape, their getaway, both of them crazy and laughing with their hair blowing in the wind when all at once Robbie raised his arms to the blue sky and yelled hurray, hurray, he didn't know why, but there he was with his arms in the air, those were his last trips with Fatalité, so thin now that Robbie put his arms around him on the road at night and felt a little scared, was he really going to melt away so fast, Fatalité and the body he had were racing for some sort of unhoped-for happiness, was Robbie raising his arms to the sky and yelling hurray, hurray proving something to heaven and earth, proving how alive and invincible they were, when Robbie's fingers slid over Fatalité's skin and pierced left nipple, who said they couldn't laugh and sing anymore cracked the insolent Fatalité with his hands on the handlebars on the windy highway, who says, eh Robbie, and that was the moment of unbridled happiness when Robbie lifted his arms, raised his hands to the sky and yelled, free, they were free, and Robbie told Fatalité faster, faster, there's no cops out here to get in our way, they'll want to stop me from entering Trinity College, they'll rough me up in the school bus, and in the back it says "No faggy boys wanted here," beat it Mick, we don't want you here, the rough, uncouth students had scrawled graffiti all over the back window of the school bus to insult and intimidate him, despite their violent homophobic words I won't let them discriminate against me or harass me thought Mick, I'm the son of a well-known novelist and a historian, not like them, also the son of the Prince, yes him and only him maybe, he walked with a dancing step and had on his black leather pants, shiny black shoes, pearly white gloves, or else his brother, the Prince's brother, the coolest look, the sexiest dance steps, not effeminate, no way, I'm all about good looks, the best, and yoga champion if I want to be, but they won't let me into the classroom 'cause they're jealous, that's right all of them, because of my parents who are very smart, not the best parents maybe for Tammy and me, but the others, the big, vulgar kids have another kind of parent, ours are open-minded, liberal, maybe not the best parents, okay, they don't know what to do with Tammy and me, the new kids, not effeminate like they say, just bursting with good looks, I'm Mick and I look like me not them, who is that now, bisexual maybe or transsexual, eh Mick, so who are you my parents ask, you can tell us, we'll understand, and at least you're not like your sister, starving herself up in her room or in the hospital where they have to force-feed her through a tube, yes at least you're not like her, that's really contemptible, disgusting to your mother and me, and one day this thick-headed student at Trinity College hit me in the head as I was getting off the school bus, so who are you Mick, tell us and we'll stop hitting you, all you have to do is tell us, well I managed to throw them both on the ground and my head wasn't really injured, then I knocked them down again 'cause they're heavier than I am, so you think you can scare me guys, well you're not going to, and if I can't take the school bus like everyone else I'll walk, that's all, maybe I'll even dance my way there if I feel like it, but they're not getting to me, besides I can walk for hours in the sun, and you're not going to get to me or shut me out, and I won't even take revenge either, I learned from the Prince and his music, it's me and so is this planet, me, Mick, Tammy said you can't go out like that this morning, it's exam time, you just can't, a little lipstick, some mascara, hat down over my eyes, a really daring dance and the sexiest look, so tell us Mick who are you, then we'll stop hitting you in the head when you get off the bus, go on Mick, tell us, then we can all have a good laugh, so are you gay, transsexual, you want us to strip you, that way we'll finally know who you are under all that pricey gear, probably women's undies, right, you know we're gonna find out Mick, we don't want you here, not on the bus, not in class, nowhere, that's what they keep saying over and over those yahoo creeps, even the younger ones always grabbing stones to let fly, throwbacks to the days of bullying and self-destruction, you've gotta know how to defend yourself, I told Tammy that this morning, and when you're a strong young male, well I'll fix them with judo or karate, then they'll stay away from me in the hallways, in a private school even the nurse and the psychologist aren't going to put a stop to it and I'm not about to throw myself off a bridge like that young musician and promoter after those student criminals outed him, and he thought they were his friends, his good buddies, nothing but lies and tricks, like any college or university, sneaking propaganda and gossip, but not me, not Mick, neither victim nor martyr, and that's what I told my sister this morning as she watched me leave, all afraid and saying Mick, couldn't you at least wait till evening before you go out like that, and I said nighttime, why, I want to live and sing in broad daylight, not in the shadows, and I'll pose for a magazine, he thought of his prince-brother in Neverland, now a zone of devastation where lone children wandered among the elephants and lions, the lone survivors of the paradise from which its monarch had been banished, when's Papa coming back they asked, when, well someone else will have to stage a revolution first, but for now they had to be content to dream in there with the animals and whatever the Prince managed to finish on his Neverland farm before he left it, more like a ranch thought Mick, the Earth is for everyone, elephants and tigers and monkeys, you could still hear his music played live to an empty hall, the Earth is for all you children of the world, it's all yours, he sang into empty space, so he sang it to Mick, you are not alone, "You Are Not Alone," to an empty house under red spotlights, and when he recalled the music, Mick felt he had nothing to fear, nothing, and if they stopped him getting on the school bus, well he'd walk that's all, a long walk in the sun but he was invincible, right, invincible, as Daniel continued waiting in the terminal for his plane to board, he saw an eleven-year-old girl sleeping propped up against her bag, legs stretched out over her father's knees, long, thick legs covered in mosquito bites, the seat was uncomfortable so her father had arranged the bag around her head as a pillow, how gracefully affectionate and protective the care he gave his little girl, half-lying on the seat, legs unfolded on Daddy's lap while he spoke in a monotone on his cellphone, constantly mindful of the sleeping girl, the entire scene touched Daniel in its simplicity, he'd experienced moments like this travelling with Mai when she was little, mosquito bites on the legs and all, the utter passivity of the sleeping girl who might as well be dreaming in her bed at home, when she shifted herself and lifted her legs, the father unthinkingly arranged the hem of her red dress, all at once seeming to Daniel an oversized child himself, mindful of her decency, pulling the short dress over her knees, then a caressing hand through her hair and over her neck to straighten the gold cross on this brown-skinned child madonna laid out across her father's knees, sensuality already apparent on her sleeping lips, the picture of youth nearing its full bloom and so full of promise for her father, and though Mai was a few years older, Daniel couldn't help thinking of her, a similar face and lips, and what an awakening underlay this corporeal blossom that was already emerging, never dormant even when she herself was, such trust between father and daughter, the days of mosquito-bitten legs, of afternoon naps in hammocks long gone, thought Daniel, the springtime and summer of our children's vitality and our own as well, so short-lived in the face of either the revolt and disobedience to come or some other wild behaviour unexpected by a father still in the thrall of childhood charms now suddenly extinguished, seemingly forgotten by those who lived it, or perhaps better forgotten, though rich in so much their parents had given them, refusing nothing, so strange this cut-off and how does one get over it, he mused as he watched the sleeping girl, how can one believe the heartache this girl will cause her father or mother with a spree of wild adventures, especially since it couldn't be otherwise, no one's fate was meant to please anyone else, and here it was that the shadow of Augustino, so far off in India, passed before him, one day so close by and the next nowhere to be found, couldn't he just write books in his room like his father, be more of a homebody and raise a family, but that was not how he saw a writer's life, no, it would take orphanages in Calcutta and slum kids who slept in the streets or asking why the Ganges was the most worshipped river in the country, what Daniel needed to know was how was his son able to fuse commitment onto action wherever he went and still be so rootless, how could one reconcile standing up for the wretched and untouchable with writing about them in the comfort of one's own home, a father's home, Daniel as a writer and ecologist still gave a few lectures and conferences in order to feel less sedentary and more anchored in his over-arching mission, as much simply human as he was nomadic, but Augustino was different, he could find a way to be useful no matter where, even if it wasn't always with a very open disposition, he ordered his brother Vincent, who was studying medicine, to send him emergency packets of biscuits, a hundred of the nutritional ones rich in proteins, vitamins, and minerals, in fact why not come himself and help save lives, wasn't studying a waste of time after all, this troubled Vincent, who couldn't drop out now and wrote, I'm sending the rations for your orphanage but you realize I have to work and study extra hard because my bouts with asthma hold me back, though at least they're less frequent now, but I can't up and leave like you, timid words to which Augustino replied, you're going to end up like so many of your colleagues, insensitive to real pain, though perhaps the real lack of sensitivity was Augustino's towards his brother, considered Daniel, he the committed writer working in so many of the worst situations in the world, so generous with those he didn't know yet the most execrable towards those closest to him, his own family, as Lou left her mother's house at six o'clock she was on her way out for Friday supper with her father, and Ari considered this his weekly reward, but since she often went to eat with Ingrid, herself often too rushed for evening meals, it was more a duty than a reward in Lou's mind, her parents always forgetting that Friday was her night to sleep over at Rosie's, now that was a reward, to see neither of her parents for a night, for Lou they were both just a harassment to be avoided, yes of course they loved her, but for ages they hadn't loved one another and Lou preferred to stay away from them and go to Rosie's instead, there she'd be woken in the morning by babies crying, Rosie had lots of brothers and sisters, yet she only had to be away for a few hours to miss Ari or Ingrid fiercely, as her mother said, she was still rather immature, despite her precocious air and the increasing resemblance to Ingrid, one thing's for certain she said, you're going to be tall and well developed like me, oh and even more beautiful than your mum, Ingrid kept busy with lots of things, mother, Catholic school commissioner, real estate agent, but Mama no, you're the most beautiful, Lou reacted, she usually had little good to say about her parents but once in a while she was capable of being kind to her mother, after all they were both women and as such more fragile than men, whereas men weren't Lou decided, and going out for supper with Ari was no fun because he wouldn't let her eat fries, just soup and salad, booooring, that day he reached for his sketch portfolio and pulled out Lou's report card and then, denying her dessert, he said she was getting a bit too plump because your mother lets you gobble down anything you want, but I'm not bringing you up that way, okay, besides your grades aren't terrific he said authoritatively, pretty good but you can do better, especially now you're in the gifted class and I'm paying for it, so you could do better, he fixed his gaze on her as she played with her bread, her hands tanned and ringed with bracelets made of hearts, she was bothered by it and pulled up the tie she'd borrowed from Jules and loosely put on over her T-shirt the way they were doing these days, Ari noticed with irritation, wearing her brother's ties when he was almost an adult, how could Ingrid put up with her boyish hairstyle too, he wondered, was the bohemian effect her mother's doing, and he told her you need to be more like before, more feminine, you're prettier without your brother's tie though I'm sure it's normal at your age to try things out, gee she thought is he going to give me a little more leeway, yeah maybe with an eyedropper she thought, if only he would stop with all this old-fashioned stuff, okay, okay, let's get back to the report card, you're tops again in math and drawing, I told you don't cut your bread like that, and look at me when I'm speaking to you, it's time you stopped acting the way your mother brought you up, she brings me up fine came the reply, now she doesn't make me go to church with her and I don't have to get up so early either, great, just what we needed grumbled Ari, you going to church with her when you need to stay away from religion and not fill your head with all that garbage, but you're Buddhist aren't you she said without raising her eyes to meet his, you do as you like and so should she, it's not her fault if she's Catholic, she got that from her mother and her grandmother, her whole family Lou said, her face beaming, all right let's get back to your grades Ari said, you know you really could do better, you're at the best school in town and in an advanced class too, so what's the deal with sleeping at Rosie's every Friday night, okay Papa I really have to go Lou said, you can just drop me off at her place, but you used to spend Friday nights with me at my place with your own books and videos, and I haven't seen you all week Lou, was he going to beg when all she wanted was just to leave, too chubby for dessert was what he said, geez he was self-important and tiresome these days, and she'd loved him so much till his mistress Noémie kept him in New York all the time, no she no longer loved him with his white hair wavy down the back of his neck, why couldn't he stay handsome and young, he still had manly charm but that harsh sharp way he spoke to her and above all this new conformism, no, he wasn't the same anymore, and what a liar she thought, he'd definitely changed, and there was no way of knowing if he had other mistresses besides, he no longer talked to her about such things, no, he wasn't truthful anymore with her or Ingrid or anyone, what a sneak, besides Lou knew how much he loved women, he even smiled at the waitress, everyone, and it was always that same winning smile, and this only served to torment and embarrass Lou, so now the long and eventful love story they'd shared was over, because he was ageing no doubt, yet he still seemed alert and sailed as well as ever, he had even finished building a new studio, he'd promised they'd go to Panama but when would that be, he'd forgotten no doubt, look Lou, Marie-Louise, he corrected himself, I'm not unhappy about this report card of yours but I would like a little more next time, promise me? she was certainly not going to answer that, I mustn't reassure him she thought, and her father felt the coming storm of her bad temper, a climate of anger that would soon break out, spreading far and wide, and he'd say yes, you're disagreeable that way Lou, I don't recognize you anymore, it's like being with your mother again, as Lou sat there with her eyes lowered to her tanned hands holding the bit of bread she sensed the fog of father–daughter uneasiness about to rise between them Ari worked at disarming her by asking suddenly, what's going on in that turbulent little head of yours eh Lou, tell me, I'm your friend aren't I, I can see you brought your big backpack to sleep at Rosie's, as if her parents didn't have enough kids to contend with, Ari could just imagine the jumble inside it because Lou's notion of order was to jam things in one on top of the other, that's why you couldn't get past the door to her room, what a mess Ari thought, though Lou seemed to be saying to herself you have no idea what's inside, do you, still caped in the fog bank of her forbidding mood, you want to go see some galleries tomorrow he said, see he's got everything planned and programmed she thought, perhaps if he talked about his latest drawings he'd soften up his pose as creative educator, for some days Lou wanted to become a designer after her father showed her the talented work of Alexander McQueen on the computer, and Lou sketched models wearing green dresses with bouquets of flying herbs atop their heads, nice but a bit offhand Ari said, especially the headpieces, not very practical, you need to pay more attention to detail like the great designer, because he was so adept that in his hands they became veritable constructions, works of art that reached to the sky, movable works, yes, he said, still as he looked at her drawings, more imaginative than his own, Lou was forever interested in serpents, her models often wore them as crowns with bunches of grapes or roses woven through their hair and she didn't feel the need for restraint, unlike her father in his paintings or sculptures, it was this very extravagance combined with precision in her choice of images or symbols or invention that amazed Ari, ah this generation surely wasn't his own, but where were they headed after they took over the rules of art in order to destroy them, you've got a fantastic imagination he finally told her and she pleased him with a searing look from her blue eyes, maybe the fog bank between them would thin away after all, I'll drop you off at Rosie's by eight he said in a voice that was less intransigent all of a sudden, please realize sweetheart that I haven't seen you for a week, that's a

long time for me and it's a pity you're so unfriendly when
you've spent time with your mother, really a shame, though
he might not actually say that out loud, knowing it was better
to wait for later, yes Ari had no doubt Lou was Ingrid's much
more than his own but it might not last forever, yes, perhaps.
I suppose, thought Daniel, children are led by secret motiva-
tions as we are, hurt maybe or some affliction could change
them forever, thus it was that Augustino never spoke of his
grandmother any more than his mother Mélanie did, secret
reasons for this hardening in Augustino or the sadness that
often woke Mélanie at night in tears while Daniel pretended
to sleep, he asked no questions, letting her weep as she had
to, and this would go on for months, Daniel was certain one
could not console others, at least not without a certain embar-
rassment, on the troubled surface of dreams in which one
glimpsed the dead rejuvenated by some supernatural effect
bound to surprise us, as if to say can I return, it's so good here
at home, why aren't you more welcoming, perhaps they've
seen the closed door to the room or cabin they lived in and
wonder why it's been closed up so soon after, with all the
other rooms they used to wander through, looking for us in
our refusal of death, and we who have no wish to realize its
constant presence in life, no matter if, like Mélanie, we are
gripped by our own nighttime fits of stabbing grief, crushing
bouts of sadness, this is how it was for Augustino, whether
briefly visiting his parents or working on a book in India or
living in the streets of Calcutta with slum kids, he alone knew
what he was living through with the memory of the joy he'd
lost with the one he adored so very much, suddenly no longer
a man but the child he used to be, with parakeets on his
shoulder in his grandmother's doorway bringing her breakfast
when she wasn't feeling well, or still younger when she swung
him on the veranda, they talked about the trees and plants of
Texas and she said you're going to remember all of these later
on, every tree, every plant, some of ours in the garden were

blown down in the storm last winter, always an incalculable loss when one of them dies, Augustino heard his grandmother's voice in the cooing of his parakeets, another life, another time, all gone, snatched away, even from a distance he knew it, he knew his mother's searing pain would never let up, all-consuming and her spirit forever in revolt, these, Daniel thought, were probably the keys to Augustino's harshness as he reached manhood, a writing voice imbued with anger and bile, as Robbie ran into Yinn again in the dressing room at the Cabaret, he discovered with stupefaction it had been only a few days ago that Herman's condition had worsened, a second black flower had blossomed on his right leg, and in the filmy green dress, a product of Yinn's oriental inspiration, his orange wig, bracelets, and necklaces for the evening show, he had suddenly flopped into a chair in a gesture of desperation, I'm so worn out tonight he told Yinn, and when I think that Marcus is in prison because of me and now his brother and friends can't think of anything but avenging him, and behold my remission is over, I'm not going to shake this Herman said coolly, you've got to want to shake it said Yinn, but he knew his consolation and advice were pointless when the black flower on Herman's leg rapidly grew out of all proportion, embedded in the contaminated flesh, yeah he said to Yinn with fury and desperation in his voice, no more operations now, let nature take its course to putrefaction, no more wheelchairs like Fatalité, you gotta be able to die on your feet, right Yinn, and this time Marcus won't be there to get me morphine from his infirmary, bit by bit it'll get so none of you will even know me, I'll become this deformed monster, bit by bit, and Yinn dared not look his friend in the face, you've got to will it, to want to live he said again, oh I've got a few months' grace Herman said, sure, a few months for lumps to form all over me, things growing out of me and who knows what else, but it won't stop me working, nossir, he went on, gotta get some hash for tonight, stoned is good, you don't feel anything, who says you gotta die sober, right Yinn, d'you think you could find me some my friend, maybe Captain Thomas has some on that boat of his, you're coming out for a drink with me after the evening's over said Yinn taking Herman by the shoulder, no more hash, you've already had too much, more than enough to get high Herman, too much of everything, crack, ecstasy, hash, enough, and tomorrow we're going to see your surgeon, you've got to want to live Herman, Yinn repeated, oh yeah what for came the question, why eh, not one of you is gonna tell me what to do, not even you Yinn, about to lose yet another of his friends, Yinn told Robbie, why is it, why is it eh, why so much injustice, he was looking at Herman now but all he could do was keep repeating why oh why, why, is it because we're different, we live free and without shame, just sensuous and alive, why, it's so unfair, we're the artists society needs, the ones they try to adapt to, or maybe they just want it too much, what's happening anyway Yinn went on, suddenly humbled and bewildered, quickly though, the need to save Herman surged to the fore again and swept him up, be at my studio tomorrow morning by eight he told Robbie, we're gonna drag him to hospital, don't forget, eight a.m. Robbie, between the two of us we can do it whether he likes it or not, he's damn well going to start treatment again, like it or not. Nora asked Christiensen over and over again do you really like the painting sweetheart, really, really I do was his answer, I don't just like it, I love it he reassured her, but however positive and encouraging her husband's reply, Nora had trouble believing it, of all your self-portraits this one's the most transcendent, said Christiensen with some hesitation, he wasn't sure the word *transcendent* was quite what she'd been looking for, it's got sublime qualities he added, but aren't the whites of the eyes too bright wondered Nora, who was also concerned that dinner wasn't ready, they were always having people over for meals the day before one of his trips, but this one was different thought

Nora, when this mission was over she would join him in Africa and this meeting would be a second honeymoon after all these years, finally together and alone, just the two of them and no kids, I'll go back to the country where I was born thought Nora, our wedding anniversary, uh-oh dinner's burning she shouted, and your pup Tangie won't stop getting underfoot when I'm cooking, she could do without his habit of gathering in every stray animal, especially when there was so little time for the two of them together, it really did get on her nerves, he's hungry but I'll take care of it Christiensen replied as he got ready to feed him out in the garden, but instead of eating, Tangie jumped into his master's arms and covered his face with kisses, my sweetie Christiensen said, I'm so glad you've got a healthy appetite, you're a brave little dog, beaten and abandoned, well not with us you won't be, we're gonna love you too much, yes, and who'll do it when you're away, me as usual, it sounded as though Nora was teasing him from the kitchen, thinking he couldn't hear her, he was supposed to be getting out the champagne and glasses as he always did on his nights before leaving, almost as though these time-honoured separations were actually celebrations, she reflected, but you never know, maybe they really were enjoyable to him, off there away from his family and fulfilling his own destiny with men and women at his command, an economist yes, but his missions were essentially humanitarian she reminded herself, still it was an odd sort of evening just the same, why did she have such curious intimations of fear, fear or emptiness, maybe it was the heat or the fact that she'd hardly slept, plagued as she'd been by awful nightmares, she tried to find her way back to it, a plunge into the void from unknown heights, falling and falling as a voice intoned such is Nora's end, wife of Christiensen, she's tumbling through the void, and then she awoke covered in perspiration, then calmed herself saying it was only a dream, she'd have liked to confide her terror to him but lately he'd been working late, then sleeping in Greta's empty room, sometimes when he was up late reading she ran and clung to him, with the day's international papers and books squashed between them, he'd caress her absently and say sleep now Nora, sleep my dear, then go on reading till dawn, I'm worried we might be turning into an old couple she thought with agitation, he goes right on reading even when I have these terrors, okay, all right, it's almost time to get up, I'll feel better after a dip in the pool, yes that will help, and it did, even if the worst dreams involved falling from sky to sea or emptiness as though cut loose from a parachute, it all seemed the same whether high or low, for the words coming from behind her were the same, Nora is no more, Nora, wife of Christiensen, Nora, like when her father, a surgeon in the African bush, said concentrate, you're too much of a dreamer, you'll never become the doctor I need to help me later on, no never, too much of a dreamer, Nora made for a tumble into the void, and her father's denial hurt her even more, look you have no rigour Nora, you're scatter-brained, you have no focus, yet that very diffuseness was what transported her still in her painting, Christiensen had spoken of transcendence in her self-portrait but he was generous by nature, perhaps not to be fully believed, and now she could hear the clinking of champagne glasses as he placed them on the garden table, oh this is going to be a delicious dinner she said, sober though, very sober, a Chinese salad, a dorado with lemon sauce, sherbets the way you like them Christiensen, she also realized she was jabbering too much, nervous, tense about her husband's departure tomorrow at dawn, she was always thrown off when he left and she talked too much, not knowing in the instant quite where to flee and trying to fob off on Christiensen the pup Tangie that followed her everywhere, in Africa they weren't able to keep pets because the hyenas would attack them at night, even pushing through the mosquito screens where my brother slept with his tame monkey, no it wasn't possible for us, but you're no longer in Africa, Christiensen told her as though calling back over his shoulder from a great distance, already on his way, no longer in her world but delighted at the prospect of soon being surrounded by his friends, painters, writers, he so loved seeing them before he departed, it was real pleasure, a joyful celebration when he was about to leave thought Nora, somewhat bitter, he seems to love them more than me, he's always beaming when they're around but with me he always seems melancholic, of course he's always busy night and day, the poor getting poorer, oh but this time it'll be different, we'll be alone together in the very city where I was born, this'll be a charming evening with our friends, fragrant breeze, time to forget those awful nightmares, such relief when Christiensen called my painting transcendent, sublime, so what if she herself wasn't that sure and if her husband liked it a bit too much, she had pleased him and that's what mattered most of all, though she did have her doubts, too much white in the eyes or did it make for a more captivating look, well she'd pick this up again tomorrow when she'd seen Christiensen off at the airport. When the student yahoos pushed him around and kept him off the school bus, Mick's mind projected a photo of the Prince ahead as far as the horizon and heard the voice again, courage, Mick, courage, they won't get away with it, Mick, I got persecuted too for no reason, in fact that's why they do it, because you're innocent, I remember one show, really dramatic, some sort of farewell performance at the Super Bowl in Pasadena, California, the Prince in his flowered white silk outfit over a white vest and black pants, Mick would have to learn to dress with that kind of celestial lightness, half of the Prince's left hand was bandaged and his fingers red from burns, here I am defenceless the picture seemed to say, just listen, I'm singing about hope for future generations, and soon they'll hear me all the way to China, and you too Mick, you too, arms wide open and face as greedily sensuous as it was tightly sealed, mouth trembling, eyes closed, Mick's image of redemption in happiness, the pioneer prince crucified against a screen on fire, moving frontiers around the globe, freedom, and in the face of this illuminating image nailed to the horizon, Mick no longer feared the toughs who pushed him around, besides he'd soon be able to deal with them, outfox them with his new-found skills in karate and judo, even tied to a fence he'd know how to get free, free of this perversity and humiliation, yes, this he'd learned, how to get free, but at a price he'd never forget, that of past mutilation and sacrifice, four younger students had committed suicide that year alone, liquidated along with taboos against the guerrilla tactics of school bullying in schools, colleges, and universities, the cruel new disorder dishing out new weapons ignored by teachers and profs, a few seconds on Facebook, video screen, or cellphone used to destroy the reputation of Tyler, a promising violinist who jumped off a bridge, or William, who hanged himself in the family garage, or Asher, only thirteen, who shot himself in the head with his grandfather's rifle, or Seth the passionate Bible reader who hanged himself within sight of his helpless mother but lingered on for a week afterwards, all of them, teachers, profs, and tutors, had said nothing, how was it they hadn't been able to save just one of those wondered Mick, striding in the sunlight, the coolest looks, the most provocative moves, his life would forever be influenced by those who had been snuffed out at their dawning, it was going to be a long walk in the sun, no way they'd let him ride the school bus with "You don't belong" here, written across the back window, good thing he had his water bottle on this long, hot walk, slowing down when he had to, like the Prince's waltz, for the music never left his head and sounded over and over in his ear, *No, you are not alone*, no, no, never alone, Mick also heard the violin music played by the promising Tyler, one of a circle of pure, innocent faces with William, Asher, and Seth, the gentlest despite what was done to him, still childlike, a melody played seconds before

Tyler first kissed a boy on the lips, then a companion's betrayal and the impulse that drove Tyler to the bridge and the void that awaited him, one message for all, goodbye, I'm going to jump off the bridge, sorry for the way things are, right, sorry thought Mick, for having to die, boy what irony, a kiss, a very first kiss on a boy's lips, and what heart-rending melody on his violin, at the end of that day he was betrayed, Tyler the musician commits self-murder, why bother with vigils in churches and temples, why cry, students in one another's arms, a storm wind blowing at candles in temples and churches, a howl of rage to be heard from beneath the bridge where he died, Mick recalled as he walked faster and faster towards Trinity College, the most daring moves, the coolest looks, no this was not going to be his tragedy, as Paul the trumpet-player asked Fleur and Kim, can I hang out here and improvise a few minutes, I won't be long, there's a bunch of other musicians waiting for me tonight, say Fleur would you rather hear Mozart or Vivaldi, done my way of course, always and everywhere, but Fleur's annoyed response was yeah we hear that cheap stuff everywhere, no respect for the compos-ers, TV ads everywhere all the time, even movie theatres and store aisles, it's a real shame, all Paul wanted was to play his trumpet and blend into what Fleur was playing as if wanting to bring back his smile, you know what, you're downright sinister under that hoodie of yours he replied, you ought to play in a real group like me, not out here in the street, your symphony must be ready for the contest by now, c'mon get the cobwebs out my friend, but it seemed to Kim that Fleur was determined to take this with worse and worse grace, Paul was after all a true and gifted musician and this underscored Fleur's failure, c'mon why not join us Paul said, jazz or pop, we take it all seriously, and Fleur, who'd played a long piece on the flute, looked as though he were holding his breath noticed Kim, his lips a brilliant red, glowed from beneath his hood, music's a joy we all need to share Paul went on, right

Kim, am I right, but her only response was a silent pout, still Paul went on with his praises for the new Golden Age of music soon to be played anywhere and everywhere, no more boring concert halls, orchestras were giving outdoor performances nowadays in all kinds of public spaces like parks and even under the arches of New York and places still more tucked away, no more being confined to rich antiseptic concert halls, uh-uh said Paul, our symphony orchestras are getting a new life and the musicians' strike will be over, Kim felt a sort of luminous self-satisfaction emanating from Paul, like Rafael the Mexican with his tarot cards, Paul was quite a charmer, a joyous hustler who had a house and a black mistress who was also a musician, sweet kids too that he dragged around with him almost anywhere, music is epic and luxuriant he said, and off he'd go to find his musician friends, whistling with his trumpet under his arm, such a triumphal air, his ease at being both a man and a musician darkened Fleur's mood it seemed to Kim, flute in hand he appeared to be holding his breath. Tomorrow wrote Daniel to his daughter from the terminal, which increasingly had been transformed into his office, tomorrow he typed, seated at a table in the bar under Laure's sour look, six hours without a cigarette was all she could think about, breathing its faint aroma would have brought her some comfort but there was no way around the rules, she wasn't even getting that, no cigarette, no trace of smoke, nothing, and while Daniel seemed so happy writing, Laure felt reduced to nothing, not even there she thought, there were esthetic considerations too, for she was a lot nicer when she had a smoke, more attractive to the men in the bar, really someone, still no flight announcements, when on earth were they going to get out of there she wondered, when, tomorrow I'll be in James Joyce country Daniel wrote as he reread tomorrow's presentation, oh my sweet I feel as though I should change it all from the start, after all I'm headed for the land of poetic reinvention and everything really comes to us from within, including linguistic audacity, language picked up from others and recycled as poetry or song, the writer identified with his people's suffering and all peoples' as well, that's really what I'm going to be driving at wrote Daniel to Mai, the critics called him subversive but he was right-thinking and conscientious man, what was happening all of a sudden, the text became garbled in Daniel's mind, a rush of words far too sonorous, the sort of thing Adrien would write, and he didn't like it, dear Mai he began again, I realize you've written me several times and I haven't answered any of your questions these past few days, so you've decided on the Art and Photography program and you and your African friends have a project to produce a documentary on slavery, what a horribly freighted word, why, you asked me, why an entire social system built on the humiliation and servitude of a people, the slave trade, and why in this day and age it still goes on, even children, sexual slavery too, I can't erase it from our history or world history like that, imagine, we who feel so free, the race of owners, how can we call ourselves free when we've done irreparable damage, so many men, women, and children subjugated and abused, why, he wrote back, well there was nothing I could say, nothing helpful, these are things I've dealt with so often in my books, particularly contemporary racism which is still alive and kicking, but like you I'm incapable, perhaps I don't want you to take this weight on your shoulders, the remembered guilt of masters from one end of the earth to the other, condemning the subjugation and annihilation of those they called inferior, the old photos you sent me that will be in your documentary, hundreds of slaves marching under the broiling sun carrying bales of cotton on their heads, men, women, and children in the cotton fields of South Carolina, well I look at those pictures and I tremble with disgust, the one of the old man from the Congo for instance, broken by labour on the plantations, dear Mai if only you didn't have to know all this, yet here we are you and I, your mother too, infallibly linked by a single conscience but with no idea if it will do any good, suddenly reaching a space so disturbing that Mai's questions reduced him to silence, and Mai, leaving her own email unfinished, had to go back to life as a student, courses, going out with friends, a whole social life that was hers alone, one Daniel hoped would help her forget Manuel and his father and the shadow world they represented, a subterranean world subject to the rigours of the law and one where, though Daniel couldn't be wholly certain, Mai had her first encounter with drugs and probably her first emotional and sexual experiences with Manuel, maybe even his father too, a world Daniel preferred to steer clear of, yes, the cowardice of so many fathers, he thought, willful blindness and silence, abdication before the actions of their offspring, even when those seemed inexplicably dangerous, perniciously amoral, yet still an act of cowardice in willing to forget that our children can undergo their own kind of hell as we all have done, as though such oblivion could simply erase the experience of errors past with one swipe, as though ignorance somehow redeemed our irresponsibility and what comes of it, still with the cardboard box containing Kim's dinner in his grasp, this evening, this beach, as the sun slowly dipped into the sea and an autumn breeze, still torrid, lifted the hair on his head, Brilliant hippity-hopped his way to Kim and Fleur, too bad about Lucia, his loving old Lucia, oppressed by her own sisters who threatened her with the loss of everything, house, animals, garden with its orange and lemon trees, they'd just have a word with the judge they said, after all she was constantly drunk and her memory was a wasteland, all she recalled was far in the past, not the present, not even feeding her animals, too bad, but Brilliant told her nothing will happen to you while I'm here Lucia, no, nothing at all, yes but if my sisters tell the judge I'll be stripped of everything she replied, everything gone and I'll be locked away, think of that my dear Brilliant, me in an institution for the aged or crazy, nonononono, that's not going to happen he said kissing her on the cheeks, no, never, not while I'm around, I'll watch out for you Lucia, a trickle of sauce dripped from the box onto his shorts, too bad, they were new he thought, I'll have to clean them so I'm presentable for tomorrow's breakfast shift, otherwise the boss will call on Pete or Vladimir instead, sneaky lowlifes, cheaters, far off Brilliant could see the steamers lighting up one by one like windows in a hotel, at night that's what they were, floating hotels with passengers all set to leave in the morning, all of them come so far and headed farther, the Bermudas perhaps, or parts unknown, green signal lights around the smaller boats out on the water, in an hour it would be dark, too bad Brilliant already felt drunk, it was all that time spent listening to Lucia and Maria and writing the whole time, mime-sketching in the smoky air, no need for a pencil or pen for this, when he'd run out of things to say, not the briefest idea, Brilliant thought that this was really what life is about, everything up in smoke, a solitary musician pulling his guitar out of its case breathed in as though expecting a storm tonight instead of such calm, Brilliant hailed him as he went by, just some wind, that's all said the musician, a sleeping hen rustled in her little square of green grass with her chicks beneath her spreading wings, a vagabond opens a rubber bag and tosses the hen some bits of bread like some kind of ritual, the chicks come straight to him chirping, Brilliant waves his approval and spies a straw beach mat inside the bag, looks like the only thing he owns, same as Fleur and Kim sleeping on theirs day and night hidden away someplace, the man seemed a bit cranky and growled his response, mistrustful of anyone outside this little family of his, and he went on scattering bread for the mother hen and her little ones, just one family he muttered, probably even more drunk than Brilliant, who'd rather not wind up looking like this guy, no, he was tidy and proud, he'd never let himself go like that, hey Misha, soon he'd see Misha cured of all his trauma, it had to be soon the vet said, then there'd be no separating them ever again, they were so patient with Misha there, he'd keep him in his room, though it was pretty bare since Marcus's brother had robbed him, white walls, one table, that was all Virgil hadn't taken for drug money, yes, it was going to be a strict kind of solitude from here on but Brilliant would at long last finish his endless novel, yes, tomorrow gotta remember to buy a pen and paper, his sister the painter had offered him a computer, but no, no question of that, way too much of a risk he'd get plagiarized or imitated, inspiration was as thin as air, mustn't forget the paper, right, tomorrow, the act of writing had to be consummated, that's what Lucia said, it had to come true she said as she reread his poem between kisses, give or receive, receive or give, two different things thought Adrien on his stone bench beneath the silvered palms, some late tennis players were still on the verdant green court under the evening lights, Adrien recalled when Charly still drove Caroline and read with her, Charly probably lolled by the pool amid a welter of sunscreens and creams, plus Caroline's newspapers and literary magazines plopped here and there around the edge of the pool, Charly languidly thumbed through them under the midday sun, yes, and while Adrien posed for Caroline's collected portraits of writers, when she admonished him in a very professional tone now don't move Adrien, he'd heard Charly seductively whisper, you know Adrien I really love that poem "Give or Receive" that Caroline had me read, but it's odd, why would the man in your poem feed sunflower seeds to starving crows in a snowy field, why in exchange for this gift to them in spring would he hope for one summer more she asked, well these poems were written in the cold when I visited my children, they ski downhill in winter he replied, you see Charly, it's a metaphor, a metaphor he repeated evasively, one can offer bread or sunflower seeds to the birds who are hungry in the winter snow and hope Heaven will help us to something, say another springtime or even another summer my dear Charly, you can't possibly understand, you're too young, so these are the poems of an aging man Charly said impudently, but Adrien just laughed and Caroline had to keep telling him not to move or she'd botch it, he had a photogenic profile and she wanted to bring out the decisiveness and strength of will in it, Adrien liked Caroline's paying tribute to my writerly profile while little Charly wrestled with my poem not too successfully, no matter, it's all very charming, but now as I reread it so long after that session, Adrien considered that he'd had that springtime and summer gift, and now not far from the age of old Isaac, perhaps it was time to sow an entire harvest of sunflower seeds for his own crows and possibly it wouldn't be too much to ask for two or three more springs in return, having written in a long-ago poem that it was reasonable to make an apparently gratuitous offering and still receive something in return, a wholly legitimate expectation, ah but this time he'd also ask for Suzanne to be restored to him safe and sound, regardless of Charly's laying her head in his lap, artfully caressing him as she'd done with Caroline, all the better to drag him down, this time Adrien knew better, he wasn't going to fall in, all of a sudden he felt a chill, something he wasn't used to in this tropical climate, especially wearing a blazer and straw boater, although his temples and forehead felt hot, from here on every poem pulled from his blazer pocket, every day and night, after tennis at the hour of solemn silence around him, from birdsong to the to-and-fro of cock crow, yes, from now on his poems would be written in the cold, that inner chill of desolation at the loss of Suzanne these past months, the chill of his lost youth, the chill of nighttime, he wouldn't be able to confide these thoughts of his own futile mortality to Isaac because the older man didn't believe in death, up on high where the ocean rose to meet him night and day in one eternal movement, and he came down only when it was time to care for his panthers and foxes and deer, last remnants of an earthly paradise he was drawing out as long as he possibly could, was this perhaps just a way of living seamlessly without disruption in magical meditation of indestructible beauty? Yeah, the coolest looks, the most daring moves thought Mick as he zigzagged through the streets in the sun, and what if evil was something that simply proliferated in this day and age, so maybe good had the same properties, why not, surely it exists in the college and classes and buildings and lecture halls and library, maybe there'd be one or two people he could ally himself with, yeah, the Alliance, the Pact Against All Discrimination, they'd climb to the roofs of all the schools in town and raise their blue and gold and mauve banner, or maybe only a white flag as an invitation to peace with the enemy side, heh heh, why hadn't Mick thought of this before, now to find a girl or boy to start the pact, an Alliance Against Every Form of Criminal Hate, all of them, same as Mick in his eccentric way of dressing or his odd way of walking, no keeping a Hispanic off the bus or a dark-skinned girl, no judging, no misunderstanding, no punishment for social causes, and if he did actually get to make this alliance with someone, then they could make it grow into a group united in solidarity, but where to find someone, where were all the likely ones to recruit under the banner and climb to the rooftops of schools and colleges, especially Trinity which had been such a symbol of tyranny to him, climbing up the steps of the fire escape to the third floor and the roof, he saw only an empty blue sky and below, should he fall, the blue void of roofs speckled with scarlet petals shed by the jasmine all around, over sidewalks and trees, a blue void he'd always have to flee, the enemies chasing after him would be frightened by it, and what if they fell off while beating him up, a smooth karate kick from him would upend them one after another on the cement roof, the very same ones who jostled him at the bus stop, forever the same, oh yes they'd be the ones to turn around when they were on their way up to biology or chemistry, it wouldn't take much for Mick to send them flying all the way down into the blue void, one smooth move and he'd never hear from them or their hatefulness again, their fat faces in his, forgotten during a fight up on the roof, well no, that would be a crime, besides his goal was to make peace, an alliance not enemies, now how to find that one person who'd go along with him, Mick was sure they existed, but where, maybe they were afraid to approach him and say we've been bullied too, we're with you, we want an alliance too, a pact against hate, we'll raise the banner on the roof with you, then when the persecution is over and they've hightailed it to biology or chemistry class, it'll finally be peaceful around here, then, then Mick could dance alone in the blue void where you could see the sea on both sides, hey, every ocean that exists, you could see them all clearly he thought and beneath the clear sky he'd dance alone, moonwalking like the Prince in his black patent leather shoes, just like some astronaut bouncing weightless on the spongy lunar soil, the magnetic step they'd invented as they slowly weaned themselves of their space capsule, and the Prince had adopted it as his own, maybe an astronaut in his own right slipping beyond the Earth's atmosphere, oh he'd dance that way a long time up on the roof, thinking no one could get to him up there, he was already somewhere else, then he heard voices, students below him quarrelling and fighting, yeah but there had to be one or two boys or girls who'd join his pact against hate, someone waiting, maybe afraid, and he'd find them and the first resilient link in the chain would be forged, Mick murmured to himself, the most provocative moves and the coolest look, oh, they'll see, yes they will. Naturally it couldn't be any other way for Augustino thought Daniel, his rebellious son was bound to go from one disappointment to another, one more email he'd forgotten to read, it had to be from annoyance at Laure's shadow hovering over him, it was unceasing by now, her resentment at not being able to smoke anywhere in the terminal, she'd write to them she said, they'd have to compensate her, and that's not all, she was a victim of the times, someone whose fundamental rights were being violated, no doubt thought Daniel, his eyes still fixed on the screen as Augustino's words of disappointment spread across it, as always, yesterday it was the huge oil slicks across rivers and oceans, black foam on the heads of pelicans and sea tortoises, and here it came again, the litany of man's laying such waste, disappointed that here and now in India unspeakable things were accumulating in the sacred rivers, well, which sacred rivers actually, because none of them were anymore, no such thing as a sacred city either when it came to that, industrialization was trampling and defiling everything he wrote, his father had to agree this time and for an instant they fully connected, the water from the Himalayas to the plains was rare and filthy with detritus, noble women in red saris walking for three or four hours each day to villages where the springs and rivers had dried up, the sacred Ganges had become the poisoned Ganges, no sacred Ganges anymore, no sacred city of Varanasi, and those who bathed in the waters were contaminating themselves wrote Augustino, to which Daniel rapidly replied I've just read a scientific article that suggests the rivers might be saved, and I'm inclined to believe it, there is a massive rescue operation going on, hey don't tell me you've finished your book now and under those conditions, I hope you've got a measure of comfort at least, you must look after your health dear Augustino, then Daniel's mind wandered to his conference next day in Ireland, James Joyce, prodigy or miracle, how else to describe what this ability to write means in a world where so little genuine literature is actually read, not scanned the way one automatically consumes so much electronic merchandise, educational or not, tactile playthings which demand little thought and stampede us into stunned mobility, dumbing us down softly in such comfort, numbing us more and more to one another thought Daniel, right here in this airport for instance, to each his own game perhaps, eventually forgetting the passage of time, nearly six hours in this enclave in expectation of a flight announcement, a leatherette-lined hell in which the barely conscious could survive a bomb attack and be unaware of it thanks to their individual electronic shells that formed a heat shield around them, ears deaf behind buds, eyes transfixed by the stream of images before them, something Daniel had elaborated on in his book *Strange Years*, he reproached himself for going months without writing anything, how had he become so neglectful, then he drifted to Olivier and Chuan, the one no longer writing, not even an article, and Daniel considered them vital, he'd written numerous times to tell Olivier that he missed his accusatory pieces, we need to hear your voice in journalism, my husband's grown very depressive came Chuan's reply, and we're anxiously by his side, Jermaine and I, hoping it's just a phase he's going through, dear Olivier, yes of course, a phase, a creeping psychic pain has now attacked his body too, you know he can barely even walk, we don't know what to think anymore, we've consulted several doctors, you know how affectionate he is, he says you love me and you go on loving me and I thank you for it, it's a lot for someone as enfeebled as I am, what is not known is that depression can lead to death, but I don't want to die, oh no, or end my days either like so many writers I've been friends with, still, where I used to condemn them for their suicides I can no longer do so, not now Olivier told his wife, this has me worried she wrote to Daniel, please come dear Daniel, I beg you, whatever the sadness in our lives, please come and see us again as you used to, our family would be overjoyed to see you, I don't know why dear Olivier feels this kind of chronic dissatisfaction, especially when up-and-coming generations have such admiration for his political and social courage, he was one of the very first black senators elected in this country and he's always fought hard, maybe too hard? wondered Daniel, fought against forces that were hostile, ill-willed, and indefatigable, even early on, as a young street demonstrator they set fierce dogs on him and beat him with nightsticks back when that was still allowed, Olivier was at the beginning of a veritable evolution in the world, laws had been changed because of him, the course of history modified, so why this weariness now, yes the weariness of an old fighter, when after all the struggle had only just begun thought Daniel recalling how Chuan had danced the night away on Mère's birthday, oh yes, I'm going to dance all night she decided on that summer evening, it was in the house and orient-scaped gardens she'd created around herself, a light luxuriousness Mère had called it, oh how good it is this airiness around one, even then Olivier often stuck to himself in the cottage by the sea, talking to his wife and son by phone, already a recluse drowning in dark thoughts Daniel realized, Chuan's work often kept her abroad, Paris, Milan, Hong Kong, and they phoned each other several times a day, Jermaine had come back from California to be with his father, such love between them, such loyal affection among them all, and then a veil was drawn that darkened Olivier's spirit, the naked misery of a spirit suddenly disarmed and drained of all initiative, and although it pained Chuan and their son they still danced all night at Mère's birthday celebration, both of them with the same smile, the same slanted eyelids, and in those days Jermaine dyed his hair blond, Chuan said tonight I'm going to do what I never do, I'm going to have some ecstasy with my son, you know I don't let him use it but one day they stop being our kids, simply big young people who do what gives them pleasure and makes them feel free, maybe we should learn from them and be less rigid, more relaxed, yes that's right, and Daniel suddenly wanted to pick up this conversation with her again, such a refined woman and one who so loved Mère and Mélanie, old friends until she dared not leave her husband alone or invite those she was close to with all this sudden internal tension, yet how she loved a laugh and a dance, surely it was unfair for her to assume this despair so foreign to her, considered Daniel, and as they continued their taxi ride Robbie and Petites Cendres spied Herman strolling along with the other girls before the eight-o'clock show, this was no longer Herman triumphant on his tricycle who went yelling "victory" through the lines of bikers with his lace cape flying behind him, no not anymore, what was going on here anyway, did Petites Cendres even want to know, was the flowering gangrene blossoming on his leg again, then why not let them amputate it if he wanted to go on living, so if he had an artificial leg who would notice under a long dress, he needed to put up more of a fight, and Robbie was afraid Herman really was stuck in a rut with heroin now, a way of avoiding suffering, the same with any other substance Marcus had given him, that's what got Marcus thrown in prison, now too stoned to fight, Herman vanquished was what they saw before them, like a marionette with broken strings, helpless in the puppeteer's hands, this is what Petites Cendres saw in tonight's procession a bare few hours before Robbie's crowning out on the platform by the sea, Petites Cendres wasn't even expecting Herman to be there with the others, probably leaning up against the wall of the bar with one hand on his cane for balance, he kept it hidden beneath the folds of his wispy green dress, his face held high and imperious under the orange wig in the last glow of dying day, it was a festive procession that night and Herman had no intention of missing it, weary as he felt, he'd admitted as much to Yinn, weary, very weary, he'd spent a long time staring at Cheng and Cobra and Santa Fe and Geisha and Triumphant Heart, who called Know-It-All his sweet love ever since lifting his cap and kissing his face, all the girls stunning in their outfits, high heels and all, Herman ate them up with his eyes in fond regret, couldn't really miss what was already behind you, such a pathetic look that Petites Cendres could have wept if it weren't that Herman's courage and bravery outstripped his own, every night and for many more to come at the Cabaret shows said Robbie, then at the tail-end of the night when there was no one left in the pale light of dawn, Yinn would oh so carefully carry Herman downstairs in his arms and place him on the red sofa, saying there my friend, you've used again haven't you, you've got to stop doping yourself, please, c'mon wake up, from under the long eyelashes Herman's green eyes would shine, greedy for the good things in life as Robbie put it, and Herman said to Yinn don't worry brother, I was just having a little nap, really it's not hurting so much now, oh yeah how good that feels, and if Yinn had been honest at that very moment, if he'd felt a bit less pity for his friend, he'd have exploded and said what he was really thinking, that for years Herman had been reckless and without respect for his health and body, first roasting on the beach from the time he got up till noon, despite knowing for years that in his quest to get browner the skin he called too pale was already stamped with cancerous cells, without a thought to what was eating him up from the inside, white men don't look good he said, pure vanity was Yinn's answer to that, look what it's got you, you and your noon beach-bathing under a harsh flaming sun, in that same pale light of day Herman's mother would appear in the Saloon doorway, a young woman with red hair and every bit as valorous as her son, I've rented a room with a veranda nearby she told Yinn, that way Herman can sleep a few hours and won't have to walk so far for tomorrow's show, Yinn listened, knowing that the weight of this mother's sorrow would soon crush her and he grasped her hands, covering them with kisses, we're heartbroken he murmured, yes really heartbroken, it is possible he did not actually dare say that but she could see it in his terror-stricken eyes, later at the Saloon he said humbly this hasn't spared us, it really hasn't, we're bewildered at the way things have turned out, speechless, then between Yinn and the courageous mother of the boy with curly red hair asleep on the sofa there was nothing but long moments of silence in which they bonded in desolate comradeship. I know, I know I was probably wrong to take those two in and make them my apprentices, thought the Old Salt on the deck of his boat, watching for the grey heron: odd though, he hadn't seen it today, he dislikes the northerly winds I suppose, either that or the two apprentices Yvan and Lukas had scared him off and he'd stopped coming around, of course he knew they were lobster poachers and squatted in the homes of people who expected to be evacuated in the next hurricane, criminals and thieves but youngsters just the same, it was the duty of men like him with some experience to give them a break, one little chance is all, nobody else was going to put a roof over their heads, it's not that he was a pushover, he knew this and figured everyone deserved a chance, the Old Salt had welcomed them as fishermen on his boat but these two boys tattooed from head to foot, Yvan and Lukas, didn't even obey the rules of autumn fishing, and now he was afraid the Coast Guard or some other officer of the law was going to haul them off to prison, and maybe they shouldn't get out either, no, Eddy the Old Salt was probably wrong, he'd done right taking them in when they had nowhere to go, what didn't look good was that no one else would have them, no, now what was it that gave the Old Salt those mean thoughts, tomorrow Kim would show up to clean the boat, but Fleur wasn't the boy for her, nossir, wouldn't stoop to anything manual except flute-playing and that wouldn't be enough for the woman she was turning into, not a good idea to hang out with a boy who keeps to the streets, a deadbeat in a hoodie and a coat he never cleans, always barefoot, the Old Salt had Kim's bicycle waiting for her shining in the sun, he'd repainted it yellow just this morning and it was dry, Eddy could imagine the surprise on her face when she saw it all done over tomorrow, this spelled new freedom for her when she went off with her dog, holding the thick cord as she rode, those sneaks Yvan and Lukas had been asking who's that for old man, you want us to sell it for you, we're on our way into town for beer and we could take care of it eh, well it's illegal to poach crab and lobster, especially when you sell them over the market price, and if the lieutenant ever found out you'd be in serious trouble boys, it's illegal and that's that said the Old Salt, and Kim's bike isn't for sale either, oh yeah said the tattooed ones, and what you keep hidden in that old sea-chest, the key's well hidden, don't you worry he replied, you fellas are way too curious and I'm not telling you anything, enough questions, time for you to get your beer, then to himself Eddy thought I got pictures of my wife and kids in that sea-chest, nothing else, I've been gone so long I guess none of them even remembers me, just the pictures and a few banknotes for later on, nothing to interest those two nosy delinquents, what about the lobster they leave to suffer in the traps, oh well I'll be happy enough when they get back with at least a dozen beers, some for me and the rest for all of us, can't ask more than that thought the Old Salt, now that's weird Kim thought, all day their stomachs hurt from hunger and here was overexcited Brilliant, chatty as ever while heating their food on the grill at the beach, okay settle round the picnic table where the grill's smoking hot he said, how come you're always parked on those straw mats with your dogs, c'mon, there's enough for everyone, even Damien and Max, let's go doggies, I just fed good old Lucia's dogs too, see, dog and cat biscuits, I get followed through the streets, one day I'll even give my apartment to Lucia so she's protected from her wicked sisters, I don't need it, hey we're young, what do we want with cruelty to old people eh, we've even got champagne, okay maybe not top-notch, but still, and Brilliant looked his friends up and down and they seemed haggard, what a nasty, rotten day said Kim, yeah but it's evening now, then a night of the full moon said Brilliant, right, supper's ready and I haven't forgotten the lemon or the sauce, nope nothing, too bad I got a stain on my shorts but I'll clean it tonight, the boss wants us spic 'n'

span or else I'll be out of work like all the others and it'll be
those illegals Pete and Vladimir instead, hey what's wrong,
you got no appetite, oh nothing said Kim, he's tired from playing flute to nobody all day, he's just tired that's all, he plays
and plays and nobody even notices, Kim wasn't about to say
it was her period and lately it had been getting painful and
messy so she did feel tired all of a sudden, the smell of cooked
fish spread through the cooling air, I didn't forget the herbs
either said Brilliant as he sprinkled some over the grill, and
here's some butter, I wonder if there's any blood on my string
she thought, wait the beach showers are still open and the
cops on those magnificent horses aren't around, so who was
going to see under those giant Australian pines, for a moment
as they all assembled around the table with dogs underfoot
she felt as though they were a family, never mind that Brilliant
was going to keep bumming around all night the way he
liked, though she had no idea where Fleur was going to sleep
or if he'd sleep alone in his cardboard box with Damien as
usual, she should have been content with that, for tomorrow
she and Fleur would head off to the Old Salt's boat and clean
the hull, that was the day he'd give her the bicycle, then they
could go anywhere, so what if people didn't like to see the
homeless riding bikes, just like Jérôme the African with all his
bric-a-brac, the green and red signal lights were shining on
the boats, they were free and they were together beneath the
Australian pine trees and not many people could say that in
this world thought Kim, listening but not listening to the
waves, they had no hut to sleep in but they did have the
beach and the sea, so harmonious and beautiful when there
was no torrential storm, out in the open too, and you could
still hear music close by, maybe it was the trumpet-player Paul
and his group, yes maybe it was them, his joy was so contagious, why hadn't she followed him, they'd have some laughs
when all she did with Fleur was cry, she couldn't understand
why, probably it was her destiny to be with him even if he

pretended to push her out of his space saying it was his part of the sidewalk, but she had to cling to him or she'd be chased away, raped by the other homeless, oh she knew them all and she didn't trust them, drug-pushing, not even knowing quite what they were doing, and it was always the same story, women were the victims, young ones and not-so-young ones, even the human ruins in their filthy swimsuits, bald, toothless women, miserable witches, at least as a family they were safe from those dangers, still clean and acceptable thought Kim, the Old Salt said she was a pretty girl and who knows, maybe it was even true, if she was then why was Fleur so cool, really, why she wondered, all this tangle of feelings and ideas was what came of her period she thought, otherwise she'd be eating hungrily after longing for it all day, Brilliant kept telling her how delicious it was, c'mon eat up, the tightening wasn't in her stomach like this morning, no, it was a feeling she couldn't explain, yes, some sort of violent emotion, this squeezing whenever she thought about their future and how could she explain it to Fleur or Brilliant, Fleur had flipped back his hood and now she could see the face he hid from her, or maybe it wasn't that, this disturbed feeling, then suddenly they all fell to with voracious appetites, there was no holding back, it was stronger than any of them, Brilliant smiling broadly said delicious, am I right, and what about our doggie friends under there, ready for more, see that, all that's left are Lucia's biscuits, never mind, I'll get her some more tomorrow, and Brilliant swept them up in his good humour so they all started laughing for no particular reason, Kim too, regardless of how she was feeling, they were alive she thought, that's it, and together, a family, of course and thank heaven the cops on their proud horses weren't there to see them, no, nobody at all but them and their dogs Max and Damien, no one would show up on the beach tonight, we've got the Earth to ourselves said Brilliant and it was true thought Kim, all was beauty and harmony around them, three kids and their dogs.

When they get here with the beer I'll give them what for, thought Eddy, I'll say, er, if I'd known you were poachers, yeah if I'd known I'd've turned you in a long time ago, the lieutenant's up there in his helicopter, I used to run into pirates long ago all the way up to Saint-Louis Bay, all over the seas and oceans, and it was them and lobster poachers and other kinds who'd never let the flying fish just live and breathe as they hovered over the water, now there won't be any left pretty soon, what with sailing regattas and water-skiing, nope, no more, no dolphins or sea turtles that I can see from the deck every day, the seas and oceans'll just be garbage dumps and rejected fish will be getting stuck in our nets, drugs changing hands and captains on the run, just heaving their syringes and needles overboard by the hundred into the crystal waters of the Gulf, along with shoes, beach sandals, the works, to wash up on the beaches along with what's left of the makeshift boats left by Cubans, nobody asking what happened to the men and women on them, same with the Haitians, the river of death swept them out of sight and out of mind along with drifting whale corpses, shoes and flip-flops, that's about all I'll see from now on, whoops is that them back again, here come the boys, yep I can hear them below in the cabin talking about something, okay time to let them have it, boy if I'd known, I want no poachers on my boat, well first maybe just a nice quiet beer with no talking, then tomorrow I've got Kim and Fleur coming, and the bicycle, the bright, shiny yellow bike and who knows, maybe, just maybe a surprise visit from the grey heron, he's probably changed his timing, could be because he knows Yvan and Lukas are around and he's not too sure, what with not being keen on the northerlies and whatnot, ah that huge bird's a gift from Heaven, a messenger from out of the clouds, an archangel of the waters, you never know, maybe he'll come thought Eddy, yep I know he will, Kim was wondering about Rafael, why was he so hyper with his tarot predictions and all that, and why didn't he tell Fleur

he would leave and have lots of musical success far from Kim
and the street, no, back to the great cities of Europe where it
had been so good for him before as a child prodigy, and close
to her, to Clara the virtuoso violinist, in fact he said there was
an echo of her and her music in his own compositions, Clara
at the violin, yes, oh if only he had a studio like Paul the
trumpeter, some real technology to work with, if only, he'd
shut himself up all day and never stop working on the voice
mix, the strength of the chorus, and far off the strident notes
from Clara's violin, and there he would be, and there he
would, Kim knew he talked that way when he'd had enough
bad champagne to get drunk or when he smoked bad pot,
Brilliant supplied that too for a lot of poorer folks like them,
he didn't sell it, it came from his strolls through bars on
Bahama Street, as well as his black panhandling friends and
the unemployed vegetating on their front porches, oh here it
was, you could hear the noise of the bikers making their entry
into town for the week, not too close yet thought Kim, but
enough to startle the hens that hadn't yet fluttered up into the
trees, the big heavy bikes were shaking the walls already as
they parked along the edge of the beach, yes now you could
hear them alright Kim said to herself, yes, now Rafael was
usually so calm, a hopeless optimist, so why, she wondered,
was he so disturbed when he told her not to get on that boat
tomorrow, and Eddy too was remembering his nightmares,
they came and went, those begging soldiers, old friends still
wearing their helmets and blowing up whales and schools of
sharks with grenades in the Pacific, then the chase, when suddenly one of them said to him the hour has come for you too
Eddy, he had his hideaways, cubbyholes in the shadow of the
rocks, he woke up uneasy these nights with the feeling he
was being watched, spied on by some ghost or other, this was
a recent thing this vague sense of fear, he'd always lived safe
and sound on the boat, his haven of peace, nowhere could
he be freer than he was here, remote and serene in his

travelling home, just a modest boat he'd fixed up himself after a storm, he hadn't looked at the pictures of his wife and children for ages, he had them wedged between pages of a book in his sea-chest, so long their features must have dissolved, how was life for them far away without him, he'd had no girls, just boys, less trouble that way, and they were getting by without him, no longer boys, they must be men by now, he could no longer imagine their faces or their bodies, and in the pictures their features had been washed away as if by water, and maybe they had, water soaks up everything the way it does a shipwreck at sea, strange though, no visit from the heron on the gangplank today, not even a trace of him circling the waves, it always got a bit choppy under the hull about this time, what were those boys talking about down in the cabin anyway, nope, Eddy hadn't given it enough thought before letting them on his boat, he'd been warned, they just got out of a juvenile detention centre, they're squatters and thieves, other sailors nearby had told him but Eddy never acted except according to his lights, luck is for everyone not just one man, and up till now he'd never made an enemy with his charitable principles, and who else could brag of being so happy living up to them for so long, a free man on his boat, the Old Salt could certainly crow about that, too bad about those nightmares though, but they weren't that frequent after all, they just sort of came and went like the waves, not too high nor that often really, and Adrien could see the officer who said from atop his horse, Mr. Adrien, sir, the tennis court is closing soon, you know I never noticed this grillwork fence before answered Adrien in astonishment at suddenly seeing a man on horseback next to him, what a magnificent animal, I'd so love to ride one as lively as this, Mr. Adrien the officer repeated, we're closing any minute now, besides, what are you doing here at this hour well after sunset, well you see replied Adrien, for a writer time is nothing but an illusion, I was so absorbed in writing this poem, in fact I was trying to think of a title, giving account, time to settle accounts, you see officer, for us time doesn't exist, no but the law does replied the policeman still in the saddle, and it exists for everyone sir, even you Mr. Adrien, and there's no escaping from time, the hands keep moving around the dial for everyone sir, then what am I to do asked Adrien, well you ought to think about leaving before we shut the gates said the officer in a threatening tone this time, fortunately a white butterfly had landed on his notebook and woken Adrien up, indeed the horse was a magnificent animal, a pleasant apparition on waking from a nap on a sleepy afternoon, what could be more reassuring on opening one's eyes, except that it was an illusion, there was no man on horseback giving orders while Adrien finished up his poem, sitting there in complete innocence on his stone bench in the cool shade of the silvered palms as he did each evening, how was it then that he no longer dreamed of Suzanne, where had she gone, was it in the hope of finding her in his arms that he drew out these naps at day's end, so this was it, she was no more, not even in dreams, his confidante and best friend, she added verve to his thoughts and without her his books on Voltaire and Racine were boring, and nothing was more painful than a boring author he thought, it may be that his students still owed him a debt for his discoveries but it was Suzanne who had stood up for Cyril when he produced the musical comedy of *Phaedra*, what an outrage, that which is divine cannot be a musical comedy Adrien said, what pretentiousness on Cyril's part, who does he think he is, just because his lover is a great poet and only a passing affair at that, Frédéric was Charles's one and only passion, Suzanne had silenced Adrien, saying Cyril was a gifted young actor and director, part of an avant-garde that was way over Adrien's head and his opinion was really old hat, and as for the affair, well, if it brought Charles's inspiration to its highest level, yes a peak in his sexual life too, why not, perhaps forgetting that Adrien was her husband, Suzanne came to Charles's defence as if he were the misunderstood spouse and sole object of her ardour, yes well let me tell you, Adrien cut in with his natural insolence, let me tell you my dear Suzanne that if God exists that would suit Charles to a "T" because he's most certainly closer to Him than to the company of men, and what is a man of his high intellectual calibre doing with Cyril eh, the flattery of adventure perhaps, untrammelled sex with an adventurous young man, nothing more if even that, while God, if He exists, and nothing proves He does, God would really be much more to his liking, at least he would be speaking the same language and be on an equal footing with Him instead of wandering in a desert composed of no one but ourselves, when he considered Suzanne's defence of Charles, Adrien remembered all of them, loyal couples, sure an occasional fault here and there, like Jean-Mathieu and Caroline, Adrien and Suzanne, Chuan and Olivier, Charles and Frédéric last and possibly least thought Adrien, who saw his own as one of the most sublime in all its secular legitimacy, indeed Adrien and Suzanne, when she was no longer there, not even in dreams, had no doubt admired her friend Charles and been on the sunlit path that led to him, united now in the sphere where spirits convene in mutual agreement, forgetting Adrien who was much more down-to-earth, much lower on the scale of knowledge, especially spiritual knowledge, something virtually unknown to him, Adrien was moved by the turtledoves cooing this late in the evening only a few feet from his bench. I should tell someone it was a mistake to fire the math teacher, thought Lou, but which one should I tell, Mama or Papa, José had been taken away in handcuffs by the sheriff and a detective and she wondered which one to tell, Ari or Ingrid, maybe I should just keep quiet and say nothing, still he'd be in jail for nothing, without pay for a week or a month, they said an investigation at school showed he had touched an eleven-year-old on the hip, but I know the kid and she lied, Sophia always lies, but the principal said we cannot tolerate such behaviour in our schools, maybe I should tell her Sophia's a liar, she said he put his black hand on my breast and my hip during volleyball, yes he touched me a few times, there and there, well I was right there with her and it's definitely not true, not true at all, he's been unjustly accused, now it's in the paper so they aren't going to believe me, they've written everywhere that he's guilty, no, we can't tolerate this sort of behaviour in our school, not just a school, we're really more of a family the principal said, it's the law of the county and the nation, this must not be allowed to go on, in getting rid of an undesirable teacher we have our students' best interests at heart, they arrested José on Wednesday and he won't be getting out for a year, it was just friendly he said in his own defence, I've never done any of those things they say I did, he touched me inappropriately on the leg said Sophia, she couldn't remember exactly where though or even how and began getting mixed up in her lies thought Lou, yes lies, while the accused man's career went into limbo maybe forever, what else was it she said, something moved in his trousers while he touched her here and there, though exactly where on her body she couldn't really remember anymore, was it an erection, maybe, yes, she even said the word while everyone listened in amazement, everyone, the principal, students, sheriff, and detective, and had he raped her, but Sophia could only answer, rape, what is that, she'd accused José the math teacher she disliked of all sorts of horrors but she couldn't really say what rape was, Lou knew perfectly well that the man who had supposedly touched Sophia on the leg, breast, and waist had done nothing of the sort, but how could she stand up in class and say no, he's innocent, I was with Sophia and she's just a liar, but he had an erection right in front of the child the principal said, we just can't allow that in our schools, and three other girls besides Sophia had lied on the police report, yes we saw it all and it's true what Sophia says, we saw the whole thing, no, none of it was true thought Lou, not a thing, all three of them lied when they said José touched Sophia just above the knee, how to tell one and all it was totally untrue, will Mama or Papa believe me if I tell them, Lou had said it to the female officer who questioned her in the principal's office, Sophia's lying, she's just a liar, Sophia's got it in for him, she always said she didn't like him or his smell or the colour of his skin, she never did, she always said what's someone like him doing in a good school like this, no, Sophia's lying, none of it's true, none of it, but she was the only one so nobody believed her, not the sheriff or the detective or the lady officer, they decided Lou was Sophia's enemy in school, who could she tell now that the man had been arrested, yes it had to be Papa or Mama or else no one, there were men just as vulnerable as the most fragile of women it turned out, so nobody gets much justice she realized, and lies could kill, what would Papa say, that Sophia, like his Lou, was rather precocious, and Mama, well she might say it was all because of that private school, she'd never wanted Lou to go there in the first place, Ari and Ingrid had intolerable arguments about it again and again, right over her head, her parents hated one another, it was always like that, harsh words between them and what with Sophia's lies they wouldn't want to hear about it so she said nothing, it was unfair to José but already the female officer had disbelieved her, no, the real reason for Sophia's lies was the C grade she got in school, José had no choice but to put that on her work because she never did her homework, so this C was why she now claimed he had touched her several times above the knee and under her skirt, or was it that she couldn't remember which lie she had told before, and it wasn't the first time she'd done something like this, once on a trip to Cuba she'd accused a man of having sat her on his lap and no, you couldn't say out loud what he'd done, that had been her first lie, and her father, Cuban himself, had beaten the man, Sophia always managed to get someone else punished in her place, must have been carrying on like this for a long time, because if she didn't get enough attention Sophia went to a very dark place and started lying, yet no one ever realized her accusations were false, and now because of her José had been humiliated and arrested in front of the whole class when the real reason was that she lied and no one would listen to or believe her otherwise, her killer lies stood thick in front of the truth, no, not even Ingrid or Ari or anyone else could see through them. As he set off to pick up his daughter at Rosie's for the week, Ari wondered when Asoka would be back, for only he, her godfather, could have a healthy influence on her, the tranquility of positive thoughts without artifice, this was how the pilgrim monk had once described himself writing from Sri Lanka, well you see, said Ari, I'm kind of volatile and so's my daughter, between the instability of Ari's love affairs and the split from his wife only this Buddhist monk could fathom the life of a man, an unchaste man forever unable to feel the exaltation towards goodness, a man like so many others, not to mention an artist's dissatisfaction with his own black marble sculptures or painted aluminum ones, could Asoka still be travelling through Russia without a coat, not that he possessed anything even at the best of times, his modesty no doubt had let him accept a coat from his Russian disciples, ephemeral is the life harboured by one's body he had written to Ari, who immediately reacted inwardly, no, no, no, one needs to be more resilient and appreciate one's own vitality, and behold a message from Asoka in Uganda, fragile as he appeared, Asoka must have this all-embracing resilience because there he was alone and fighting side by side with those stricken by malaria in the giant swamps infested with crocodiles and suffocating lilies and papyrus plants that propagate the parasite, he wrote my dear Ari, blessings on you and Ingrid and Lou and bless you tenderly for remembering me and for your material help my dear Ari, it has allowed me to buy hundreds of mosquito nets for children in the refugee camps near Lake Kwania, here the swamp mosquitoes are deadly indeed and feed greedily off human flesh, eventually the survivors go back to fishing in the swamps and promptly get reinfected, between the malaria and malnutrition a great many babies die each day wrote Asoka, towns are gradually being decimated, we do have medical centres and quite a few volunteers, bless you Ari for not forgetting me, I shall soon be joining you and your daughter, but when would that be Ari wondered, with calls for his work as a monk from all over the world, and how would he explain Lou's imperfections to this exemplary man, her bad moods as puberty drew near and her personal secrets were pulling them apart, perhaps the little girl and her father bent over a sheet of drawing paper or solving a puzzle on the computer were gone forever, a new era of suspicion had crept up on them, faced with this precarious imbalance, Asoka might remind Ari of his own flightiness, womanizing and other indulgences he might disapprove of, well even Ari considered himself to be indulgence personified, and how could an artist in constant search of new forms be otherwise, the positive thinking espoused by his friend just wasn't enough to assuage the thirst that drove him, it's surely too late Ari thought, and what was a positive thought anyway, could it even exist in the middle of all this tumult we call modern life, still it would truly be a joy to see his daughter waiting in front of Rosie's for him, Lou had probably tired quickly of all her friend's brothers and sisters, Papa, she'd yell coming towards him and that's how their week together would start off, cranky or sweet or maybe constantly on the cellphone to her mother, I'd rather be with you Ingrid, what sort of disarray were they bound for, somewhere between love and betrayal, yes when you thought about it Asoka would have been good for Lou, for both of them, a healthy influence on Lou, were all the fathers of this world doomed to dwell in lack of understanding and exasperating solitude Ari wondered, these hard little heads, so quick to anger, always ended up outstripping their parents though they might never know it, of course it hurt to feel oneself left behind, in fact what Lou really needed from her father and didn't get was severity, so Ari would be stricter, a bit late he thought, especially after spoiling her so and providing no tangible direction, now this kind of severity would be a bit like trying to stop a wild pony in full flight, yes, there it was he thought, when Adrien glanced back over the poem "Giving Account" he caught himself wondering why he had been so hard on Augustino's writing, such a charming young man, always scruffy and badly dressed, was it his appearance that made him a target, perhaps more so than his actual books, as to that, Adrien had to admit he'd hardly read them and scarcely remembered anything of them, a superficial reading was inexcusable, and as for Cyril, well, Suzanne had been right to remind him in dreams that he hadn't been very flattering in that regard either, be it Cyril himself or his stagings, his librettos, the contemporary fluidity in his creations so praised by other critics, but to remove Phaedra from her myth, her ancient foundations in Euripides and Seneca, not to mention Racine's tragedy, with her drama of fatality and predestination and turn her into an incestuous biker-lover, well that really was an abuse, you couldn't just drain all the classicism out of her, really Cyril had gone too far, this wasn't uncharitable on Adrien's part; he was right, he was merely defending the great against the crazy, as he had always done with integrity, oh but here was his wife again, she'd returned to his dreams and was asking him, really now wasn't there some repressed nastiness in those reviews of yours Adrien dear, better yet, perhaps you were jealous, yes of course, that's it isn't it, jealous of Augustino and of Cyril, jealous that they had, each in his own way, so much imagination, always he awakened from these vexing dreams just in time, some vague sense of guilt dogged him and for the longest time he thought he heard Suzanne saying again and again in his ear Adrien, my dear Adrien, as the young and beloved face she wore in these apparitions faded into the mist, he'd seen himself too in all the ardour of his twenty years, oh what a trap these dreams were, leading you to reach out to air, nothing, Suzanne fading into the far distance with her own preoccupations, for she seemed to have a lot to do, what could that possibly be in motionless time, what was Adrien himself thinking of every night and day when he waited for her during his afternoon naps under the silvered palms right after tennis, yes, Adrien waited tirelessly for Suzanne with such longing, would he ever realize his wife was never coming back, not tonight or tomorrow, he was so unused to pain that he thought his soul would always be full of joy and confidence, that any moment Charly's convertible would pass by in the glow of the setting sun, and as for the poem, well, he'd change the title, this one was too heavy, too nebulous, there would be no accounting, no judgement for his mistakes, the weight of them laid him low, and then he felt a sudden relief, he mustn't forget to visit old Isaac on his island, no he'd not forget, one must visit one's friends when there are so few of them left. Hit me, that's what they did, thought the Old Salt, what did they do, they hit me with an iron bar, yeah Yvan and Lukas, now I never should have, no the others warned me, there's no iron bar anywhere on this boat, or was it the broom or a weapon and maybe they took one look at my long scrawny neck from behind while I was at the wheel wondering if the grey heron would be back today, they said get the old guy, but no blood said one of them, just one whack will do it, we just want to knock him out, no busting him up any more than that, find the keys, he keeps them on him or in his rain-slicker pocket, it's up there on the nail in the hold, just one whack or maybe two with the iron bat thought Eddy, his eyes were giving him trouble, no I never should have invited them aboard, have they done me in or can I get up now, all they're going to find are some yellowed old photos of my wife and kids, some banknotes, the bike, let's take the bike too Lukas had said, don't rough him up, he's old, why not just finish the job said Yvan, like those lobsters in the trap, they're old so why not put an end to him now, he won't feel a thing, we'll just paint the bike black and make it look battered, maybe change the tires said Lukas, don't forget the money in the chest, hey stop hitting him will you, we don't want to leave any marks on him, see he's barely breathing already, right so let's finish him off said Yvan, that way he can't talk, I'll do it, you'll see, it's easy, boy my eyes are really acting up thought Eddy, something fierce, like waves are starting to cover me up, geez why did I ever let them on here, never should have, I wanted to give them a chance and lookit how they thank me, are they going to kill me, help he murmured, help, but the words wouldn't leave his lips, no voice and no words Eddy thought to himself, leave him on the gangplank Yvan said, like he fell asleep after his beers, yeah right, like he's sleeping, c'mon quick, let's go said Lukas, we've got to get out of here, he's still alive, either gasping or crying, who knows, now see that's why I wanted to finish him off said Yvan, enough said Lukas, I just wanted him out of it, do you really want to get us accused of something serious, no, no way, let's take the money and the bike, that's it, hey that's enough, let him alone, he's old, c'mon before it gets dark on the water, c'mon will you, how is he, asleep, only sleeping, good so let's get out of here. My girlfriends the rappers from New Orleans will be there Robbie was telling Petites Cendres, they've been at it for ages, it's a good way for ordinary folks to get the word out, revolt and the joy of living need to mix it up and explode in the body somehow, for a rapper like my friend Fred it's a way of life, even existence itself, hip-hop artists live at this fine edge of dance Robbie said to Petites Cendres who from the taxi was reacting to the haggard face of Herman under his orange wig, then his thoughts turned to Robbie's friend Fred who had danced and sung so much of his life in the hottest shows and videos and in all the hottest places, there was no keeping track of time or thinking about retirement, he just went on singing and dancing without letup, while Herman, still young, was definitely on his last run, however courageous and formidable he might be he weighed very little and had to be virtually carried onstage by Yinn, such a shipwreck this life of ours thought Petites Cendres yet he held on to it just as tight as Herman, he willed himself with all his might to dream of what he'd long forgotten swinging in his hammock and refusing to get up for all these months while Mabel watched over him like a mother, the sheer voluptuousness of being alive, it was now coming back to him along with his taste for things of the night and the memories of so many giddy times with his friends at the Porte du Baiser Saloon, my rapper friends will be there tonight for my coronation said Robbie, what a party, oh yes and Fred up on the stage as wicked and wired as ever, and perhaps Martha was right when she told her son the Music Council and the jurors would be a little too wise for Fleur, he had no fixed address and lived in the street amid all that filth, would he be brave enough to submit his composition to them, these people are too sharp for you she said, great conductors and musicians, and what you've given them is a sombre story of demolition, is it even music she said, his mother, who had once been so proud of him and bragged to one and all, now seemed to enjoy humiliating him, there's this older musician Franz, I've heard his *Requiem*, well they say he gives a hand to young composers and lets them conduct his symphony orchestra, even young women who he says will provide the next generation of conductors, well, that is when his musicians aren't on strike, Fleur had gone and sat on his beach mat wrapped in his coat a short distance from Kim and Brilliant while Damien stood guard by his side, as always in a stoic position with his ears upright and paws straight out in front as he sniffed the air, the same as he would in the street, good dog murmured Fleur, where would I be without you, Kim could just hear the murmur of Fleur's voice as he repeated, good dog, good dog,

Kim had never known him to speak this affectionately to the dog and confide in him like no one else, especially Kim, she also heard the sound of the waves and it reassured her, yet still she felt that sharp inexplicable fear in her breast, no point in thinking about tomorrow or the future or even Fleur's plans of which she knew nothing, all she did know was that the only reason he went to his mother's was to work on his music in his old bedroom covered with posters of him when he was a little boy with Clara and her violin, Fleur wondered about the musicians on the council that supported modern artists, if only two or three of them could understand him, and his mother's words came back to him, they're merciless in their verdicts and they won't be on your side, son, reading and listening to music all day on your earphones, you've joined the ranks of the self-taught with no real training, you have no idea what you're dealing with, just a shiftless soul flitting from one thing to another said Martha, to them you're just an ignorant barbarian, you mustn't forget you're a street kid now, unwashed and barefoot, and when they set eyes on you they'll be let down, but Fleur was thinking at least one or two must have been exposed to music when they were kids, yeah sure I'll dress properly with shoes when the day comes, they won't even guess my street life, it'll be a day of rebirth, they mustn't find out and I'll tell my mother that too, we're surrounded by demolition, nothing but demolition, the space shuttle and the astronauts blowing up in the sky, the glaciers too exploding and sliding down into the depths with the polar bears, implosion and destruction wherever you look, even the air I breathe is loaded, you do realize this don't you Mama, don't you see the song of Clara's violin is going to be the one note of purity and hope, I can hear the solo even now, yes, crystalline and increasing in speed as it weaves in and out of the other instruments as the orchestra comes in with cadences, and rapidity, while the voices provide structure to it all, a high-pitched ascent for anxiety to be felt, yes thought Fleur from under the hood, we need the effect of speeding up so the instruments can provoke an uneasiness, the rhythms must be troubling too and any harmony between instruments must seem unusual, they'll explode in dissonance and autonomy, yes one or two of those judges will understand me if they were exposed to music as kids, yes they'll understand he thought, now if Lucia's sisters go on mistreating her this way what's going to become of her, Brilliant wondered still standing by the smoking grill and watching the sky darken over the waves, Lucia my lover just wants to have some fun once in a while, get out from under them, the reign of those tyrant sisters, they want to steal her away from me she said, and take away everything I've built up over the years, my store and my business and my jewels, lock me up and take it all, it's a scandal, a crying shame thought Brilliant, ah but never fear, I Brilliant will be her protector and defend my beautiful and righteous friend, I'll fight for you like a son, don't you worry, Misha and I will always be there to look out for you, the vet says he's doing much better, then we'll never be apart, no, now Misha's survived floods and hurricanes and we'll soon be together again, and there isn't going to be any Third or Fourth Great Devastation, nossir, I can go back to my room and they won't always be hounding me, all these dead and drowned people begging for rescue, even my brother, my black Nanny's son, never again to see his blue coveralls ballooning up amid the foam, no and I no longer see his face either now, his face eaten away by the flood, no longer see my mother walking across the stinking water, elegant and denatured and pious enough to send her birthday flowers back to me, sure, walking on the water and aloof from the sorrows of all those bobbing drowning heads, walking, even running and laughing and saying to me it's your own fault Victor died, I don't ever want to see you in my house deviant son, that drumming, what is it, must be Jérôme the African with his metal buckets summoning people to us at the edge of the sea to hear his wounded chants and rhythms, *bang, bong,* it gives me a start like the far-off thunder, yes tomorrow I'm going to see Misha and bring him home, yessir my future's with Misha and Lucia, gotta get my loving Lucia out of there, she who so loves kissing me, kissing the stigmata scars on my arms and saying what abominable hellish mother could force her black servant to whip her son, yes there now, a few kisses more and you'll feel better, a kiss and a caress here and all will be forgotten Brilliant, my lovely Brilliant, I'm not crazy about your sideburns, they look old on a young man like you, oh I do it to look more like Misha, Brilliant said, yes we've gotta get Lucia out from under their surveillance, those sisters of hers are up to no good, so that's what I'll do, I'll talk to the judge, then Misha and I can finally go home with them following us, the drowned ones still gasping for breath, everywhere, under the stairs, yes Brilliant thought, there will be no more devastation, then Kim came and sat next to him on the mat while Max closed in on the grill for a sniff as the salty air took on the smell of smoke, Brilliant was hippity-hopping and laughable, Kim thought back to Rafael the clairvoyant spreading out his cards, here for you Fleur is the best card of all, it's the World, and for you my sweet Kim, he abruptly fell silent and covered up the Ruined House card with his hand, what a stinking stupid day thought Kim, first thing in the morning you find a dead bird lying on the sidewalk, then you know it's going to be a dumb unhappy day, yes you do, first you try and lift up the little head, but it just flops back and you wonder how it happened, he must have been singing at dawn, yes I think I heard him, the first one in the frangipanis, guess I'd better put him somewhere out of the way where no one will see, let him rest in a bush, as she caressed the little ball of feathers, you knew that was it and this was going to be one stinking stupid day, yes, a sign and a bad one too, you just knew it when you saw the nestling stiff-legged and on its back, took it in your hands to warm it up knowing it was pointless, even a little consciousness, regardless of its position, and it would have been aware of Kim's kindness, and if it had managed to fly away it would remember yes remember, she thought, then she'd have the impression she could still hear him singing in the frangipanis again, okay maybe not him but an earthbound echo of his spirit, Rafael the Mexican clairvoyant had told Fleur, you get the best card of all, the World, this card is the supreme victory, oh yes it is, and Kim had felt from the morning as she led Max to Fleur's spot by his crude rope, not really a leash at all, that this was going to be some stupid stinking day, she absolutely knew it, and here it was evening, nearly nightfall, and the green starboard lights of the boats were coming on and maybe she was feeling a little better about it, though the sensation of fear was still there in her breast, Brilliant said you really need to get another leash for Max, doesn't matter if he's a mutt, he should have a nice new one, you and me and Misha and Max ought to go to the bicycle races, I bet we come in first, c'mon let's have some more champagne Kim, but what if Fleur were to leave she thought, they'd no longer have a family, I'll buy a leash for Max Brilliant said, and Kim was no longer thinking about Fleur alone and hiding under his hood again so far from them, and Kim barely heard Brilliant's voice, always the same funny hippity-hopping guy telling stories that Kim had no way of knowing were true or false or maybe just the crazy poetry of a writer who'd had too much to drink, he always did in the bars and taverns along the way, you couldn't really make a family with him anyway because before long he'd be off at night bumming and wandering with words tripping off his lips, words from books he would never write, well maybe he would, no way Kim could know what the future held for any of them, even Max and Damien, no, no way to know, there had to be a bunch of you to make a family, dogs and all, the dogs needed to be on guard in the street whether they were lying down or not, uh-huh and what if Fleur left, he'd have to, like the nestling with its head thrown back she'd be dead, yeah, that or hang out with Paul the trumpeter who flouted his happiness under their noses, with him joy was contagious, it really was, then there was this fearful feeling in her breast, nope, no way to know what would become of them all, while she listened to Brilliant laugh she looked all around them into the night, no, no way to tell, but at least one thing was certain, tomorrow they'd be off to the Old Salt's boat, just like every Saturday, and hating that sensation of fear when he put his wrinkled hand on her head and said I know you don't realize it yet but you really are a pretty girl and such a hard worker too, and here's the bike I promised you, yes it's for you Kim. What if, what if the reason for the delay is something really serious Laure said to Daniel as he typed on his computer in the terminal, as always she used her plaintive cigarette-deprived voice, I can't stand it, seven hours, that's right, that's how long we've been here, seven hours, what if, say, the president or vice-president of some country's been assassinated and that's why we're being held up here, did you ever think of that Daniel, maybe it's something that serious, well then you can be sure we're the last of their worries, and smokers last of all, forget 'em, just folks with nasty habits, all they have to do is give it up, simple as that, they're poisoning and stinking up the air for everyone else anyway, tough, I bet that's how they think of us, me, you don't smoke, do you, yes I can see that, sure for something really critical like some big politician they might leave us stuck here for days, who cares about a bunch of plane passengers, borders'd be closed anyway, ever think of that Daniel, all these flights delayed and now they're closing the airport, could be something really big, look how nice it is outside, she was agitated and yelling by now, then Daniel answered her the way he would one of his children, whatever it is we need to stay calm, there's no good in getting worked up like this, it'll all pass, just keep believing we'll leave soon said Daniel, paternalistic as always, the man and father had no choice but to speak to the annoying woman as though she were his daughter though they were probably the same age, how condescending thought Laure, they're all alike, this was why she was still single she reminded herself, they're always patronizing like this one, oh he was likeable enough, maybe not irresistible but likeable enough, too wrapped up in his own thoughts though, well he was a writer wasn't he, maybe not quite as patronizing as she made him out to be, maybe just being polite and exercising his curiosity as a writer, she believed he considered her interesting, he might find her exasperating but not necessarily attractive and this was the first real flesh-and-blood writer she'd met, he's not like anyone else and he's brought a pile of books he's constantly dipping into and making notes, quiet and fully absorbed, worst of all, when he wasn't at his computer, he wasn't about to have a smoke either, that's what really riled her because he couldn't understand the hunger, the thirst she suffered, he couldn't even share with her that little wavelength she was on longing for a smoke, let alone offer to sneak her one, but this imagined discussion got on her nerves even more, you think something like that could've happened he asked her, I mean a president for instance, and they wouldn't tell us first of all, and as he said that she managed to catch his eye under those substantial brows that expressed his wordless perplexity even when reading or writing, despite his uncertainty, and she realized she'd troubled him without meaning to, all she wanted was for him to listen, to see that the situation might be a tragedy in the making with some unknown repercussion about to blow up in their faces, instant annihilation in seconds, or maybe she was it, because here he was calmly reading from his computer, so here she was alone again and feeling the boredom and irritation rise in her, along with the desire to smoke of course, god it was awful she exclaimed, not knowing Daniel had heard her anyway, he always did and he too wondered what they were all waiting for, possibly nothing at all, if the worst came to the worst his final thoughts would be of the little pink baby and the golden curl on top of the tiny head held close against her mother's breast while the pink legs protruding from the travel bag as both danced so she'd go to sleep, a last recollection of Mai or Rudy when their parents carried them that way, dancing to get them drowsy, one foot then the other, a soft cadence, a little jazzy and a little slow, what a last thought that would be if one imagined the worst as Laure was doing, her conscious chaos actually took several forms, erasing all their existences with a fiery arrow, whether this were actually to happen or merely apprehended, Daniel's next thought was that he was too young and unfulfilled to die yet, okay there were his books and his kids, but what else had he accomplished that was so overwhelming he could leave the world and feel contented, well, really nothing all that tangible, nothing to compare with Olivier's scale of grand social and political transformation, true he was Daniel's senior by several decades and no longer able to manage his exhaustion or his corrosive fits of depression, such was the bitter fruit of a life dedicated to all, already fighting racial segregation as a young student in Birmingham, watching so many black houses, churches, and businesses being firebombed, now a man of laws living with the constant threat of violence, even chained and beaten, no Daniel would never be that kind of liberating militant, odd he should be thinking of Olivier now paralyzed by depression, barely able to get out of bed in the morning, as though the burden of bile from burnt churches and schools in his native Birmingham still crushed him beneath its weight and the thought that despite all the sacrifice everything might possibly go on as before, had he lost faith in the redemption from ancestral hate, it tortured and oppressed him this overwhelming hate of one part of the Earth for another pondered Daniel, then words from Samuel shone out from the screen, Papa, dear Papa I've got a second dance in mind to follow the one you saw in New York, I'm writing this while Rudy plays with his toy planes on the table and sends them gliding around the world as though counting on a smooth landing on the kitchen table again just for him, Rudy loves it and it'd be true they're everywhere we want them, this autumn I'd love to see everyone on display in this choreography, disinterred from their asphalt and cement tombs: Tanjou, our good family friend and dancer-administrator of our group who went down with one of the towers that day, Our Lady of the Bags, sent flying off to the park where she used to panhandle with her Bible open on her lap and her pleated skirt, bursting out from under the piles of earth and taking up where she left off in life, a mere stone's throw from death when everyone was swept up in the current of swirling people in the stairwells, a random stone's throw, crushed and forgotten at the foot of the tower after spending the night in the park, she needs a park, a garden for her momentary resurrection, see Papa, everyone could appear to be taking flight through the barred windows dressed as they were that day, all of them from gaps in the windows out towards their families and their lives before the massacre, angelic yet united in one burning brazier of humanity, the music, the music would need to be a cantata, where are you Papa, in Ireland by now I guess, please write me when you arrive, your son Samuel, kisses from all of us, Rudy, Veronica, and me, you see Papa, what I want to capture is all the intensity and feverish and unquenchable thirst for life, the ineffable love that gathers and unites all those lives, Samuel who loves you, reading this message from Samuel, Daniel scolded himself for not having written these past months, as well as for his inability to follow the rather sombre path of Augustino, then there was the void at home left by Mai, and he was no longer there waiting for her to wander into his office when she came in late or fell on her skateboard or her skates, wonder what she's doing at four in the morning, has she got back in touch with Manuel, for the longest time he'd thought of no one but Augustino and Mai, relegating Samuel to his own independent life, but he needed him too, ironically it might be Samuel, the artist and ground-breaking choreographer, who was closest to him in this kind of writing solitude, Samuel had been the first to grow up at his side amid the jumble when he was writing *Strange Years*, the ghost of his Great-Uncle Samuel, soul-blasted as he emerged from his snowy grave, shot dead in Poland, shot dead on his knees there in the snow, whose name Samuel now bore, his sensitivity too perhaps as he plumbed the depths of hell, Samuel's right perhaps, we're never just one person each, we each come from everyone, our collected experience new or old may not always have been gleaned with love, though Samuel believed it did, in fact we may even be repulsed by our first urge to belong to a single community of the living, still for Samuel to be slightly naive was normal, as was his idea of love reigning over a humanity in peril, how like a young man to think that way Daniel realized, feeling suddenly like a patriarch, what fun to get crowned Queen of Carnival Week Robbie exclaimed to Petites Cendres, they'd lowered the taxi window and had already seen the beginning of the street parade, oh boy there's nothing you won't see these next few days, Robbie was already wired by it all, you're gonna see hundreds of Adams and Eves out on the sidewalks wearing nothing but a hanky, even puffy traditional couples, skinny ones, whatever, who just take it all off and dance with a hula hoop, what a gas, we're gonna have so much fun making the rounds of the balls and masquerades and parties all day and night, watching will give you a pick-me-up Petites Cendres, such naughty wild stuff you'll have a great time, and when I'm up on the stage with the royal family, you'll be clapping your hands, Yinn's going to announce what time the crowning will be and when the ball's to begin, being the queen of the burlesque celebration isn't that big a deal, but I, Robbie, am gonna be so proud up there wearing my crown, and Yinn says all the proceeds are going to Acacia Gardens and to medical research, it has to be a smash, you hear me Petites Cendres, the coronation and all, it's gotta be, and it better not rain on all our nice costumes and fetishes and whatnot, that would really be a disaster, all those men and women with their bodies painted a thousand colours and all kinds of wild designs in the pouring rain like one big fish-bowl Robbie ran on, with only one parrot on her shoulder Mabel felt bad that there were so many tourists in town, though it was good for business, lemon-and-ginger-drink sales, displaying parrots, nope no longer two, one to mourn, to treasure and spoil and love, but she'd soon be getting some doves, oh Petites Cendres was going to like that if he still lived there, not sure about that though because of his health, what was this she was hearing about special care, he was lazy, that's all, nothing wrong with him, lethargic all these months, sure, apart from that what did he have to complain about, Mabel buried Merlin in the sand at the cemetery, no crying, she couldn't afford to stain her nice travelling dress before the trip to her daughter's in Indiana, she'd had to bury her beloved parrot, the most beautiful imported from Brazil, killed by the Shooter, and now all she could think about was revenge if she ever caught up with him and dragged him to court, oh yes she'd avenge her beautiful bird from the tropical savannas, bloodied by that Shooter, Jerry the remaining bird on her other shoulder said are we going Mama, are we going, don't mess up my hair she said, and don't pull it, she felt his plumed head soft against her cheek, all right we're going, let's go along by the docks, still without Merlin I'd rather they didn't have any Carnival celebrations this year, he was their favourite, the kids loved him, even the small ones, and on top of that all my boarders are going to be dead drunk tonight and throwing up all over my furniture by dawn, you're all I've got now Jerry, only you, are we going Mama he said again, where's Merlin, where's Merlin, yep said Mabel, throw up all over the place, they won't even remember how drunk they were, dancing the night away practically naked and probably randy as well, if only the Lord Jesus could see them, but on Carnival nights it's like He doesn't see a thing, no point wasting time on what goes on around here, and when these folks get back home, they'll be oh-so-good like always, hey Jerry, remember how brilliant Merlin's crest was, everywhere on the docks come see the one who'll outlive me a few years, come see Merlin, yeah I laid some roses over his wings before I piled the sand on him, none left for us to sell today, at least Petites Cendres' anonymous benefactor pays well, we don't have to do without, do we Jerry, let's go Mama came the reply again, always harking back to his first owner, a shrimp fisherman and captain of his own boat, Jerry couldn't help missing those days, white as snow my parrot Jerry said Mabel, quit pulling my hair, c'mon now Jerry, you don't want to hurt this old head of mine do you, remember the brown lines he had around his and that piercing yellow eye, Mama let's go he said again, it's nighttime Mama, let's go, let's go, yes Jerry we're going she answered him, you know I'm going to sing in the Ancestral Choir said Mabel when Dr. Dieudonné gets back, Dieudonné man of God who never asks the poor folks for one cent though he takes care of them all, he's getting a medal of honour from the town and Eureka's going to conduct our Ancestral Choir, we all get to sing in her church and you Jerry are going to be right there on my shoulder, with that Shooter around we got to be careful, I'm keeping you safe with me the whole time, Merlin, Mama, Jerry suddenly stridently demanded, where's Merlin. I'm going to tell all those musical bigwigs, those teachers on the Music Council, thought Fleur sitting on his straw mat facing the ocean, which now looked dark and threatening as night drew on, I'll tell them sure I composed an opera when I was thirteen, like Gian Carlo Menotti, its theme was the little Hiroshima girls the way we might have heard them if they'd just sung their sadness that day on August 6, exactly, maybe they were on their way to

school, none of them, no really none of them expecting
what . . . singing on their way to school and still singing when,
when . . . it's a piece for children's choir and violins, three
violins, and I'll tell them just like Gian Carlo Menotti I was
thirteen when I composed my first opera, I've still got it in a
drawer at my mother's place, at least I used to, I hope it's not
burnt, hope my mother didn't decide to get rid of it, no wait,
the manuscript's still intact, I remember now I moved it myself,
ah how bright the stars are shining, but not aligned for all of
us though thought Fleur no, but I'll tell them, I'm sure at least
one of them's been exposed to music since he was very young
and he'll understand me, not many people around me would,
yup wrote my first opera at thirteen, just like Gian Carlo
Menotti, but still the stars in the sky aren't aligned for all of
us, Ari said to Lou I prepared this vegetarian meal specially
for you, why aren't you eating it, salad, strawberries, lemonade, I thought you liked strawberries but all you do is look at
me with your elbows on the table and eat nothing, now I've
told you not to hold your fork like that, haven't I, it's not polite
to sit at the table like that, I drank my lemonade Lou said, I
can't eat the salad and the strawberries because you told me
I was a bit too tubby, I said you needed to eat healthy, not
like at your mother's, that's what I said Lou, he replied sternly,
Papa I want to tell you about a girl at school called Sophia,
you have a new friend called Sophia, he asked, still discour-
aged by her lack of manners over his vegetarian meal, no, Lou
changed her mind, no, okay then what asked Ari impatiently,
what is it, no, never mind, nothing said Lou, nothing Papa,
nothing, it's nearly bedtime said Ari, time to go upstairs and
go to sleep, yes Papa I know, I've already got my pyjamas on,
she said getting up, good night Papa, you're sure you don't
have something you want to tell me before you go to bed he
asked, like you love me a bit at least, no, nothing Papa, good
night, her face was so glittering sharp and cold that it worried
Ari, those blue eyes under her blonde bangs, he thought, okay

if your homework's done, up you go he said, she didn't even kiss me good night, she no longer loves me he thought to himself, must be her mother's doing, sure it is, I thought a coffee martini was your favourite Robbie said, if I had some scissors I'd slice strips out of your jeans he told Petites Cendres, like the partygoers in the street, go ahead try your martini bro, then we'll go find their highnesses the princesses up there attending my coronation, look every man on Earth has his hill to climb day in and day out, so you're just going to have to do the same he said as they sipped their drinks on the terrace and looked out at the celebrations over the water, canoe races, parachutists sailing over the boats, Sea-Doos bouncing across the waves, now that's something isn't it said Robbie, too many people, too much noise Petites Cendres said ignoring his cocktail, okay it's Carnival time said Robbie, what the hell universe are you living in anyway, the lower depths of limbo or something, just then Robbie had a flash of himself on this very terrace with Fatalité, though that one had been drinking his champagne too fast and laughing too much, that was his escape, but Petites Cendres didn't even crack a smile, then Robbie saw Herman in his orange wig leaning on his cane in front of the Saloon, this was Robbie's night, his special event, and he expected to be so very happy, he wondered about that, what was it with these sourpusses ushering in their twenty-fifth queen, he'd be swapping his paper crown for a gold one, imitation gold of course, still very impressive as it sat on his head of long brown curly hair, he was the one who'd given Herman the orange wig so no one would see how much of his red hair was gone treatments he'd had, under the wig that won't show thought Robbie, but why were they so uptight on his special night now he'd finally become Yinn's successor after a run of several years, though Yinn hadn't planned it that way, he just kept getting re-elected, sort of a Queen Mother, a title customized to his own lofty beauty, now a hesitant smile surfaced on Petites Cendres' lips, we gotta go he said, they're waiting for us onstage, right, the royal family laughed Robbie, let's go brother, and he took Petites Cendres' arm, all right, let's go. When exactly was it that Nora got the uneasy feeling he was never coming back, perhaps during their dinner beneath the gumbo tree with its sweet-smelling flowers that fell to the table while they were eating, all friends and painters and writers raising their glasses to toast the health of Nora and Christiensen, a perfect and adorable couple with such generous friends, or was it later during her nightmares that she felt it so clearly, the more she tried to pin it down the more diffuse it became, and today what struck her was the undefinable tenderness with which he embraced every one of his friends, especially the women, was that when she finally realized, or when she was alone in the car after she drove him to the airport and held him in one final long embrace, like in the old days when they were young thought Nora, the day he said your painting has sublime qualities, yes transcendent, those were his last words in the garden weren't they, as they lingered fingers intertwined after their guests had left so they could have some time together, he'd never described any of her paintings that way before, sublime, transcendent, she'd be absolutely glowing with happiness if only he were still there by her side, if only his journey had been a different one, if only he'd been less impetuous about this mission, why are you so worried he asked her, I'll be back in a week, and she repeated once again I have a premonition that you shouldn't go this time, this journey was the space left for the love that would last till the end of their lives, without him there was no certainty she'd want to go on living, was it really possible for one country to contain so much war, violence, and internal divisions, oh Africa, bereft and torn Africa, no this time you mustn't go, think of your children, you're taking greater and greater risks, but I'm not a soldier, I'm a diplomat, an economist was Christiensen's reply, this can't go on, the poor are forever more destitute and it's always the same people who have to pay, no they mustn't, and he cast a teasing look, a slightly detached and mocking glance she could never forget, the same one he'd given her at supper as though resigned to a sudden unwished-for distance between them, even as they kissed and said goodbye at the terminal he found himself asking the same question, was his departure unexpected, yes, then was it desirable, perhaps not, the air was charged with heavy storm weather as Christiensen once more mentioned how much he liked Nora's painting, this only confirmed the intuition, the presentiment behind Nora's dreams and her plunge into the void of the vision, the fear was that Tangie, the little dog, like so many other animals her husband brought home, often the ugliest and least wanted, that Tangie, being a loud barker and having followed Christiensen all day, even running panic-stricken up against his legs, even after Christiensen had taken him in his arms for reassurance, this little animal too, this fluffy ball of hair standing on end, was barking and wagging his tail to express his own terror at his master's leaving and it was so obvious, so why hadn't he picked up on both his wife's and his dog's terror in the air that hung so heavily about them, yes it had to be a sign, oh why did he never listen to her, Nora had the same presentiments and premonitions as if she were an animal, despite her childhood in Africa she'd never liked animals, in fact she feared them, and when they were accepted into the house she managed to develop a subtle feminine jealousy of them, as though they'd conquered the heart of Christiensen before her, possibly the memory of hyenas pushing in the mosquito screen and killing the little monkey that slept with her younger brother, that one with its screams and howls and an unconsolable brother that made the hot air so stifling all of a sudden, that was the reason for her mistrust, even hostility towards animals, especially ugly abandoned ones like Tangie, Christiensen brought him home for her to look after, then off he went again, that was why, was it reason enough though, but how could anything be as petty as jealousy or envy, she'd always warned her youngest don't be jealous Greta, it's an ugly sentiment sweetheart, she looked at the dinner table beneath the gumbo tree, the silk tablecloth wrinkled in the storm, folds swelling under their coating of petals, she could still hear their friends' voices as they raised glasses in a toast to their healths, far off the cellphone was ringing, ma'am it's concerning your husband said a foreign male voice, please don't be alarmed, it's only an incident, you see your husband in his own modest way was not what you thought, that is, he was a political agitator who was visiting the ambassador for lunch at the embassy itself which is on the outskirts of town, there were no guards or security people that day however, the embassy has not been able to afford such things of late, I do apologize for burdening you with these details ma'am, there have been threats in the past and it is easy enough to get in through the rear of the building through the greenhouse next to the back wall, the ambassador's wife was once seriously wounded, your husband was here to destabilize the economy, hence his meeting with the ambassador, well, remarks were made in confidence, illegal plots, the target was the ambassador and his wife, not your husband, no, not again, not this time, what he had planned was well known, but Nora said no it's not true, my husband wasn't mixed up in anything secret, he talked a lot about squandered fortunes, about justice getting back on its feet, financial justice, I mean his life here with our family was an open book, yes totally open, what you don't know, what you don't know said the foreign voice is that your husband, your husband, well it is only an incident, now I don't want you to be alarmed ma'am, then the voice fell silent, I've got to get this tablecloth cleaned up Nora thought to herself, fast, if the rain hasn't already ruined it, I've got to, she froze beneath the gumbo, yes the children, I must tell them, I must, that their father had a secret life that we never suspected, their father was, no, it's not true, he sleeps in late up there with his papers and books and things that concern him and keep him up at night, first a dip in the pool then I'll lie down beside him the way I always do, his burning hot body, yes that's what I'll do she thought, yes. The whole of Samuel's passionate future would be channelled into dance and choreography thought Daniel, his son's future was already present, far beyond the realm of mere promise, his bold and brilliantly creative friend Arnie Graal appeared on his screen and far out beyond the airport glass and even the apparently calm skies and waters where millions of screens connected, playing or replaying all the scenes in the world, for the terminal windows saw all that he could not hide from himself, the future that belonged to all the young who had no future, legions of them without a future, Augustino among them, yes of course he was, they have no taste for weapons but theirs would have to be the art of tearing their geographic capital from the hands of despots and dictators, the art of revolution, but for many of them with souls so primal this art and philosophy would have to be studied and refined while they were still under the very perfidy of oppression Daniel realized, and the most perfidious of all was to keep them in ignorance so that they would not revolt, not be enraged, this art would have to be acknowledged, and brutal without finesse or delicacy, it would mean killing and pillaging just those who now held them down, power lying only in the knife and the revolver held to a head, yes thought Daniel, all these young people with no future would soon be engaging in the most brutal of executions, no qualms, no trials, no nuances, so pitiless towards their oppressors, just as they had been during those springs and summers of flaming revolt and ceaseless ransacking, pure they were and unalloyed in the butchery of youthful revenge, the destruction of their animals and their archaeological heritage, their attacks, the tanks of coalitions having wiping out all traces of an antiquity that mattered little to so many with no future, the Islamic art with the camels, the horses, the sheep, all of it thought Daniel, under the boots or the bare feet of the legions of the young with no future, the ragged princes of countries yet to be, built with their blood and reconquered with blood tomorrow as well, an art of revolution with no subtleties or scruples where brutality alone reigns supreme, revolutions never to be denied them, fertile in fanaticism and religion, abusive of women and children and rights and freedom of thought, oh yes thought Daniel, Mélanie might well weep beside him the night she lost her mother, almost in silence though, not for him to see, and weep she also did for the fate of women crushed beneath the weight of revolution and war, precious few were born like her to privilege and rights already won, what flaming scandal and injustice when so many other women were born without as much as the right to live, much less vote or join a feminist group or play a role in government, these women she said, oppressed by the religion of their fathers and husbands and brothers, born with only the right to be killed at their first slight mistake, such as a leaning towards freedom or loving or adultery or flouting of custom and barbaric tradition, for guilty they will soon be and no doubt punished, stoned perhaps or shot by their own fathers, brothers, friends, and by what right, what right indeed, the right to die, the right to be killed, of course, of course Mélanie's tears that night were for them, tears falling on those who would number more and more to be spared less and less, oh yes, Mélanie cried for all of them that night, all. Well my hour of glory's here cried Robbie to Petites Cendres as they climbed the steps to the platform above the roaring mob of Carnival Night, and look at them all here with me, though Robbie had no idea who even the closest one was because they were all disguised and masked, some with heads like birds under haloes of branches, almost a moving wood weaving its way through the streets, where are Mabel and Merlin and Jerry Petites Cendres worried, why haven't they come to Robbie's coronation, they should be right up front with all the other bird-handlers, I hope this isn't going to be a letdown thought Robbie, these high heels are killing me, I can feel my ankles wobbling already, once they're all up there Cheng's going to dazzle everyone, the young Prince of Asia who Yinn's been training to dance, but a modest sort of dance, subtle even austere, that's right, that's the way Yinn wants it, if all these kids with pierced ears gravitate towards me it's because I'm a father figure, no, more like a brother to them Robbie reflected, quite a few have shown up to admire their mysterious Queen all aglitter for her crowning, okay let's not get carried away, I'm a brother to them that's all, I wonder if they notice that the pizzas are beginning to show around my waistline, Yinn's been telling me to lay off them, of course he could eat about twenty and be just as svelte as ever, Puerto Rican big brother, that's all I am, and tonight Queen as well, these kids still tied to their mothers' apron strings, are usually surprised when they spend a night with me, then find themselves getting married, bunch of spoiled kids, oh well that's life isn't it, this is gonna be a street banquet and what a party, I think I'll keep this mole near my lip, it's sexy, Yinn says I'm getting sexier and sexier, yeah well, okay, like Fred, always out there onstage, yep gotta slim down a bit, you see, when Fred shakes her ass when she dances or does her rap thing she shows a little too, don't get me wrong, she's been a beautiful queen for quite some time and everyone respects her, specially when she tells everyone in a real haughty way that she's not hiding a thing, no closet for her, she laughs when we clap for her too, everyone's going to be there, even the sugar daddies that broke my heart, though I don't want to see them said Robbie, and Petites Cendres watched them all appear on the platform in order of nobility, Yinn in his white beaded dress and heels so high he might teeter if someone brushed by too close, Yinn took the limelight of course, though Petites Cendres made like he didn't see him, he was that weak from emotion, much as

on the red sofa in the Porte du Baiser Saloon when Yinn
danced all night for him alone until the greenish glow of
dawn, the erotic ghost of Yinn or maybe even Yinn himself,
how to tell, a ravishing dance that swallowed Petites Cendres
in its slow fire, Yinn always danced slow, very slow, and there
was Yinn as he guided Cheng the second Prince of Asia,
Cheng was no longer called the Next One but he had some
childlike skittishness under that silken outfit so Yinn's guid-
ance was still needed, still the master, thighs seeming even
darker through the slit in the oriental dress Yinn had pulled
together in a few days, Geisha and Triumphant Heart were
beaming, inseparable as ever, then Know-It-All and Santa Fe
with all the other princesses, then following them all, stepping
gracious and slow in his orange wig with his cane beneath his
wispy dress, the last of all, Herman, a few more moments and
Yinn had opened the ball and crowned Robbie with gold,
whispering in his ear that beauty spot on your lip, you should
get rid of it, Robbie remained motionless in his regal pose,
he'd soon have to say something about the recipient of the
night's proceeds, he added that he'd be visiting the orphans
on Christmas night though it wasn't in what Yinn had written
for him to memorize, still he figured as Queen it was his pre-
rogative to be Robbie the Charitable and in his magnanimity
do the town proud, he'd take food baskets and Christmas
feasts to the families on Bahama Street, to women whose
husbands were out of work, he finally realized it was time to
shut up when Yinn signalled him, for never had a queen been
so chatty, often all they did was let themselves be admired
and bat their wild-animal lashes, then suddenly Robbie heard
something weird and everyone turned to see, Herman had
fallen, Yinn ran over to him and said what is this, stoned
again, oh no not again, not now, Robbie's mind was scram-
bled, he had a feeling something was going to rain on his
parade but with crown still on his head he ran like the others
to where Herman lay stretched out on the stage, wispy dress

and all, his mother was there too, saying to her son sweetheart wake up, you've got to wake up, it all happened so fast and she asked for him to be taken to the house with a veranda she'd rented specially near the Saloon, that's where he wanted to be she said, no hospitals, no nothing, just his mother, brother, and sister in their little rented house so close he could walk to work at night, he'd thought of everything and told his mother, now Robbie with the crown still on his head found himself with all the other queens of bygone years and princesses of tonight and Yinn in his white dress and high heels in the rented room where Herman was to breathe his last, though they were not to know this yet, all they knew was that he was stoned, absolutely stoned as Yinn said but in fact his heart was stopping, and Yinn said if he knew that was going to happen when he got stoned, so be it, that's the way he wanted it, that's right said his mother, that's what he wanted, though she hoped against hope he'd come out of the coma, probably the only one who knew in advance, she knew her son that well, she'd even asked her other children to get coffee and tea ready just in case, sandwiches too, she'd thought of everything, expecting friends to be in the house, in a sense it was for this night that she'd rented it, words, what words, forget about words, especially *final night, party night, coronation*, thought Herman's mother, not last, no, not a last evening, not a last night, then in an instant the rented house was filled, an army of friends invading first the veranda then the small living room, the kitchen, and the bedroom, if Herman had known he'd've been delighted to see all these people around his bed, why such a small one, well it was a child's bed and Herman filled it completely, leaving him on his own like that, so very far away and totally stoned thought Robbie as he sat on the bed energetically rubbing and massaging Herman's icy and inert hands, Geisha, Santa Fe, Triumphant Heart, Know-it-All trapped in a whirlpool of vertigo and looking at Herman in bewilderment, what just happened they murmured, tears and mascara running down their cheeks, then Yinn took them to one side and said we have to revive him, we've got to, we simply have to, he jumped on Herman's chest and began pressing as forcefully as he could with his hands, pushing and pushing with his palms till he was exhausted, no breath came from Herman's mouth, nothing, not a whisper, and Robbie's loud sobbing broke the silence, no Yinn said, think of his mother and brother and sister, I'm choked up Robbie said, then he sobbed louder than ever, he can't do this to us, no he can't, he really cannot, you'd think he was an angel thought Petites Cendres, for the panels of his dress were raised up around his thin body and creased sharply from the weight and the pressure of Yinn's fingers, so they looked like the wings of an angel or a giant bird, now if it was me with Yinn's fingers sliding across my chest I'd wake up just like that thought Petites Cendres darkly, oh I feel it already, and where is Herman going like this, but with Yinn, ah Yinn, what sort of angel are we talking about, the angel of life or of . . . no, no it was the angel of life, sure, it's this idiot Herman who refuses to wake up, Herman whose mother was saying to them all, no, let's not disturb him anymore, it's useless she said as she moved closer to the bed and stroked her son's forehead, good night my little boy, good night, then a moment later Robbie placed his gold crown on the pillow next to the bony head now that Yinn had carefully removed the orange wig that framed the hollow cheeks, so ascetic-looking now, Yinn and Herman's mother weren't crying, no, it was as though the need for rigour had taken hold of them for this contained ritual that would keep them by Herman's bedside for a few hours yet thought Petites Cendres, perhaps till dawn. Surely the most discreet of his sons had to be Vincent, Daniel reflected, it was he who soon would be curing, consoling, and alleviating pain, but first he must conquer his own acute crises and physical hurt before he was ready to care for others, his latent suffering, his shortness of breath, but the son he'd once thought was not long for this world had doggedly made it through school and would soon be conducting research with the same determination, he with the worst prognosis was the most vibrant of Daniel's sons, the most confident in the gift he'd been given, treasuring every second, and the most grateful to his parents for having saved his life so often, certain of a future honourably fulfilled, odd that it should be so, we would never have guessed, Daniel thought how little we really know our own children, that was when he felt a hand tap him on the shoulder, whew at last we're leaving said Laure, aha you didn't hear them announce it did you, we're leaving in a few minutes, like all those people perched on uncomfortable chairs watching football on multiple screens, Daniel found his way back out of a deep dream, got up and stretched his legs, nope didn't hear a thing he told Laure, it's time to board she said, friendly all of a sudden, what a pleasure it was meeting you, actually you've been very patient with me, perhaps we'll meet again some day, yes perhaps indeed said Daniel with that same spontaneous warmth that one can muster for a stranger, still his gaze wandered far off, towards a young man in a black suit being escorted without handcuffs by two customs officers and two policemen, he was piously leafing through a book he held in his hands, but no he would not be getting on the plane, not this plane, not this passageway, he was tall and thin with an expression that seemed fixed but harmless and he dared not make the slightest movement without being squeezed in even tighter, Daniel thought this was Lazaro but was he sure it was Jermaine's childhood friend, the one Olivier had rightly worried about, he'd been suspected of violent crimes, or maybe it was the bunch he hung out with that committed such heinous acts, maybe not, perhaps Daniel was wrong and they faintly resembled one another, sure, that could well be, Kim gathered up her backpack and told Max to follow, each one of us going off alone into the night she thought, the sea was rumbling under a starry sky, sure, each one alone, she with her dog to watch out for her but each one alone, well tomorrow she'd see Fleur on the Old Salt's boat, yes she would, wouldn't she.

Acknowledgements

With great thanks to Kelly Joseph of Anansi and Gillian Watts, to my sons Olivier and Antoine, and to Jocelyne.

— Nigel Spencer

About the Author

Photo by Jill Glessing

MARIE-CLAIRE BLAIS is the internationally revered author of more than twenty-five books, many of which have been published around the world. In addition to the Governor General's Literary Award for Fiction, which she has won four times, Blais has been awarded the Gilles-Corbeil Prize, the Medicis Prize, the Molson Prize, and Guggenheim Fellowships. She divides her time between Quebec and Florida.

ABOUT THE TRANSLATOR

NIGEL SPENCER has won the Governor General's Literary Award for Translation with three novels by Marie-Claire Blais: *Thunder and Light, Augustino and the Choir of Destruction,* and *Mai at the Predators' Ball,* which was also a finalist for the QWF Cole Foundation Prize for Translation. He has translated numerous other works and films by and about Marie-Claire Blais, Poet Laureate Pauline Michel, Evelyn de la Chenelière, and others. He is also a film-subtitler, editor, and actor now living in Montreal.